William Peace is a retired business executive and management consultant. He is American and is married to an Italian chef. He has travelled widely and lives in Wandsworth, London. This is his ninth novel.

Other Novels by William Peace

Fishing in Foreign Seas

Sin & Contrition

Efraim's Eye

The Iranian Scorpion

Hidden Battlefields

Sable Shadow & The Presence

Seeking Father Khaliq

Achieving Superpersonhood: Three East African Lives

William Peace

GRANDUNCLE BERTIE

AUSTIN MACAULEY PUBLISHERS™

LONDON * CAMBRIDGE * NEW YORK * SHARJAH

A CIP catalogue record for this title is available from the British Library.

ISBN 9781398438767 (Paperback)
ISBN 9781398438774 (ePub-e-book)

www.austinmacauley.com

First Published 2022
Austin Macauley Publishers Ltd®
1 Canada Square
Canary Wharf
London
E14 5AA

Chapter 1
Mother's Funeral

I'm not sure I should have accepted this assignment. But my nan's older brother, Albert Smithson – we all call him 'Bertie' – asked me to help him write his memoir. I'm not a writer, and there's almost five-decade age gap.

He looks like Michael Douglas playing a friendly pensioner wearing brown trousers and an off-white shirt, but he's also like an insecure student sitting an exam for which he hasn't studied. He's unspiritual and a bit of a hypochondriac, but now he may have some kind of a real illness.

We've been partners for seven years now, writing popular picture books for kids: he's the writer and I'm the illustrator, because I studied art at university. He's straight, conservative (with a small c), he always votes Labour; and I'm a gay female, pretty alternative, and I vote Green. We argue sometimes about who's got the better ideas, but fortunately we've got plenty of them, and we both love kids, and kids love him. In fact, deep down, I love him, too.

We're sitting in his second-floor office that used to be his daughter, Elizabeth's loft bedroom with a view over the Wandsworth's southwest London rooftops. He's got the stuffed easy chair, and I've got the swivel-based desk chair. There are a notebook and pen in my lap. I reach for the audio recorder, press the button and the red light comes on.

"Where do you want to start, Uncle Bertie? Maybe about age seven?"

"No, Sarah, I'd like to start with my parents' passing."

"Why there?"

He reflects for a moment. "Because that's where the real problems started. Before that, things were pretty much on an even keel."

"OK, fire away."

"I had a terrible dream just before my mother's funeral. I was sitting in the office of a doctor with a grey crew cut. The office was bare except for three framed certificates. He looked at me compassionately over his steel-rimmed glasses. 'I'm sorry, Mr Smithson, but your headaches are the result of this tumour.' He pointed with a pen at an indistinct image on his screen. I suddenly felt as if I was falling into total blackness, blind, with an enormous roaring all around me, icy cold. His voice followed me. 'The tumour is malignant. Inoperable. Months to live.' I woke, shouting 'No! No!' My twisted nightshirt was damp with sweat. Still I was in darkness.

"'Bertie! Bertie, what's the matter?' My cries had awakened Jo, and feebly I took refuge against her. 'A nightmare, Jo, a terrible nightmare.'

She switched on the light and considered me, as if she were focusing her concern on a child weeping by our bedside at 2 am. She stroked my head. 'It's all right, Bertie. It's just a nightmare. It's gone now.'

"But the nightmare isn't gone."

His shadowed eyes meet mine.

"What do you mean, Uncle Bertie?"

He looks out the window, making hopeless gestures. "It still comes back."

"Do you know why it keeps coming back?"

"It comes back..." He straightens his spine, hands gripped in his lap. "...because I'm terrified..." His voice fades away.

"Of what?"

He looks at me and away as if it's a secret I can't understand; his eyes have filled with tears.

"Tell me, Uncle Bertie."

He turns to face me. "Of death."

"But..." I wonder if, unknown to him, this is secretly what his memoir is about – a terrifying struggle to live with impending death. What have I gotten myself into? I bite my lip. Several rebuttals come to mind; none seems appropriate. I put my notebook on the table.

"Uncle Bertie...what can I do?"

He studies me with deep concentration. "I have enormous admiration for you, Sarah. You are strong, resourceful, you have great insight into the façade of things. As a young person, you have a different view of the world than I have, and I think you can help me see things in a new light. Besides, I don't think Jo could help me write this memoir. She knows me too well, and it would turn out just as she knows me, without my struggles."

So, he wants his memoir to reflect his inner struggles, not just his life as we all know it – a good life of a very good man, who overcame plenty of difficulties. Can I do this? It's a bigger job than I thought. Not just writing. It will be exploring unknown caves in the mind of a man whom I care about. Can I do this? *Yeah, Sarah, let's do it.*

I sit up in the chair, pen poised over my notepad. "How did this fear get started, Uncle Bertie?"

He looks out the window for several moments. "It started with my father's death. He was a union man, very strong, in the building trades. He knew plumbing, bricks and mortar, electrics, but mostly he was an organiser, a promoter of the union shop. He was no friend of the construction companies, but they respected him. He expected both sides to do things right: a good day's work for a fair wage.

My father took off his tweed flat cap when he came home by six, we'd have supper, the five of us, and he'd tell us his interpretation of what happened during his day. I'd listen and I'd think: *he's so wise, figuring things out.* On Saturdays, he'd take us out into the park. We'd kick a football. When I was small, I'd ride on his shoulders, looking down on the world. He'd tell me stories about what it is to be a man. He was like a god to me – only better – because I knew he loved me.

On Sundays, Momma took the three of us to church, but he'd go and play cards with his mates. I missed him on Sundays, not understanding why he couldn't be with us. He said, 'I don't believe in that religious hokum, it just makes things complicated.' I think he saw religion as a set of training wheels on an adult bicycle. But what was complicated about it? It was just being a little dressed up and sitting in church with your family like it was a special occasion.

Papa was a smoker – a pack a day of Gold Flake, and he had the smoker's cough to go with it; but he took a certain pride in not going to see the doctor, so I can remember when he got sick. His complexion turned grey, he didn't have much energy, he was coughing constantly, and he complained of chest pain. I'd never heard him complain about anything before. He said he just needed some rest and stayed home for a week.

There was a commotion one morning when I was about seventeen. Papa came down the stairs all bent over and coughing with a bloody handkerchief at his mouth. Momma shoed us kids away and hurried him out of the house. Carol-Ann, Jason and I didn't know what to think. Jason and Carol-Ann started to cry, we just hugged each other. Momma came home and said he was in the hospital. I heard her talking to the doctor something about 'cancer'. Nobody ever mentioned that word. People whispered the phrase 'the Big C'. None of us dared to ask Momma about it. We were lost in a cave with no light.

Papa discharged himself from the hospital and came home. When I went to see him, a district nurse was just leaving. She was shaking her head. 'He don't want me to help him!'

For a man who was so sick, he wouldn't sit still. He would jump out of bed and stalk around the room, swearing like a sailor, blaming the doctors, my poor mother, and even me. Then he would dissolve into a fit of coughing and slump into bed. I couldn't believe that this was my father, my hero.

In a matter of days, the cancer had apparently spread to his brain. He started shouting and cursing. 'No decent god would do this to me! Damn you! I want to live! Don't you dare let me die, you bastard!' And he would go on for half an hour like this, then collapse, and start again. I was stunned into numb disbelief; my mother sat nearby, wringing her hands, tears streaming down her face. He didn't recognise any of us who were there with him.

In about a week, his strength deserted him. He lay in bed muttering, slipping in and out of consciousness. And then he was gone."

Uncle Bertie looks into the distance. I see there are tears running down his cheeks. I feel my tears starting too, and I find my hands clenched between my knees.

"Papa was fifty-one when he died," he continues. "Momma was a widow for thirty-seven years. She was seventy-four when she died; I was fifty-four then, when I had that nightmare for the first time.

"So, you thought the dream was an omen," I say. "A warning that you, like your dad, would die in a year in utter agony."

"Yes."

"Is the dream still an omen for you?"

"Yes, but it doesn't have that time limit." He chews his lower lip. "One might think no time limit is good. On the contrary. It could be five weeks or five years. You don't know, and the nightmare returns, again and again, to remind you that you will have to face the horror."

"Tell me about your mother, Uncle Bertie. What was she like?"

"My mother was dedicated to the church, her family and her circle of friends. Nothing else, other than her antique Christian principles, mattered to her. She would stretch herself for people she regarded as good and despise those who were lazy or wicked. I loved my mother – particularly as a child – though as I grew older, the puppy love matured into affection and respect for a kind, strong woman, in spite of our clashes on social issues.

I remember her funeral very well. As I passed through the peaked stone entrance of St Bartholomew's, I could see Momma's off-white coffin resting near the altar, and though her death is, for me, an anticipated event, a sudden failure overcame me, and I stumbled on a bit of loose carpet. I was too old to weep and too young to have made sense of the passing of so many: the loved, the friends.

I took my seat next to my younger sister, Carol-Ann, who was dressed in sombre black with a white carnation, our mother's favourite. I touched her hand as she turned to acknowledge me with a suppressed smile, and her glance from my face to an old navy-blue suit and green tie told me she was glad of my presence but disapproving of my hasty choice of dress. Could my mother – wherever she is today – possibly disparage my choice of the ten-year-old navy blue over the purchase of a funereal version that costs three hundred pounds, and which would inevitably be subject to the attack of moths until it is my turn to be horizontal at the altar?

The organist was playing a welcome hymn softly, the name of which I can't remember. The masses of white carnations, which Carol-Ann must have requested, lifted the spirits with their insistent purity, and the scent of incense is a reminder of holiness. A rectangular patch of red and white light appeared on the floor of the transept, and as it grew in intensity, one could trace its origin through the illuminated air back to a window high in the transept. Is this really a holy occasion: the death of one old lady? To me, it seemed more like a farewell, a time of remembrance, of sadness. But am I the odd man out? Many in the congregation, faces lifted, were looking at the life-sized crucifixion.

Our younger brother, Jason, sat gently next to me. 'You OK, Bertie?'

I patted his knee. 'Yeah, Jace, I'm good.'

A glance at his face told me he had been weeping. I confessed that his emotional excursions into joy or sadness were foreign to me: for almost fifty years, I had marvelled at his joy in life and failed to understand his overwrought misfortunes.

Turning to the pews behind me, I saw Josephine, my lovely wife, with our three adult children; she returned my smile, and I noticed that she, too, was in black with a carnation, a low white hat and mesh veil. Probably quite fashionable, but not too expensive, I hope. There also was Raymond, Carol-Ann's second husband and five years my senior. Unsurprisingly, Ray was dressed for a day at the Ascot races: a light plaid sport jacket and red tie. I suppose that as long he presented himself at family events, on time, in reasonable attire, he remained beyond Carol-Ann's reproach. There, too, is Geraldine, Jason's partner, my age, who was conservatively presented in navy blue, whereas when she is pulling pints at the Dog and Duck, I suppose she wore sleeve garters with her generously scoop-necked blouse.

There were many parishioners who were unknown to me, mostly old women in doughty dress with oversized handbags; I suppose that they, like Sarah, my mother, were charter members of the Women's Institute – well, not charter members: they would have to be older than God, but surely, they all produced copious quantities of warm and useless knitwear.

St Bartholomew's was the Anglican church my mother took me to as a child, but I later drifted away and married Jo, a genuine Catholic, with whom I sometimes attended St Christopher's. So, I didn't know this vicar, wearing a heavy gold and white brocaded robe and elaborately embroidered stole, over which her blonde hair cascaded; she couldn't be more than thirty-five. For me the idea of young, female priests in the Church of England was a revolution similar to the introduction of the iPhone, but my mother had never mentioned her. I wondered what Jo is making of the vicar: probably, as a Catholic feminist, torn between solidarity and condemnation.

The service began with solemn chanting and swinging of the smoking thurible. I know that incense is an ancient symbol of sacrifice – better to burn resin than sheep – and the smoke symbolises prayers rising to heaven, but why was it necessary? Leave out the sacrifice and let any prayers rise on their own.

I was unable to focus on and comprehend the words or the symbols of Christianity; it all seemed so foreign to me that I might as well be in a mosque. *Shame on you, Bertie! Pay attention!* But my heart was heavy, and my brain was numb.

The vicar was offering a eulogy of my mother, complete with life history. Where did she get all this? Actually, I wouldn't be surprised if my mother wrote out her own obituary – not for any newspaper – but to plant in the memories of the attendees at her last farewell. It would have been a necessary part of 'putting things in order'.

The vicar was praising my mother for her dedicated love of six grandchildren. Just a minute! She wasn't so dedicated to all of them. In the case of my three children, she ignored Jeffrey, our oldest, while lavishing time and resources on Michael, our tearaway. Elizabeth is, after all, 'just a girl'. Jeffrey suffered from low self-esteem, and he would have benefitted from his nan's attentions. Neither Jo nor I succeeded in bringing Michael's excesses under control. Mother tamed him. I never thanked her for her resourcefulness with Michael nor tried to shift some of her attention to his brother. Too late now. Mother, if you're listening, thank you for Michael and sorry about Jeffrey. *Silly, that thought; she's not listening.*"

I interrupt. "Excuse me, but how do you know she wasn't listening, Uncle Bertie?"

His hands make flustered gestures and he looks from me to the window. "Well, I...I mean...it's just a figure of speech. After all, when you're dead, you're dead."

"Would your mother have agreed with that?"

"Probably not."

"From all I've heard: certainly not. And if not, wouldn't she have been disappointed that you choose her funeral to criticise her?"

His hands flutter again. "Well...I also said that she did a wonderful job with Michael." He looks sadly at his outstretched feet. "I guess I was feeling kind of down, and I was focusing on the negative. Sorry, Sarah."

I give him a nod of acknowledgement. "If you were giving your mother's eulogy now, what would you say?"

He takes a deep breath and focuses on the ceiling for a long moment. When he turns to face me, his eyes are brimming, and tears spill down his cheeks. "I miss her so much. She loved me, and she was a bulwark which kept our family together when my father died. And her faith was a large, deep river. Nothing could stop it, but it always stayed within its banks. It was astonishing: this seventy-four-year-old widow, suffering the physical pains of her cancer, taking morphine every four hours, but otherwise completely at peace with herself and the world. I would be blubbering and screaming for Jesus to appear and save me."

He turns back to the window. "The soprano soloist was singing the first verse of *Abide with Me* and the choir joined her in the last line, 'Help of the helpless. O abide with me.' The hymn continued with a different soloist on each verse. In spite of myself, there was a tingle coursing down my spine. The voices were splendid, subduing the organ, and the raw emotion conveyed by the faithful, suppliant singer was electric. I have to admit that music and art are two of Christianity's most persuasive recruiting tools.

About ten days ago, Mother had said to the three of us, 'Now, I don't want you to be parcelling out assignments for the service. The vicar will be in charge and if somebody wants to say something, they should volunteer.'

I was not surprised when Carol-Ann arrived at the lectern without notes, smiled at the congregation just as Momma would have done, and, after a pause, said, 'My mother wasn't a saint.' For several seconds, she surveyed her audience. "But that's only because the Church of England doesn't create saints. The only saints we have are in our hearts and the only saint I have is my mother, and I know that is true for many of you. She was a servant saint, serving her family, her friends, people in need and our Lord Jesus. You and I were lucky to have her. Today, we give thanks for her, and we wish her well in God's company.'

I worried that Jason forced himself to ignore the word 'volunteer' as he tearfully read the twenty-third psalm without comprehension. And I was surprised when Elizabeth, Momma's youngest grandchild, my eighteen-year-old daughter, rose from her pew, took the lectern, looked the congregation in the eye, and read a classic, emotional poetic tribute to her grandmother.

The cemetery was half a mile from St Barts, and since most of us lived nearby, we elected to walk, nearly keeping pace with the hearse, with its coffin blanketed in white carnations. The sky had turned London dreary grey again. The city was respectfully quiet, as traffic and pedestrians slow. Most likely, they were thinking, I wonder who it was. Probably, somebody unimportant who can't afford limousines. This reminded me of the beautiful old hearse, a glass display case on four wheels, all glossy black and draw by a placid pair of white horses. It was the central feature of some local funerals, and I had noticed it attracted gawking admiration: 'that important fellow is going out in style!' I suspected, though, that the fellow was the old Greek barber whose five sons took out a loan to finance the display.

Stretching along the rail line for most of a mile, and nearly two hundred yards wide, the cemetery was a reservoir of unexpected calm. The perspective was a long vista of grass, punctuated by grey headstones, random trees, shrubs and a surprisingly generous sprinkling of red, white and yellow flowers. There were slow-moving visitors here and there, pausing at their vital site to rearrange or water flowers, or perhaps to savour a memory.

We were led by a thin old man, in a black cloak, hat and cane, to the grave: a precise, yawning pit which had been carved into the ground, and its earth piled under a carpet of artificial grass. The undertaker's sombre crew placed the coffin, in startling white contrast to its surroundings, onto belts suspended above the pit.

The vicar began the final service. Listening to her tone and observing her gestures, it was clear to me that she truly believed the Church's message of spiritual resurrection, in spite of all the immediate contrary evidence: the pit, the sealed coffin, the grey skies and the gloomy guests. 'Earth to earth, ashes to ashes, dust to dust,' and 'Death where is thy sting?' I could tell you where the sting is; it's in my heart. A horrible heavy hopelessness. In light of my agnosticism, these religious platitudes do little to convince me of the verity of Church's message. Nor does the sight of my weeping brother releasing his handful of earth onto our mother's coffin."

"Can we stop for a moment, Uncle Bertie?"

"Yes, of course."

"I want to ask you what effect the recollection of your mother's funeral has on your fear of death."

"It intensifies my fear of death," he says, without hesitation.

"In spite of the fact that your mother herself had no fear, and your sister and the vicar both expressed the belief that she is with God?"

The muscles in his jaw are working as he grits his teeth. "I find it very difficult to believe."

I can see now that at least one of my challenges will be to find that spark of belief that will illuminate his inner struggles.

Chapter 2
Funeral Reception

Uncle Bertie continues his description of his mother's funeral. "The Unite union hall was also a short walk and was more appropriate than a pub or restaurant; my parents' home, while spacious, would never accommodate seventy people. Besides, this union hall was where we held my father's funeral reception, even though Unite (which aspires to represent everyone) was not his union. The chairs which usually fill the ground floor hall had been folded away, and a waitress was placing plates of tea sandwiches, scones and cakes beside the coffee and tea urns on the trestle tables. The barman in his white apron was ready to serve beer, red or white wine. The usual array of spirit bottles had been hidden away.

There was an eagerness to talk among the guests streaming in, a desire to release the bottled feelings which had been accumulated in silence during an intense hour and a half.

'Wasn't that a lovely service?' said one WI lady.

'Yes, I think Sarah would have liked it,' said another.

From my point of view, would it have made any difference if Sarah hadn't liked it after having written the specification? In fairness, I suppose the WI lady meant that <u>she</u> liked it and is predisposed to something similar for herself in the very distant future.

A grey-haired black man with huge alert eyes and a cleft chin approached me deferentially; though he seemed familiar, I couldn't place him. 'Mr Smithson, have you noticed that the concept of family seems different now that your parents have both passed on?'

I considered him for a moment, startled by the abruptness of his question. 'No, I haven't, and I'm not sure what you mean.'

'Well, what I mean is that when we have parents, there is always someone to refer to, particularly emotionally, someone to blame or to ask for support. Now, for you, that reference point is gone, and <u>you</u> become the reference point for your descendants.'

'Oh, I see. No, I haven't experienced that feeling yet, but perhaps I will. Have you any experience of it?'

'Yes. It can be another subconscious form of grief…of loss, actually; another stage of life we must pass through.' My attention drifted across the room. His hand touched my sleeve. 'I believe your mother—God rest her soul—was the matriarch of the family. What does that now make you?'

I paused and gave him an indulgent smile. 'A patriarch? Why would I want to be patriarch? The family can take care of itself.'

'There are two points about this, Mr Smithson. The first is a sociological fact: families do not take care of themselves. They tend to self-destruct as a result of conflicting interests. Think of any historically prominent family. Where is it now? What is required is the firm hand of leadership to promote values and vision. The second is that a successful leader is highly valued, even loved, and he or she feels a great sense of fulfilment.'"

"Uncle Bertie, you must have picked up on that right away."

"I didn't, actually, Sarah. I didn't have enough respect for the Professor at that point to pay any attention to his advice. But I told him that I would think about it and then to compensate for my insincerity, I asked, 'Would you tell me your name, sir? I have seen you before, but just can't place you.'

'My name is George Jenkins. I'm retired from Arriva Busses—used to drive the 28, the 44 and the 270N. I live in the Prince Henry Estate, and I'm what most people would call a busy body.'

'Did you know my mother, George?'

'Yes, I read about her untimely death in the local *Courier.*'

'And do you have any family, George?'

'Not anymore. My wife and daughter left and went back to Jamaica.'

'So, you're a sort of reference point for the neighbourhood?'

'Yes, exactly.' And he moved toward the refreshments.

My sister approached, violin case in hand. 'Who was that you were talking to, Bertie?'

'That was George Jenkins, a retired bus driver from Jamaica.'

Carol-Ann frowned. 'Did he know Mother?'

'Yes, and he said he read about her death in the paper.'

She gazed into the distance. 'Come to think of it, Mother once mentioned a black bus driver from Jamaica. She called him *The Professor*.'

'But surely,' I protested, 'he doesn't have a degree.'

Over her shoulder, my sister suggested, 'From a prominent secondary school in Jamaica?'

I suppose driving a bus could be a very educational experience.

My old friend, Dr Mortimer Ramsden, spotted me from across the hall; he hurried over, glass of white wine in hand. 'How are you holding up, Bertie?'

'I'm all right; just a bit sad, that's all.'

'We don't want you to be getting depressed. It can run in families, you know.'

'I do have a little trouble sleeping lately.'

He stepped closer. 'I can write you a prescription.'

'I'll be OK, Mort.'

I know he means well, but he seems to think I'm a bit of a hypochondriac."

It seems to me that 'a bit of a hypochondriac' is an understatement. The family makes jokes about Uncle Bertie's aches, insomnia, neuralgia, gastritis, arthritis, lumbago, and being 'generally indisposed'. He's perfectly healthy, we all give him a hug and tell him that. He's never been in the hospital and Doctor Ramsden seems to cater to his worries, which, I now suspect, may derive from his thanatophobia (fear of death).

"I'm standing at the bar," he continues, "a pint of bitter in hand, as people drift around the hall. Jo arrived beside me. 'You OK?'

'Yes, now that you're here.'

She gave me a sunny smile. 'It was a lovely service, don't you think?'

I considered for a moment. 'In a way, yes, but it's too bad Momma wasn't there.'

She looked around the hall. 'She was there, Bertie, and here, too.'

'I know you believe that.'

She tilted her head in acknowledgement, and I noticed that the hat and veil were gone – just the lustrous, tightly coiffed, black hair. 'I'd like a chardonnay, Bertie.'

When I returned with her wine, I found that she was in conversation with our oldest granddaughter, JoJo, aged five, a child of our older son Jeff, named for his grandfather.

It seemed to be a Smithson family tradition that given names are re-used a generation or two later. In my case, the given name, Albert, came from my great-grandfather, who, in turn, was named for Queen Victoria's prince. Unfortunately, however, the prince failed to pass on to me that essential addition to his name: money.

'Gramma,' JoJo asked, 'Is Grand G in heaven now?'

'Yes, sweetheart.'

'How do you know?' she asked; this query was a recent addition to her old reliable *why?*

'Well, sweetheart, I felt that her spirit was here today.'

'What do you mean, Gramma?'

'Let me ask you, JoJo, have you ever been in a room where you felt there was someone else there, but you didn't see them?'

JoJo was biting her lip in concentration. 'Yeah.'

'Well, for me, it was like that. It felt like Grand G was there even though I couldn't see her.'

'But, Gramma, how does she get from here to heaven?'

'Do you know what a spirit is, JoJo?'

'You mean like the Holy Spirit?'

'Exactly! When you're a person but you have no body, it's very easy to get around, like the Holy Spirit.'

JoJo's cherubic face shined with enlightenment; she dashed off. Jo took in my sceptical look. 'You don't believe a word I said.'

I lifted one shoulder in acknowledgement. 'Of course not, but that hardly matters. You convinced JoJo, and Father Anthony would be very proud of you.'

'Oh, Bertie, don't be like that.'

'No, I'm serious, love, I say earnestly. It's far better to start out in life as one of the believers, because the Catholic Church installs barriers of faith in young minds so that that they have a basis to resist the tragedies and disappointments which life will throw at them. If they began their lives with a blank script, as I have, they would be at a disadvantage.'

She took my arm and hugged me. 'We've got to find you the right script writer.'

'If you say so. By the way, I like your funeral hat.'

'It's not just a funeral hat, Bertie; it's also good for weddings.'

'If it doesn't get misappropriated. Right now, your granddaughter seems to like it. It's a little big, though.'

Jo turned to look. 'Oh!'

JoJo's mom, Cathy, had made the co-incidental discovery, and was also converging on the cute little miscreant.

The persistent clinking of a glass brought a hush. Carol-Ann was standing, unsheathed violin in hand, in front of three other musicians, another violinist, a violist and, a cellist. 'As many of you know, my mother enjoyed classical music, and while she didn't play an instrument, she read music and was a soprano soloist in the church choir. With her encouragement, I took up the violin, and with three talented colleagues have formed the Wandle String Quartet. This afternoon, as a tribute to my mother, we would like to play some of her favourite pieces for you.'

The musicians arranged their folding chairs in a semicircle around their music stands, all attention on their instruments and sheet music. The guests eagerly formed another, larger semicircle; the children, quiet now, were watching intently. Carol-Ann nodded several times and as the bow crossed her instrument, the music began to pour out, swell in depth and intensity as the others joined in. It was something magical; the sweet, glowing sounds that stringed instruments could make, sometimes lively, occasionally mournful: the gamut of human feelings.

Though I had heard the Wandle play many times, I didn't know what they played; I know Mother had a particular fondness for Mozart, Haydn and Shostakovich. We were all entranced.

Jason detached himself from the semicircle, and, towing Gerri into the open space, turned her to face him, and they began to dance to what must be a waltz. Spontaneous applause erupted. Moments later, two pairs of elderly ladies joined, and Elizabeth had dragged her brother Jeff into action. Jason's face was lit with blissful abandon, and Gerri was enjoying his happiness as much as the dance in which she appears to be the competent leader. Thank God for Gerri. She, as much as all the medication he took, helped my brother ward off the bouts of depression which fall from his bipolar disorder.

Jason had selected Elizabeth as his next dance partner, and Gerri was standing beside me, glass of red wine in hand. 'This is quite a nice Malbec,' she announced.

'Well, as our publican, I'll take your word for it.'

'Jason is taking the loss of his mother pretty hard.' She looked at me. 'I hope it's a little easier for you, Bertie.'

I said, 'For me, the loss of my dad was really hard.'

She watched Jason and Elizabeth trying to reconcile their footwork. 'Jason told me your dad was terrified of dying.'

'Yes, and I guess it runs in the family.'

She frowned. 'What do you mean, Bertie?'

I shrugged and made a dismissive gesture. 'I just mean that…' I searched for words. '…that I have uncomfortable thoughts about dying.'

She considered me, trying, perhaps, to identify those thoughts. 'I think most people are afraid of death.'

'Yes, yes, I suppose so. Tell me, Gerri, what do your punters say about it?'

She studied the far wall for a moment. 'There was one regular fellow—used to come in on Friday nights. I think he was a psychologist. He was sitting at the bar talking to an old guy, one of my nightly regulars. I heard him tell the old guy, *You'll have to find three things to rest easy about dying.*'

'Did you hear him say what they were, Gerri?'

'Yeah. He said that you have to have a good family life, a fulfilling vocation and faith.'

'Those three things?'

'That's what he said, Bertie.'"

I hold up a hand to my granduncle. "What was your reaction to that, Uncle Bertie?"

There is silence in the room. Did he hear me?

"Well," he says. "Gerri and I talked about what each of those three things meant in practice for a good while. And the more I thought about them, the more they made sense."

"And what else?" I prompt.

He takes a deep breath. "Well, I also realised how far I was from being able to say I really had them, and how much effort it would take to achieve them."

"Were you discouraged, Uncle Bertie?"

"Not exactly discouraged. I thought, *you've got to have a plan, Bertie, for eating all three of those elephants.*"

I smile. "OK, continue with your story."

"Carol-Ann's husband, Raymond Hotchkis, was at my side, a glass of whiskey in his hand. Where the hell did he get that? 'You like classical music, Bertie?'

'Yes, Ray, I do. Don't get to hear my sister play often enough.'

'Well, you ought to come around to our place any Friday evening.' He grimaced. 'I'm a Beatles, ABBA kind of guy.'

'Do I sense a note of family dissonance?'

He frowned. 'I was surprised we didn't hear from you during the service.'

'Well, Elizabeth was my representative.'

'And a very pretty lass she is, but one would expect to hear from the oldest representative of the next generation.'

'Well, there were only so many slots in the service, and...'

'Oh, come now, Bertie. There's always room for one more.'

His half-smile reminded me of a cat studying a canary. 'It's not my style, Ray. I would have looked uncomfortable and insincere if I'd stood up there and delivered a eulogy to my mother, much as I love her.'

'Ah, yes, the old butterflies in the stomach.'

'No, it's not that, Ray. I speak in public to my workforce every day. For me, feelings are a proprietary matter.' I paused, considering, and opted for honesty: 'Ray, it's not so easy for me to tell Jo, in person, what she means to me. I can't imagine trying to convey to seventy people my feelings for my mother.'

'Well, I can recommend a good shrink for you, Bertie.'

'You mean the one who's been teaching you amiability, Ray?'

He scowled and moved off. Why does Ray behave like that? He can be selfish, disagreeable, and a put-down artist, not just with me, but with other adult family members; he doesn't usually bother with children. But why? He was independently wealthy, didn't have to work for a living, he was married to my sister, who, were she a Catholic, would have been nominated for sainthood. He must be angry about something in his life. Jo says he's jealous of me. Whatever could anyone find to be jealous of ordinary me?"

I say, "You know, Uncle Bertie, I think Aunt Jo is right. My grandfather is a little jealous of the attention that my nan gives you, because your kids are successful, and because of our partnership. He knows he can wind you up, so he does it to get even. I think he's actually a sad and kindly old man."

Chapter 3
The Old Homestead

I am looking over my notes of our last session. "Uncle Bertie, the man that Carol-Ann refers to as the 'Professor' said that families tend to self-destruct out of self-interest, if there is no one in charge. Do you agree with that?"

"No, I don't. Why is it necessary for someone to be in charge? Families are democratic institutions—or at least they should be."

"But don't all democratic institutions have someone in charge?"

He frowns. "Sarah, what does this have to do with my memoirs?"

"I think it's important to describe your role in the family," I persist. "After all, you were the oldest member."

"No, Raymond was four years older."

"OK, but he wasn't a Smithson," I say. "Most of the people are Smithsons."

"You're not a Smithson, Sarah." There's an edge of defensiveness in his voice.

Frustrated, I rub the back of my neck. "My surname isn't relevant, Uncle Bertie. This family began with your great-grandfather, who was also Albert Smithson – probably before that. Some people, like my father and grandfather were outsiders who joined the family by marriage and became part of the Smithson clan. In fact, we're just like a Scottish clan: a close-knit group of relatives; you don't need to be related to the clan chief to be a clan member."

He gives a derisive chuckle. "Are you suggesting that I'm the Smithson clan chief?"

"I guess I am, but I'm actually more interested in how you got to be whatever you are."

"I don't really know, but I suppose my mother was in charge until her death. She was the one who insisted on the big family lunch every Sunday and the two-week family holidays in Seaford every summer. If you ignored or overrode a family tradition, you'd certainly hear from her about it."

"OK. So, what happened after her death?"

"Well, we moved the Sunday lunches into my house from my parents' home, because the old home, while much more comfortable, was closed to family gatherings: it was on the market."

"I remember the home when it was Grand G's," I say, "it had a double-size reception area, and an old, three-pedestal table with four leaves. Chairs were purloined from the rest of the house so that there was seating for twenty. The small children ate in a separate shift. We were then squeezed into your house around four tables in two connecting rooms: a total of seventeen adults and ten grandchildren, although two of the grandchildren were still breastfeeding."

He laughs. "And to make it worse, family convocations do not take place only on Sundays. There are also Christmas and New Year's Day, the Queen's Birthday, and Guy Fawkes Day. So, I have to admit that I wasn't very happy with this use of my house: it seemed rather cramped. Of course, we were all used to pitching in, cooking, serving and cleaning up."

"It must have been on the third or fourth Sunday after the change of venue," he continues, "that Jason slowly ascended to his feet, listing slightly to port, a nearly empty glass of cava in his hand and dreamy smile on his face. 'So nice to see you all here today...' He went on to favourably recognise random individuals. '...I'm sure we all have a warm glow of love from keeping this Smithson family tradition alive...' This was followed by a recitation of the benefits of maintaining a close family bond: harmonious relationships, individual security, and care for each of us. There was a noisy pounding on the table of agreement. 'And I think we all owe a special thanks to Jo for putting on this most welcome occasion.'

There were calls of 'Hear! Hear!' and the family rose to its feet to toast Jo.

'That's very kind of you, Jason,' Jo said, 'and I'm sorry we're a bit cramped here, but I agree that it is good to get us together.'

His voice booming, Raymond announced, 'Well, it seems to me that there is a solution to the crowding problem to which our lovely hostess, Josephine, just referred.' He offered an ingratiating smile to Jo, for whom I have long suspected he has a particular lust and looks around the family for a response. Hearing none, he went on, 'The solution is quite simple: we continue to use the old home.'

'But, Ray,' I protested, 'the old home is for sale.'

'Yes, of course, but one of the family members can buy it and move in.'

'So, are you suggesting that one of us sell our house and move into the old home?'

'Exactly!'

'But, why would any of us want to do that?'

'For lots of reasons!' Ray was now in oratory mode. 'One of you will have a larger house, which can be suitably modernised to your taste. One of you will be able to recreate the beautiful memories of living where you grew up, and one of you will be doing an inestimable service to the family.'

I had the urge to say, 'The memories weren't always beautiful', but instead, I looked over at Carol-Ann. She had a distinctly disengaged look on her face. I suspected Ray tried the idea on her, and she said, 'No way!' Jason, however, appeared to be very much engaged with the idea. The problem with Jason was that there was no way, emotionally, or financially, he could make it happen. I glanced at Jo; there was a Mona Lisa smile on her face, which probably means, 'Don't say no just yet.'

'I have the feeling,' I said, 'that I'm being nominated.'

With apparent sincerity, Ray said, 'I can't think of a better owner for the old homestead.'

'Thanks for the vote of confidence, Ray, but I'm not sure I want to stump up the extra money to buy that house.'

'Ah, but you're forgetting something, Bertie.' Ray switched to condescending mode. 'By virtue of your inheritance, you already own a third of the old homestead.'

I turned to my younger son, Michael. 'Mike, put your estate agent hat on and tell us what you think.'

'Well, Dad, in spite of the fact that my grandparents' home is bigger, it needs renovation, and I don't think it would sell for any more money than our house. Uncle Ray has a point: a third of the value of my grandparents' home can be used either as equity or for refurbishment.'

'Sounds like the finances might get a bit complicated,' I said.

'I'm sure I could help with that, Dad.'

Dishtowel in hand as I put away innumerable plates and glasses, I asked Jo, 'Did Ray, by any chance, run his idea by you before the lunch?'

'No, he didn't, Bertie,' she said turning from the sink to face me, 'and he wouldn't dare. There never has been, and never will be anything between Raymond and me.'

'Well, he sure is hopeful.'

'That's his problem. If he steps out of line, I'll give your sister an earful.'

She stepped close to me, wrapped her bare, wet arms around my neck, and gave me a soft, bemused smile. 'I like it when you worry, Bertie. Nothing to worry about, but it makes me feel good. By the way, I think I'm going to like your parents' home.'

I sat on a kitchen chair. 'It seems to me that this implies that I'm to be something like a patriarch, and I'm not sure I want to be a patriarch in my mother's home.'

'That's a rather old-fashioned word. Why are you using it? Would *leader* suit you better?' I recounted my conversation with the Professor at Mother's funeral. 'Well, Bertie, I think that the Professor, as you call him, has a point. Families can self-destruct when they haven't a leader.' I could feel the wrinkles on my brow. 'Look at the Queen,' she continued, 'Without her guidance, it seems to me that England would be a republic, were it not for her persona and firm hand. I'll bet she's buried two-thirds of the scandals those fractious royals have gotten into.'

'Well, I'm pretty sure we don't have as many wilful members as the royal family.'

'I wouldn't bet on it.'

'Anyway, I'm not sure I want the job.'

'Bertie, I'm not sure you understand. It's either you or nobody.'

'I vote for nobody.'

She sat down next to me. 'I can guarantee you that several things will happen if you don't take the job. First, there will be some unfortunate, preventable events in the family, which will make you feel embarrassed. Second, you'll kick yourself for not having enough courage to take the job. And, third, your parents will be disappointed in you and you'll feel it.'

I said, 'I doubt your third point.'

'I know you do, but I can still feel the presence of your mother, God rest her soul, and if I can feel her, and if you disappoint her, you will know it!'

There was a long pause while I considered. 'Jo, I haven't any idea how to be a patriarch.'

Jo leant into me; there was that special smile on her face, so I knew what was coming. With the tips of her fingers, she massaged my forehead until the creases were gone.

'Neither do I but, together we'll figure it out.'"

"Uncle Bertie," I put in, "you leave me with the impression that you didn't feel up to being a patriarch." He inclines his head and gives a slight shrug. "Why did you feel that way?"

He scratches his jaw. "It wasn't so much 'patriarch' that was bothering me. I still don't know what a patriarch is. I didn't want to be the 'leader'. I didn't think I should be telling everybody what to do."

"But when you were a construction foreman, you did exactly that."

"Yes, but it was necessary as part of the job."

I think for a moment. "Did Aunt Jo's reassurance that she would help you make it easier for you?"

"Well, you know Jo; she has all kinds of self-confidence."

"Were you worried that if you were the leader, some of the family wouldn't respect your decisions?"

"Well, yeah. We've talked about how Ray liked to wind me up."

"Yes, but underneath that, I'm pretty sure Ray actually respected you," I say, "Does that make sense to you?"

He pauses for a moment, studying the bookshelves. "Yes, in a way it does, but I never thought of it at the time." He looks out the window and continues, "Jo, two of the kids and I went to have a good look at what was then my parents' home. She said, 'I really do like it, Bertie. It has good light, and a warm, welcome feel to it, but it definitely needs a good tug into the twenty-first century.'

I looked around the ground floor of the home where I grew up; to me, it was familiar, therefore timeless. Cautiously, I asked, 'What does your good tug include, Jo?'

'Well, this wall here needs to come out, the side return needs to be done to expand the kitchen, all the flooring should be renewed, and…'

'What's the matter with the floor?' I interrupted.

She stooped and lifted a corner of what is, admittedly, a threadbare carpet, and pointed. 'Bertie, look, this floor is the original pine floor, approaching twice your age, and it's more scarred and knottier than you are.'

Feigning sadness, I asked, 'Are you planning to give me a good tug, too?'

She turned, hands on hips, tilting her head from side to side, and squinted at me. 'No, I think a haircut and a new pair of jeans will do you for a while. Let's look upstairs.'

Elizabeth and Michael were prowling around the first floor. 'I don't think I've ever looked in the master bedroom before,' Michael said, 'You guys are lucky: two bow windows and what looks like a working chimney. Twice the size of Abby's and mine.' At the time, they had a newly built high-rise, near the river.

'Well, Mike,' Jo said, 'as you know better than we do, the Victorians were generous with their master bedrooms and reception rooms, but stingy about everything else, particularly bathrooms and kitchen.'

'Which explains why Victorian families were large, thin and doused in deodorant,' I added.

I was transfixed by the dark wooden bedstead whose four posts were carved with clinging vines; the headboard and the footboard were decorated with similar vine overlays. Not large – double bed size – it seemed solid and stable, meant to last more than one human lifetime. I suppose I was conceived in this bed, and I could almost calculate the date of that event. Perhaps Elizabeth would want it, and she would conceive her children in it. But I was reminded that nowadays, couples in bed prize personal space over personal contact, in which case Elizabeth – and husband-to-be-determined – would prefer a super king size, and the old vine bed would see out its days in a council flat providing slumber for two children. This thought process led me into melancholy, that state of wistful sadness in which I considered the world's perverse changes. I felt a pang for that beautiful bed at being downgraded from matrimonial love nest to children's cot.

Elizabeth was pointing up the stairs to the second-floor loft. 'Whose room was that up there?'

'That was Carol-Ann's room,' I told her.

'But why did she want to be all by herself at the top of the house?'

'Well, she certainly didn't want to be near her barbarian brothers who teased and played tricks, she wanted to avoid parental control and have her privacy.'

Elizabeth's voice came down the stairwell: 'There seems to be some kind of a ladder outside the back window.'

'That's supposed to be a fire escape. Carol-Ann insisted that my father put it in.'

'She was concerned about her safety at the top of the house, in case of fire?'

'Allegedly.'

Elizabeth hurried back down the stairs and studied me, eyes narrowed. 'What was the real reason?'

'Visitors.'

A crafty smile appeared. 'Male visitors…at night?'

'More likely late afternoon.'

'Did they make any noise?'

'I don't remember.'

Elizabeth's concentration was intense. 'Yes, you do!'

'They didn't make too much noise.'

'Grandpa didn't hear it?'

'He was at work and Momma was probably in the kitchen.'

Elizabeth chewed her lip, reflectively. 'You and Uncle Jason agreed not to tell on her?'

'We couldn't. She had too much dirt to dish out on us; besides, we liked to listen.'

'You're terrible, Dad!'

'I know. Don't let on to your aunt that you know anything about this.'

'I won't but it's funny: I never could have guessed she would do something like that.'

'Probably, it was her musical-artistic passion playing out.'

There was a wistful look on Elizabeth's face. I sensed that Jo had come up behind me and was listening.

'Dad, I think I'd like to have Aunt C's old room.'

The voice behind me said, 'You can have it, Elizabeth, but the ladder's going to go.'

'I probably wouldn't use it except if there were a fire, Momma.'

'It's the *probably* I worry about. No ladder!'"

I stand up from my seat and look out the window. "So, the ladder was attached there, Uncle Bertie?"

He joins me at the window to look where I'm pointing. "I think so. I had a hell of a time getting it down. Then Jo objected to having a loose ladder in the garden. 'Some thief will use it when we're away,' she said. So, I cut it up and we used it for firewood one winter—much to Elizabeth's disgust."

I laugh. "What else did you find in your exploration of the house?"

"My old room was at the back of the house, with a shared bathroom between Jason and me, and overlooking our tiny garden, then overgrown. There was just the one large window in front of which there was the old metal desk and folding chair. The single, metal-frame bed, covered with a faded blue spread, was against one wall and opposite was a battle-scarred pine chest of drawers. Judging by the condition of these objects, I must have been pretty hard on furniture, or at least I had no respect for its decorative aspects. But when I looked into the closet, there was a counterpoint: a hand-made balsa wood and tissue paper model of a Phantom F4 fighter bomber; there was also a smaller-scale model of a B52 bomber. These two weapons of war in the air, and others like them, were hung from my ceiling with great pride. I remember looking up from my bed in twilight at these aircraft and imagining the sorties they were on. The air fleet gently floating from my ceiling was, I now recall, the highlight for any visitors, be they mine or my parents' friends.

Frequently I was accused of having no artistic bent, but that F4, in particular, was an artistic creation, evocative and beautiful; dozens of individual ribs and splines were cut from sheets of balsa wood and glued together to form a skeleton. Coloured tissue paper, precisely cut, was pasted to the skeleton, painted with water, allowed to dry and shrink in place, forming the skin to which the insignia decals were pasted.

Nowadays, models of F4's – they're still available – cost about fifteen pounds, and they consist of die-cast plastic parts that can be snapped together and decorated in half an hour. The model of sixty years ago cost about one pound and consisted of three or four thin, printed sheets of balsa, a marked membrane of tissue paper, a folio of decals, and instructions, which I could lovingly assemble into a replica F4 in three or four days.

What does that tell us about progress? We've gotten richer (fifteen pounds versus one pound): that's good. We care more about quick results (1/2 hour vs 3 days) than we do about craftsmanship and the joy of creation: that's bad. What's more, I worry where we will be in another sixty years, when I will not be around? Will model-making and the creative joy of craftsmanship disappear entirely? Those long hours I spent making models weren't frivolous. I learnt patience, discipline, hand-eye skills, and the ability to follow instructions, as well as some self-reliance.

Jo found me sitting on my old bed, looking out the window with a supersonic F4 on the bed beside me. 'Bertie, I thought you were going to think about how these two back bedrooms could work as guest rooms.'

'Sorry, Jo, I got side-tracked.'

She picked up the F4 and examined it. 'You made this?' I gave an affirmative nod. 'It's beautiful, Bertie.' She hefted it. 'So light!'

'Gross weight four ounces. The real thing weighs about thirty tons.'

'How old were you?'

'About fourteen.'

'And you dreamt of flying in it?'

'Particularly of taking it through the sound barrier.'

She sat down beside me. 'Is moving back into this old house going to be a little too much for you, Bertie?'

I looked around the room. Above the chest of drawers was a photo of Ray Illingworth as a batsman in front of the wicket. 'You know he's still alive,' I said, 'Must be thirty years older than me.'

'This room must be full of memories for you.'

'I've been indulging myself in them.'

'All good?'

'A mixture. I was remembering when my father sent me in here, took off his belt, and threatened to give me a *good thrashing* if I ever did that again.'

'What was *that*?'

'I think it had to do with returning short-change from a shopping trip.'

'So that's why you are so careful with money.'

I took a deep breath and released it. 'To answer your question, Jo, I guess that if we moved in here without renovation, I would waste a lot of time reminiscing, and some would give me new insights about myself, but most of it would be useless self-indulgence. So, I'm ready to renovate. Besides, it makes sense to renovate the house, if we're making modifications to me.' She looked at me blankly. 'You know, I'm to become a patriarch.'

She pursed her lips in agreement. 'So, you're ready to do both?'

'Well,' I said, 'I figure you'll take care of the house renovation while I pretend to be a patriarch.'

'OK. Now then, how do we make this room into a guest room?'

'Repaint, all new furniture. Curtains for the window. Carpeting. Reproductions of pastoral scenes. A proper radiator cover, and air conditioning. This room is hot as blazes in summer.'"

"What does this house symbolise for you, Uncle Bertie?" I ask.

He tilts his head from side to side, considering. "It symbolises family – an imperfect family, with some hard times and some good times."

"What could have made it better?"

"It would have been better if my father had been more like my mother."

"What do you mean?" I ask.

"I mean that he should have been more spiritual, and not so terrified of death. As I think about him now, I realise that fear made him tough and distant sometimes."

"But you say that he was your hero."

He chews his lower lip carefully. "He was my hero because he was tough, he knew a lot of things, and he would explain things to me, and play football. But sometimes he would be angry or moody and impatient, and I just waited until my hero came back."

"That must have been difficult for you," I say.

"It hurt, and I felt very sad, because I couldn't figure out what I had done wrong to make him angry with me, until the next time he put me up on his shoulders, and I knew that my hero still loved me."

"Could you go to your mother when your father was in an angry mood?"

"Yes, but she was closer to Jason and Carol-Ann. She assumed that I was Papa's favourite. If I had tried to approach her – I don't know how – she would not have understood."

I am thinking, and my granduncle is waiting for me.

"Uncle Bertie, you said that Aunt Jo promised to help you become the family leader or patriarch. In light of what you've said about your childhood family, what does that suggest to you about your new assignment?"

He gives a derisive snort. "I guess it means that I've had to try to become a model parent."

"Nonsense," I say. "If I understood the problems in your childhood family, they were about sharing feelings openly, spontaneously, even lovingly, and that's about establishing a <u>culture</u>, not about being a model parent."

Chapter 4
Moving House

"After Jo and I agreed we'd buy the house," Uncle Bertie says, "I had to talk to Michael about making it happen.

Michael's office was a small estate agency next to an old-age charity shop. At the top of the broad window it said *Smithson's*, on either side of which was the logo: a red heart with a green door in it – a little cheesy, but memorable. The rest of the window was taken up with photos and selling points of homes, flats and apartments.

Peering through the photos, I could see that Mike and Abby were at their desks. I had to admit that they both work unusually long hours, open six days a week (except Sunday) from 8:30 until the last client left about 7. More remarkable was that they had two small children, a boy of three, who spent much of the day in a nursery and a four-month-old girl who was breastfeeding and resides in a little crib by the file cabinets. The arrangement reminded me of third-world families, but Mike said the business now had a solid position in the community and was starting to make money, which contradicted my fear that Mike would have an indolent life on benefits.

As a rebellious middle child, he showed little interest in or aptitude for school; he was a ringleader in a sports-mad, girl-crazy flock of ne'er-do-wells – until he was arrested by police for possession of an illegal knife, and was sent to a youth detention centre, where his grandmother went to see him, after I refused to bail him out. For reasons I've never understood, the two of them were like a falconer and her hawk. My mother's report of that meeting was brief: 'I poured some of the devil's own brimstone on him.' Shortly thereafter, Mike joined the army and survived two tours in Afghanistan. He came home a sober adult, and met Abigale, who, as a tough young girl trying to sever relations with an abusive family, was working in a corner chicken shop. Pretty she may be, but a chicken she is not: she would have Michael, but not until he got a full-time, paying job. Grandma sent him to get an estate agent's diploma, figuring he could put his quick social skills, and hunger for a deal to good use. He graduated and joined one on the big chains, where he was soon a prize salesman, wearing two-hundred-pound suits and driving a new Fiat 500. He understood the income side of the business pretty well, and, over time, calculated the cost side, allowing the assurance of good results on his own – with the right partner: Abby.

On entry, I saw that Mike and Abby were both busy; Mike with a customer seated opposite him, and Abby on the telephone while she nursed little Heather. I was somewhat startled when Heather was deftly moved to the opposite breast, exposing the one vacated, while the telephone conversation continued. Well, I guess modern mothers had a sense of pride and security in the intimacy of motherhood that previous generations could not match. For a male of a previous generation, it took some getting used to.

Heather seemed to have fallen asleep. Abby finished her conversation, got to her feet and hands the child to me. 'She needs burping, Bertie.'

'OK.' I took the small, warm bundle in my arms, and gazed at the placid face. Who does she resemble? I hadn't the faintest notion. To me, she seemed like a contented, healthy baby, pink cheeks and tiny mouth, who, for some remote reason, felt very dear. I moved her into a vertical position on one shoulder and patted her gently on the back. Some moments later, there was a surprisingly loud guttural sound in my ear. As she wriggled gently in my arms, I reflected on my youngest grandchild. What did she have ahead of her in life, in a world that changes so frequently and inexorably that it is difficult to know what path one is on, let alone the path one should be on, how and why. Would I change places with her, if I could start a life again in a new uncertain world? Tempting as the idea of reincarnation is sometimes, I was not so certain. What I was certain of was that I would not recommend that she step into my old shoes, though, undoubtedly, she would do a better job with the time I had remaining.

The customer had moved from Mike's to Abby's desk where they were looking at apartments on her computer screen.

'Hi, come and sit, Dad. Sorry to hold you up.'

Heather and I sat, and for the next hour, my son and I decided a financial plan that embraced the sale of one house and the purchase of another, including the contingency of a bridging loan, and the inheritance cash for Carol-Ann and Jason.

'There we have it,' he said.

'You think it's doable?'

'Yes, of course.'

As I leant back in my chair, with the warmth of his child against my chest, there was a temperate sense of satisfaction. 'Michael, I just want you to know how proud of you I am. From a teenage tearaway, you have somehow morphed into a competent businessman, father and husband. I don't know how you did it, but I know I didn't help you very much.'

'Thanks, Dad. I got some help from Grammy.' His face clouded with pain. 'I'm sorry about her funeral.'

'What do you mean, son?'

'I mean if anybody owed her a farewell tribute, it was me, but I just couldn't bring myself to volunteer, and then Elizabeth delivered that special poem.'

There was a trace of envy of Elizabeth – her easy competence – in his voice. 'I wouldn't worry about it, Mike, I'm sure Grammy knows how much you loved her and appreciated her help.'

'I hope so, but I can't help feeling I let her down, and I've let myself down by…not making myself volunteer.'

Was he talking about courage? Here was a man who fought his way through live fire-fights with the Taliban. I studied his face which had taken on a mask of shame and regret.

'Oh, I didn't realise. Maybe I could have helped you, Mike.'

'It's strange, in a way, Dad. I love talking to customers and people one-on-one. But groups—big groups—no way. I was asked to give a talk at the Chamber of Commerce. Couldn't do it.'

I said, 'Well, you might consider taking a course in public speaking—to add to your other diplomas."

I stood up, the baby still in my arms, and I realised that Abby has gone out.

'You can put her in the crib, Dad. Abby will be back in a little while. She's just showing an apartment to that customer.'"

"So, you got to know Heather at a very early age, Uncle Bertie. I didn't really know her until she was old enough to sit in a highchair at Sunday lunch."

His face clouds with sadness and he gazes out the window. "Yes, she looked up at me with those big grey eyes as if to say, 'thank you very much, Grandpa.'"

Uncle Bertie continues, "The concept of consecrating a home was not entirely foreign to me. Jo had insisted on it for our newly wed apartment, our young-children apartment, the starter home, and our recently vacated place. In retrospect, those four consecrations, certainly did us no harm, and, in fact, those homes bravely kept our loving but challenged family intact. Whether the consecrations brought us closer to the God who was asked to bless those abodes was, for me, less certain.

On each occasion, the parish priest came on a Saturday, performed the blessing and stayed for lunch. Because of different parishes and transfers, we never had the same priest twice. This time, it is Father Anthony, a grizzled, sun-burnt priest who was built like one of my bricklayers: massive neck, shoulders, biceps and thighs. One might think twice about confessing to him out of fear that he might issue a corporal punishment as well as a demand for Hail Marys and Our Fathers. From my occasional observations of him during mass, he was attuned to the hidden weaknesses of his parishioners without whitewash, a sympathetic, no-nonsense priest, for whom a reformed sinner is closer to his heart than a charitable virgin of seventy.

'Where shall we begin the blessing, Josephine?' he asked on his arrival.

Jo led him to the entrance, where above the newly repainted front door, Jo had asked me to hang a small wooden crucifix, with a tiny golden halo atop the head of Jesus. 'I think here, Father,' she said, with a vague gesture toward the crucifix.

Each of us, Jo, Elizabeth and I, were given a sheet with the various prayers and our expected responses. The boys were exempted from the ceremony this time as they had their own homes.

At the entrance, Father Anthony said a prayer for the house and its residents, and, retrieving a small aspergillum from his breast pocket, sprinkled the door and the hall with holy water. This procedure was repeated briefly in each room of the house.

Over lunch, Jo and Father Anthony discussed parish news, and he told us of a sabbatical he had taken the previous year in Monterrey, Mexico.

'Mexico must be quite interesting, Father,' I said.

'Apart from the language and the economy, it's not so different from London: the services are much the same. People have very similar problems, though poverty and crime are more apparent.'

'But, Father,' I ventured, 'I think I've read that the churches in Latin America still have vestiges of the native Aztec and Inca religions.'

Father Anthony considered me for a moment as if trying to divine my agenda. 'Well, in the villages, one does find some Catholic saints, in miniature, dressed in ceremonial native garb.'

'Did you find any instances of what we would think of as superstition,' I persisted, 'entering into the mass?'

He set his fork down and then caught my eye. 'This is not a superstition, Albert, and it may surprise you: there's more belief in the use of exorcism.'

'You mean driving out the devil?'

'Yes. People from distant villages come to the cathedral with a family member or friend whom they're convinced is possessed.'

'Who deals with these people, Father?'

'Because I've had the Vatican training, I dealt with most of them. My Spanish is pretty good, and there were native translators for dialect.'

'So, how many exorcisms did you perform, Father?'

'In the six months I was there, Albert: none.' He noted my surprise and continued: 'Of the dozen cases I saw, none of them had the classic symptoms of possession: knowledge of strange languages or of distant events, great physical strength, and violent aversion to God, the Virgin, the cross, or the name of Jesus.'

'Have you ever dealt with a genuine case of possession?' I asked.

'No, but I know of priests who have done so. It's quite a rare phenomenon—something like one in five thousand cases are genuine.' He paused to butter a slice of bread. 'The aspect of this which I find most interesting is the presence of Satan in the consciousness of so many religious people in Latin America.' I must have looked puzzled. 'For many religious Europeans,' he continued, 'there is only the loving influence of God, Jesus, the Virgin and the saints, but the Church teaches that there is also the influence of evil: Satan.'

'I suppose,' I ventured, 'that people don't want to be caught up in Satan worship.'

'But, you see, it's not a case of Satan worship. Jesus referred to Satan as *the ruler of the world* and Jesus refused to be tempted by him, so Satan is not a god to be worshipped, though some sinners seem to have done so.'

'Father, I've been aware of the idea of a devil since I was a child, but I've never paid him any attention.'

He smiled. 'I believe you told me, Albert, during our first meeting, that you are uncertain about the existence of God.' He paused momentarily to take in my reluctant gesture of assent. 'In your situation, Albert, I would pay particular attention to what may be causing events in the world. Ask yourself, was it a good or was it a bad influence that caused that particular event to happen? If you keep score for a while, I believe you'll understand why Jesus called Satan *the ruler of the world.*'

'That sounds rather pessimistic,' I suggested.

'On the contrary, I think it allows us to allocate blame for many tragedies to Satan, and thanks to God for His blessings.'

'So, you're saying that God is the source of good events, and Satan, the ruler of the world is responsible for the bad events.'

'Something like that.' He considered me for a moment. 'I understand your friends call you *Bertie.* May I do likewise?'

'By all means, Father.'

There was a pause while desert was being served.

'If I understand you right, Father, you believe that Satan is a quite active in the world, not passive.'

'He's stirring up trouble all the time, everywhere.'

'How does he do that, Father?'

There was a brief snort of mirth. 'I don't know, Bertie, but I have a theory that the human subconscious is like an accessible mailbox, and that unbeknown to us, we receive lots of mail, most of which goes unread into the junk folder, but some, because of the way we have set our filters, ends up in our inbox. The inbox messages come to our attention, and we either press delete, or we read the message.'

'Sounds like a pretty advanced system,' I said with a smile.

'You understand that I'm just making an analogy, but we've all heard of people who make catastrophic decisions which they afterwards attribute to *hearing a voice.*'

'You mean like some of those crazy shootings in the States.'

'Or even suicides.'

'You seem to get along rather well with Father Anthony, Bertie,' Jo said.

'I like the fellow. He reminds me of my bricklayers—look tough and sloppy but they're very good at what they do. In that sense, he's not just a priest, he's

36

also an ordinary bloke. He may know all the theory, but he also knows how things really are…I was surprised he doesn't consider me a complete write-off and he says some interesting things.'

'Like what?'

'That the devil is the ruler of the world. I never heard that before.'

She turned to face me. 'Do you think it's true?'

'I don't know, Jo. I suppose I may get a notion if I evaluate events, as he suggested.'

Jo was looking into the middle distance, a smile of accomplishment on her face. 'It's what I call a *forensic examination*—you're always trying to decide who did it.'"

"Uncle Bertie, you've been specific about your discussion with Father Anthony, and as Jo said, you seem to have established a good relationship with him. I wonder what that says about your agnosticism."

He adjusts himself in the chair defensively. "Well, I'm still an agnostic, but at least I can talk about it with somebody who sees my point of view. I mean, I know about the devil, he's just around the corner, but God is a pretty remote concept."

Chapter 5
Seaford

"I thought this morning," Uncle Bertie begins, "we could talk about Seaford and the Smithson summer holidays."

I nod my agreement.

He sits back in his chair and reflects for a moment. "'You don't need a new bathing suit, Elizabeth,' Jo said, 'you've got two perfectly good ones and we'll only be gone two weeks.'

My daughter had a handful of bikinis gripped in each fist. She protested, 'Momma! This one is faded.' She shook her right fist. 'And this one is way too tight!'

Jo sighed patiently. 'Let's see you in the one that you say is too tight.'

A surly Elizabeth reappeared in two strips of blue and green cloth causing Rubenesque bulges where none were needed.

Jo pressed her brow in disapproving puzzlement. 'Oh dear, how did that happen?'

'I think it shrunk.'

'You mean it "shrank".'

'Whatever,' she snarled, 'It makes me look awful.'

'OK. You can get a new suit. Not too revealing, please, and not too flashy.'

This annual beachwear inventory was a sure sign that our traditional summer holiday was approaching, when the entire Smithson family had been going to Seaford on the south coast of East Sussex for over half a century. As you know, Sarah, we liked Seaford because of the economy of rentals, its clean beach, its modest position as a small and unprepossessing town with rail services from London, and half a dozen rainy day attractions.

My earliest memory of Seaford is of a three-bedroom flat that suited us until Carol-Ann and I were married. We then rented a six-bedroom house, which served until our children were married. When Mother died and I had to take over managing the arrangements, which, by then had become quite cramped, I had to look into other options.

I remember putting on a slideshow at a Sunday lunch during which I presented three alternatives. Jo and I had a preference for an old hostel with eight bedrooms, a large bunkroom, and an enormous family room on the ground floor. The other alternatives involved two separate houses. The presentation took fifteen minutes; the discussion consumed a frustrating hour and a half. Costs, location and space were questioned in excruciating detail. The objections to the old hostel were: there were only four bathrooms, it was a fifteen-minute walk to the pebble beach, and the bunk room was not gender separate. Jo could see that I was getting hot under the collar. She managed to interrupt the discussion for a good five minutes while she spilt a glass of wine, cleaned up the spill, refilled the glass, and handed it to me with her *don't worry* smile.

I said, 'Ladies and gentlemen, the main purpose of this holiday is to be together as a family. That isn't possible with either of the two-house alternatives. I can ask the owner if he is willing to partition the bunk room in half: one side for the boys; the other side for girls.'

Jason said, 'Can you also ask him to put in an outside shower? That way we don't have to queue for the indoor showers when we return from the beach.'

There were shouts of 'great idea', and surprisingly, Raymond said, 'I call for the motion.'

A motion for the rental of the hostel passed with two abstentions.

From that experience, I learnt that running a large family can be very frustrating and it requires patience as well as a lot of thought and personal effort. But it was not without reward: Jason, Abigale and Anne all personally thanked me for the selection. I began to think that being a patriarch was something like being a scout leader: sometimes you had to deal with juveniles.

'Brucie and Margaret are going to join us on Sunday, the third of August,' Carol-Ann informed me on the phone.

'That's a day later than the rest of us who are taking the train on Saturday morning,' I said.

'Apparently the council needs Margaret to attend a departmental meeting on Saturday.'

'That's ridiculous!' I said. 'When does the council ever do anything on Saturday? Why doesn't Brucie come with us, and Margaret can join us after the summit meeting?'

I already knew the answer: 'Because Brucie wants to come with Margaret.'

Aged nearly forty, Brucie – never 'Bruce' – was Raymond's much-adored and only child from his first marriage. Aside from Margaret, the battle-axe, there was also a ten-year-old son, Nelson, who was named for our great war hero, but, like his father, was a sweet, conformist taking his direction from Margaret. It must be a wearisome existence for Margaret to form suitable ideas and opinions for three people, but she worked in the council's benefits department whose charter was to know what everyone needs to get by. Brucie, by contrast, worked as a scheduler in the highway department; his role being, presumably, to plan the beginning and the end of innumerable road works.

'Carol-Ann,' I said, 'this is not right. The dates of our holiday have been known for months. No one is indispensable at the Council—particularly on a Saturday. But Margaret and Brucie are on the rota to serve Saturday's dinner. That means that Jo and I will have to do Saturday, and Margaret and Brucie will take our first turn, so they will have to do an extra dinner. OK?'

'I'll tell them.'

When Brucie and company did arrive, trudging down the beach, carrying an umbrella, towels, buckets, shovels and a mesh sack full of beach toys, they found the rest of us in good spirits: the sea was cool, but moderately clean, it hadn't rained, and the sun had appeared for a good five hours.

Raymond leapt to his feet to embrace his son, greet his daughter-in-law with a remote kiss, and offering to take Nelson to get an ice cream cone.

Margaret approached me to protest their extra dinner assignment. I said, quite audibly, with a definite shrug, 'Sorry, Margaret, your last-minute change in plans screwed up the rota. Were you expecting that someone else would do the extra duty?'

Margaret turned, grumbling to herself, and began to lay out towels and beach toys.

Aunt Jo brought us some tea, and I considered my own experiences of the beach. Seaford was a special opportunity to really know other individual family members, their values, their characters, their troubles, and best of all, to achieve that strange and wonderful feeling of mutual connectedness. I could remember a long conversation I had with Aunt Cathy, the ambulance driver, Uncle Bertie's older daughter-in-law, that led to a special fondness for her. She described wonderful and heart-breaking experiences on her ambulance in a way that made me feel as if I were there with her, her little inner *I'm going to help you* promise when she first saw each patient. Her feelings of agonised failure at a tragic death and her joy at an unexpected recovery. I marvelled at her ability to ride that emotional rollercoaster every working day, but I began to understand her as an extraordinary, yet quite ordinary, caring person who radiates peace and self-effacement. In fact, I am closer to her than to my mother.

And as a child growing up in the Seaford environment with about a dozen assorted cousins was a great gift. Yes, we saw each other every Sunday, but this was like a hundred Sundays all at once. You were free! Free of nearly all parental supervision. Free to invent new entertainments (some of which are subsequently sanctioned). Free to test old friendships and grow new ones. Free to shed childish foibles and try on more mature behaviours. Freedom, in short, to learn and grow. The bonds we formed flying kites, building sandcastles, laughing and teasing were incredibly strong."

Uncle Bertie takes a first sip of his tea. "After dinner, Margaret asked her husband, 'Are you going to try out your new jogging shoes tomorrow, Brucie?'

Brucie hung his head in confession. 'I've put on about eight kilos, so she's got me exercising.'

'Never believed in it myself,' I said, tongue in cheek, 'I understand it can be quite hard on the knees.'

Brucie ignored that. 'Do you suppose that one of your kids would like to run with me, Uncle Bertie?'

'We are a pretty lazy lot, Brucie, but it doesn't hurt to ask.'

There was a low-stakes poker game in progress with Raymond and four of the young husbands, apart from Brucie. That was generating enough noise that Carol-Ann intervened to urge less raucousness so as not to wake the grandchildren. Jason and Gerri had invited Elizabeth to accompany them to the local disco, of which I have no knowledge, but Jason assured us that the 'music and lighting are awesome'. Surely, this would necessitate a visit at least every other night, with Elizabeth's motivation doubtless being the investigation of young male attendees. Brucie and Margaret were playing Scrabble, at which Margaret was a semi-professional. Which left me with my wife, my sister and four young married women, who seemed to have formed a huddle about child management. I opted into the poker game, hoping to escape my persistent bad luck.

Breakfast was chaotic with adult family members appearing, drowsily, in pyjamas, to brew coffee and to make sure the children were actually eating cereal rather than last night's chocolate cake.

By nine-thirty, the first hardy souls began the trek to the beach, burdened with towels, an umbrella, an assortment of small implements for moving sand, and a bag containing suntan cream, snacks, extra shorts, shirts and underwear, and an ad hoc first aid kit. The early expedition staked out a Smithson claim to about two dozen square metres of prime pebble beach just above the highwater mark. The small children congregated in shallow water or on wet sand and co-operated on various short-term construction projects and experiment with the floatation or water-carrying properties of various toys.

Abigale and Jennifer, Carol-Ann's daughter-in-law, had arranged themselves sitting on adjacent towels, in the sun, with a view down the beach to the children's activity zone, while being within easy reach of their babies, who were sleeping under a shared umbrella. In this arrangement, they could continue their conversation of the previous evening on paediatric maladies, their diagnosis and remedies.

I noticed that Elizabeth, clad in her new blue and green wonder, was standing in knee-deep water speaking to a clean-shaven young man wearing miniscule black shorts over his enviably dark tan. I decided to join the grandchildren at the water's edge to better appraise the situation, and I was soon engaged in a tidal suppression project under your direction, Sarah, with physical labour supplied by JoJo and your brother, Robbie. With the background murmur and chatter from the beach, it was difficult to catch more than phrases, but I nonetheless drew several conclusions. The young man, who is quite good-looking, had spent his summer at Seaford, probably working as a waiter. He seemed to be quite attracted to Elizabeth (he was not a complete dolt). Elizabeth was interested, but not sufficiently certain as to introduce him to some of the family horde. They strolled off down the beach.

As Elizabeth meandered off, Brucie appeared, clad in a newly minted runner's outfit consisting of T-shirt crammed with logos, black shorts, white socks and black trainers. He was jogging in place to demonstrate his eagerness. 'Anybody ready for a run?'

'Where are you going, Brucie?' his wife asked.

'I don't know. Eastbourne and back,' he smirked. As it was over ten kilometres to Eastbourne, this would be a very ambitious first jog. My suspicion was confirmed when he headed off in the opposite direction, toward Newhaven, about three kilometres away.

During a conversation with my son Jeffrey, I surveyed the beach to my right for a glimpse of the returning Brucie, thinking that he would arrive soon, sweaty and triumphant. I noticed that Raymond was standing, shading his eyes, and trying to make out the arrival of his son.

I spotted his garish T-shirt two hundred metres away, not running, but weaving as if he had just won a drinking contest. There was a shout from Raymond, who was now running. Brucie had fallen. I said something to Jeff, got up and started running, too. There was already a small crowd around the fallen figure, some kneeling, trying to talk to Brucie, some standing, observing and perplexed.

'Brucie, what's the matter?' Raymond shouted as we approach.

One of the kneeling men said, 'He's not talking. Something's wrong.'

'I'm his father!' Raymond flung himself down beside his son, grasped his shoulders, and shook him. 'Brucie, Brucie, what's wrong, son?'

Brucie's face was a waxy pale white. His eyes were open, but unmoving and his body position was awkward, suggesting sudden collapse. This was not a good situation, and no one seemed to be in charge.

'Brucie, Brucie, speak to me!'

'He needs CPR!' a bystander said, and, kneeling next to Brucie, he repositioned the fallen man's head, checked his mouth and began to rapidly press down hard on his chest.

'An ambulance is on the way!' someone shouted.

A woman at his head said, 'He has no pulse!'

My hands were clasped together in horror. *No pulse! How can that be?* I crowded a little closer and watched, paralysed with foreboding.

Frequently, the first aider closed Brucie's nose, and delivered a lungful of breath, mouth-to-mouth. 'His airway is clear. He's not choking.'

The crowd around increased. Nelson squeezed through, dropping at his father's feet. 'Dad, what's wrong? Dad?'

Margaret appeared, observed her husband and the CPR with great agitation, trembling as if in a seizure, and clasping her hands to her compressed lips. She spoke to Raymond, who answered in non-sequitur phrases from a stooped position, his eyes fixed on his son's face.

Nelson was clinging to his mother and wailing miserably. An approaching siren could be heard.

Oh, my God! This is really serious. I was trembling.

The observers were no longer focused on the patient and the first aider; now they were exchanging looks, glancing at their watches and whispering briefly. Brucie fell over five minutes ago.

Two paramedics in day-glow orange pressed though the crowd. They questioned the first aider while examining Brucie. They cut away the sweaty T-shirt, attached electrodes to Brucie's chest, and delivered an audible and visible shock with no apparent result. One of the ambulance crew stepped outside the wall of spectators, and spoke into a mobile device. Several more siren-equipped vehicles arrived. A grey-haired woman wearing a hastily donned orange jacket hurried from a blue-light vehicle to the crowd. Her jacket said 'Doctor'. She talked to the ambulance crew and examined Brucie. Getting back to her feet, she looked around. 'Next of kin?'

Margaret's face looked to have aged ten years, and still shaking, she said, 'I am his wife. Are you going to take him to the hospital?'

'I'm sorry, madam, there's nothing we can do.' Margaret opened her mouth to object. 'I'm afraid he's dead.'

Dead! My God he's dead! But he was alive ten minutes ago. I stifled a convulsive shudder.

Margaret and Nelson collapsed together, moaning and wailing, to the pebbles. Raymond, a desperate figure, tried unsuccessfully to raise her, and protested, 'But, doctor, he just went for a short jog.'

'I'm sorry, sir. His heart has failed completely.'

Confused and numb, we picked up our things and trekked back to the house. We needed the shelter of privacy and family. The weeping trio of Raymond, Margaret and Nelson, clinging together for mutual support as they shuffled silently up the beach, resembled beaten soldiers stumbling through the Russian snow of 1812.

The house was quiet out of deference and respect. Carol-Ann, ministering to the stricken trio in a corner of the parlour, had assumed the duty of sharing their torment. Now and then, an adult Wishert (Anne, James, Albert or Jennifer) would join the ministry, but four of their children, sensing that an incomprehensible and terrible tragedy had occurred, required solace and loving attention.

Jo and I ventured in from time to time, sharing a hug and the sorrow with Raymond, Margaret and Nelson. We brought them cups of tea and listened to their agony.

My children and grandchildren were shadows in the background, whispering among themselves: questions, observations of the happening, and theories as to the cause. We, the adults, were shocked, saddened and confused by an event – death – in which we would play the lead role, and which we all had relegated to the distant future, but which has suddenly and forcibly overtaken one of us."

"Uncle Bertie, Brucie's death must have been a tremendous jolt to you."

He takes a deep breath and releases it. "I was a grieving wreck, Sarah. My heart was racing, my limbs didn't function well, I hurt all over, and I felt sure that my heart, too, would stop. I felt sorry for Raymond, seeing his son die in front of him. Poor Raymond, what a dreadful tragedy. And for Nelson, seeing his father – whom he adored – die on the beach as if he had just been shot. It was terrible! But also for me. I just <u>knew</u> that my nightmare was going to come true, and it would be sooner rather than later. Look at Brucie, dying at age thirty-nine!"

We take a break from the loft. Uncle Bertie and I leave the house and walk slowly around King George's Park until he feels able to continue.

"A day later, in the privacy of our bedroom, Jo and I could talk, share our impressions and feelings. Jo was sitting next to me on the bed. There were circles of exhaustion under her eyes and her arms hung limply at her sides. 'He must have had something wrong—a thrombosis, maybe—which caused a stroke or which blocked his heart. I wonder if he knew.'

There was a knock at the door.

'Come in.'

Elizabeth asked, 'Is it all right if I go out?'

Her mother smiled. 'Where are you going, sweetheart?'

'I was going to the disco to meet Robert, but I thought I'd better ask.'

'Is he the guy you were talking to on the beach yesterday?' I asked.

'Yeah.'

'You want to tell us about him?'

Elizabeth sat somewhat rigidly in a nearby chair. 'Well, he's really nice—and fit. He's a desk clerk at the hotel, and he's taking a course in hotel management so he can get a better position. He lives in Eastbourne, and he has a motorcycle. His family moved here from Somalia when he was six.'

'So, he's a Somali?' I tried to restrain my reflexive bias.

'Yes.'

'You understand, Elizabeth,' I said, 'that he's from a different culture with different values?' I know this comment will not go down well and that I'll be accused of racism, but I feel that it has to be said. At the very least, we know nothing of this man's background.

Elizabeth raised one shoulder nonchalantly. 'He seems like a regular guy.'

Jo was ready to issue instructions. 'OK, sweetheart, I want you back here by midnight, in this room, by midnight, waking me up. And, under no circumstances are you to get on that motorcycle with Robert if he's had anything to drink. You understand?'

'Yes, Mum.'

'Have a good time.'

I certainly agreed with Jo's instructions, and I recognised that enlarging on my point about race and culture would be counterproductive. I'd just be told she had to be free to explore and make her own mistakes.

The post-mortem report was issued. 'The patient died of a sudden rupture of an aortic aneurism.' It went on to say that the patient's GP had prescribed medication for high blood pressure, but there was no record of the prescription having been filled. The report concluded: *Since most cases of aortic aneurism are hereditary, next of kin should be examined for this condition.*

'I didn't know he had high blood pressure,' Margaret protested. 'If I had known, I would have insisted he take medication. But it was difficult to get Brucie to go to the doctor. He was afraid of doctors and didn't like medication.'

For several days, there was uncertainty about where the funeral service would be held.

Margaret explained, 'Raymond and Miriam, Ray's first wife, never had any interest in church so Brucie thought that church is optional at extra cost. I managed to drag him with Nelson and me some Sundays, but I doubt he would have wanted a religious funeral.'

Raymond suggested, 'Look, we're all here, except for his mother and a few friends. We can have a simple remembrance service at the crematorium and invite his mother and anyone else who wants to attend.'

'What about his ashes?' Carol-Ann asked.

'He always liked to come here,' Margaret said, 'Can we just scatter them on the beach?'

Raymond said, 'Mmm, I don't think so, but it's perfectly OK to scatter them at sea.'

So, Albert made the arrangements for a remembrance service at the crematorium. We can all attend. Raymond and Margaret prepared a joint eulogy. Nelson was being tutored by Raymond to read *Crossing the Bar* by Alfred Lord Tennyson, though he broke down in the middle of it. There was a guitarist who led us through some of the songs that Brucie liked, including *Wind Beneath My Wings*.

Miriam (whom I'd never seen before) showed up at the crematorium, wearing a black silk dress, black patent leather heels, and a sculptured hat with a severe veil. It was as if she was repenting her maternal sins as much as grieving the loss of her son.

Albert also took charge of hiring a small boat and captain, leaving from Newhaven, that would take a few of us out into the Channel where Brucie's ashes would be scattered.

I was afraid that Albert would have to do the job alone, but as it turned out, Raymond, Margaret and a curious Nelson went along.

As we settled into our seats on the train back to London, I said to Jo, 'You remember that Father Anthony recommended I should decide whether a good or bad influence was behind major events?' She turned to give me her full attention. 'Certainly, the death of Brucie is a major event, but I can't characterise it other than that it was a bad event.'

'It's not the event itself that you should evaluate, Bertie, it's the <u>cause</u>.'

'OK, that was the aneurism.'

'No, it didn't <u>cause</u> the event."

'That was the rupture."

'Which was caused by?'

'High blood pressure.'

'Which could have been prevented by?'

'Taking the medication he was told to take.' I paused. 'But what caused him not to take the medication?' Jo offered no reply, just a mysterious smile. 'Come on, Jo. So what?'

Relenting, she said, 'At the point where you've traced it back through human hands as far as it can go, you have to ask yourself, what other superhuman influence could have been involved?'

'You mean like God and the devil?' There was no reply. 'You mean that one of them influenced Brucie not to take the pills?' I considered this. 'I don't think that God would do that, but I don't see how the devil would do it.'

'Do you remember what Father Anthony said about mailboxes in the mind?'"

As it seem important, I decide to pursue this further with Uncle Bertie. "After your conversation with Jo, what was your view of Father Anthony's theory?"

"Sarah, I was hung up on this mailboxes part. So much depends on that."

I say, "But weren't mailboxes just metaphors for a means of spiritual communication?"

"I get that, but how would it work?"

You see what I mean about him being literal-minded?

"Uncle Bertie, have you ever had a thought enter your mind that you thought *where did that come from?*"

"Yes, of course."

"OK. Well, I think what Father Anthony is saying is that some of those stray messages could come from God or the devil, and I'll bet that Aunt Jo would say that, as a forensic expert, she can tell who sent what."

There is a giggle from my granduncle. "You're right, Sarah. She certainly knows who sent what."

"Anything more about Brucie when you got back home?"

"My old friend Dr Ramsden left me a voicemail expressing his condolences for Brucie's death and asking me to make an appointment. When I saw him, he asked how I was coping with the death; I said I was all right.

'Bertie, if you're feeling down, I can give you a prescription.'

'I think I'm OK, Mort.'

'Well, you just let me know.' He turned to look at his screen. 'I see that your nephew died of a ruptured aortic aneurism. Perhaps we ought to have you tested.'

'He wasn't a blood relation, Mort.'

'We've seen a lot of these conditions, Bertie. Maybe we're just more aware of it. Wouldn't do any harm to have an ultrasound exam. Shall I arrange it?'

Of course, I was worried when I went to the hospital for the ultrasound. They put that grease on your chest to make sure the reflected sound can get back to the probe. I was sweating so much that the grease is redundant. The technician started the exam, frowning. He moved the probe around, clicking buttons, looking closely at the screen, shaking his head. My heart was going at least twice the normal rate. *He's found something really wrong.*

Finally, he pushed back his chair, and said, 'Everything's normal, Mr Smithson.'

I went home and had a double Scotch.

Between our sessions, I looked through my notes. I was curious about this Professor fellow; something about him didn't seem quite right. Why would people address a retired bus driver as Professor, and why would he want to come to my great grandmother's funeral?"

"Uncle Bertie, you mentioned the Professor for the first time when you met him at your mother's funeral. Did you encounter him frequently after that?"

"I wouldn't say it was frequently, but he and I seemed to like the same coffee shop near the station; they have wonderful fresh brioches. I would be reading the *Guardian* and I would hear, 'Hello, Bertie. Mind if I join you?'

'Of course, Professor, have a seat.'

He looked me over. 'I read about the tragic death of your family member.'

(He was referring to Brucie.) 'Yes, his death was a shock.'

'How is his missus coping?'

'As well as can be expected, I suppose.'

'I haven't seen her lately, but she's the one who normally handles my benefit claims. I understand there's a son.'

'Yes, that would be Nelson; he's ten.'

He seemed to be studying the traffic moving along Garratt Lane. 'I've seen that missis wears a cross, so I assume that she is a religious soul.'

'Yes, I think she is.'

'That's very fortunate. She can show Nelson the faith that he will need.'

'Sorry, Professor, but I would have thought he'll need other things more than faith: a good education, for example.'

"You're right, Bertie, a good education is essential, but one needs the counterpart of knowledge to be a whole person.'

'You're saying that faith is the counterpart of knowledge?'

'Yes. If we say that knowledge is the understanding of the concrete and tangible—the aspects of life which can be proven, or which we accept as proven, faith is the understanding of the unproven aspects of life: spirituality, religion and theories of life. In effect, it is the fourth dimension of being alive.'

I pushed my coffee mug away. 'Well, I grew up without having any faith.'

'I believe you're speaking about religious faith, Bertie, but I feel confident that you had many unproven theories about life, and you probably thought about ghosts and such.'

'Yes, I remember wondering whether my grandfather could still communicate with me after he passed away.' I retrieved the empty coffee mug and signalled to the waitress.

'Would you like a cup of coffee, Professor?

'Yes, I would.'

I stirred the fresh cup of coffee, watching the latte art in the milk blend away. 'But why do you think faith is so important for the boy, Professor?'

'Because it helps him live in that fourth dimension which is otherwise unknown. For example, Nelson probably understands some of the medical science of what happened to his father, but he will be wondering where his father is now, and, like you, whether there can be any communication, and how death will eventually affect him.'

'But how can he ever know any of that, Professor?' I protested.

'Ah, and that's my point, Bertie: one can't know it, but one can reach an understanding which fills a need which all of us have. One can feel whole, though not completely secure.'

'But, Professor, that understanding you mention is likely to change over time.'

'Yes, of course. In that sense, our faith challenges us and we challenge our faith. That's what I call living in the fourth dimension.'

I took a long sip of my coffee, enjoying its robustness and the conversation. 'In your experience, Professor, how does this process of challenging one's faith work?'

He leant back in his chair. 'I think one has to start with the concept that faith is necessary, rather than optional. One has to ask oneself the existential questions: what's the point of the universe? Of life? Of me? Is there a god? What kind? One then has to sift through the possible answers, based on what one has read, or observed, or learnt, and choose a panoply of answers with which one is comfortable. And, as you suggest, the comfortable answer is organic because it is subject to the pushing and shoving we all experience in real life.'

'But you're suggesting that in the religious dimension, for example, people should not necessarily follow the script of the church.'

'What are we, Bertie? Seven billion people on the world? I can assure you that there are seven billion different versions of religion.'

We lapsed into chit chat. He told me that just a year ago, he received an MBE for community and local services. As only about two thousand people are awarded MBEs every year, I wondered how this retired bus driver, this black gadabout on a state pension, made it into the two thousand.

'Well,' he said, 'The council recommended me for it.' He paused savouring the recollection. 'I went to Buckingham Palace and the Queen pinned it on me and said, Thank you!'

As I was walking home, I was trying to figure out how much of this MBE story was true, and I decided to call my son, Jeff, who was then an elected Council representative.

'I checked, Dad. It wasn't last year. We recommended George Jenkins for an MBE some years ago and he received it.'

I reflected. *After all, the Professor is an older man, and seeing the Queen is a memorable event. Maybe so memorable that it seems more recent.*"

Chapter 6
Elizabeth

Uncle Bertie says, "I don't know whether what I'm about to tell you should actually appear in my memoir."

"Well, we can always decide to take it out later; why don't you go ahead?"

"OK, well, about a year after Brucie's death, Elizabeth plopped herself down on the living room sofa, and I would be unreservedly happy about her arrival were it not for several alarm bells. First, the phone call asking if we would be home on Saturday afternoon as she thought she might 'stop by'. Second, the fact that Warwick was still in session, and her trips home had always coincided with term breaks. And third, the nervous chewing of the inside of her cheek. Had she been caught using one of those online paper writing resources?

'Umm.' She looked from Jo to me and back again. 'I thought I ought to tell you that I'm pregnant.'

I had been runover by a heavy lorry: bump, thump, whump! I felt as if I was doing bodily summersaults; my brain definitely was. Jo's face recovered from teeth bared in horror to a mask of forced patience. 'Is Robert, the boy from Seaford, the father, dear?' Elizabeth inclined her head in assent, biting her inner lip. 'You're planning to get married?'

Elizabeth stiffened and looked away. 'I dumped him.'

Jo stared at her daughter, wide-eyed. 'You dumped him?'

'Yes…I couldn't…'

'You couldn't what?'

Tears slowly rolled down Elizabeth's cheeks. 'I couldn't stand him anymore.'

'What happened, Elizabeth?' I asked.

She looked at me, took a deep breath and looked away. 'When I told him I was pregnant, he said, that's your problem. We had a terrible argument and I left.'

'You were at Seaford?'

'I wish I'd never gone to Seaford.'

There was an uncomfortable pause. Softly, Jo inquired, 'Are you sure you're pregnant, dear?'

'Yes, Mum. I bought two different kits.'

Jo said, 'But, Elizabeth, we talked about this.'

'Yes, I know, Mum.' She took another deep breath and looked at the ceiling. 'I didn't want to start on the pill until I was sure.' She took in the puzzled look on her mother's face. 'Mom, I didn't want to be on the pill as a reason for saying *Yes*.' Another pause. 'He came up to Warwick three or four times to see me, and he stayed at the student union; they have strict gender segregation. He kept asking me to come to Seaford.' She bit her lip trying to control a surge of misery. 'He was so nice and so much fun.' Weeping overtook her. 'I really liked him.' She wiped her cheek. 'So, I said *yes*, and I knew he had access to rooms at the hotel.' She looked from one of us to the other. 'So, I started on the pills.'

Jo groaned audibly. 'I should have told you it takes time for the pills to take effect.'

'And I guess you felt there was no need for the morning after pill,' I added, lamely; then: 'Elizabeth, I think you did the right thing to dump him.'

Jo was counting on her fingers. 'So, it'll be November.'

Elizabeth said, 'It would be the twenty-first of October. I've seen the GP.'

'You'll probably have to skip some of next year's classes,' Jo added.

'Guess I would if I had the baby.'

'What do you mean *if*?' Jo demanded. 'Of course you're going to have the baby.'

'Mum, I came here to talk about it.'

'What's to talk about?'

'Do you both think I should have the baby?' Elizabeth looked from one to the other of us.

'Jo,' I said, 'I'm sorry but I'm not going to agree with you. I think she should have an abortion.'

'No!' Jo exploded. 'I'm not going to tell my daughter to kill her unborn child!'

I paused long enough to allow the silence to take hold, knowing that my wife had, without warning, been forced to defend a position to which she was morally committed, but about which, as a woman, she may have doubts.

Defensively, I said: 'I'm not proposing to tell Elizabeth to do anything.'

'You just said she should have an abortion.'

'That's only my opinion. She should make her own decision.'

'Based on what?' Jo demanded.

'Based on a number of things. First of all, there will be no father until in a few years' time some princely fellow comes along and is willing to take on Elizabeth and her toddler.'

'She can always put the baby up for adoption,' Jo said.

'Is that what you want to do, Elizabeth?' I asked.

'Not really.'

I turned back to Jo. 'Her social life will be affected; she'll be the odd one out with her friends. And there's her university life which will be altered: as a minimum, she'll graduate in a different class from her friends, if she's able to keep up with her studies. To me, it seems like the pro-life position, at the end of the day, punishes a woman for her perceived indiscretion. But, in Elizabeth's case, she is a totally innocent victim.'

'Are you finished?' Jo asked sourly.

'No. There's one other point that I think Elizabeth should consider: her life will be entirely different from what she may be hoping for if she doesn't give the baby up for adoption.'

'What do you mean, Dad?'

'Well, if for example, you wanted to go to medical school, it will be a lot more difficult having a baby that needs your attention.'

Jo said, 'But that's where you and I come in, Bertie.'

'I accept that, but we're just grandparents, not the mother.'

Jo had turned quiet, her arms folded across her chest, she looked into the distance. She looked at Elizabeth and then away. Her lips were compressed and turn down in the corners. Elizabeth moved close to her. 'Mum, I know how you feel about this, and I know this is important to you.' She managed to take one of her mother's hands in both of hers. 'But I'm not ready to be a mother, and I really don't want a child right now. It would really set me back. Try to understand, Mum,' she pleaded, as tears slid down her cheeks.

Jo looked at her daughter, whose tear-stained face was turned to her. Jo casted a heavy sigh, and slowly wrapped her arms around Elizabeth, pulling her close. "I'm so sorry this has happened to you, sweetheart.' Slowly, Elizabeth drew back. They gazed at each other. Jo closed her eyes and nodded.

'Dad, I have to ask a favour of you.' A hesitant Elizabeth had reached me on my mobile phone at work.

'Of course, sweetheart, what is it?' I ducked into the office portacabin to get away from the construction noise.

'Do you think you could come with me when I have the procedure?'

Perhaps I should have expected this. Jo would be the go-to resource for any medical handholding, but under the circumstances, that would be a very big ask. 'OK, Elizabeth. Where and when?'

'Well, that's part of the problem, Dad. I can't find a centre with a waiting time less than six weeks. That will make ten and waiting that long really upsets me: a lot of development has already happened by then. The GP says I can go private, and if I do, Birmingham can take me next Thursday at 1 pm.'

'I'm not sure if our insurance will cover it. If not, do you know what the fee is?'

'The surgical procedure under local is six-fifteen; the medical—that's the abortion pill—is four-eighty. I want the surgical; the pill causes a lot of bleeding.'

'OK, sweetheart, why don't you sign up for Thursday in Birmingham? One way or the other, we'll sort out the finances.' There was a sigh of relief at the other end. 'Shall I pick you up at your hall?'

'Yes, please.'

'I guess you won't be staying overnight.'

'No. They say I can leave by about five.'

'OK.'

'Dad.' A long pause. 'What are you going to tell Mum?'

'I don't have to tell her anything. She knows you're going to have the procedure, and I'm sure she'd rather not know any of the details.'

Once inside, the abortion clinic in Birmingham could be mistaken for any local NHS clinic, except that is one of several dozen run by a private company and funded, in part, by the NHS. There were two receptionists, busy but empathetic uniformed clinical staff stride purposely down the gleaming corridors. Nervous women in street clothing sat, fidgeting or trying to read, in the soothing-music and live-plant-enhanced waiting area. There was one other male visitor, an acne-marked boy of about twenty sitting alongside his girlfriend and doubtless wishing he had been swallowed up by the earth.

Elizabeth, thankfully explaining that I was her father, went through a consultation with a nurse, to confirm data from an earlier visit, and identify current health issues. There was a brief chat with a doctor, intended to pacify jangled nerves. Elizabeth donned one of those horrible surgical gowns which normally put your bum on display, though she had tied the rear curtain closed.

I sat, facing my daughter, holding her hand and watching her face, taking no interest in the several clinicians, who were busy between her elevated and spread legs and whose focus was thankfully hidden. She was resolutely staring at the ceiling, biting her lip, occasionally allowing a tear to slide down her cheek, and responding to the clinicians in monosyllables. I didn't take in the meaning of what she was saying, and I avoided speculating on the function of a softly buzzing motor and various video monitors.

We were done. Elizabeth was offered a bed and some tea; she declined the former, and sat, chewing on her cheek.

'How are you feeling, Elizabeth?'

'OK. A little shaky. It really wasn't too bad. Right now, there's only a little pain, and I'm packed solid.'

There was little occasion to talk on the way back to Warwick. What could I say that was neither obvious nor trivial? You are a brave girl? or do you have classes tomorrow?

Elizabeth dozed most of the trip.

At her student hall, she hugged me. 'Thanks, Dad. You made the horrible tolerable.'

She looked around, as if to be sure she wasn't being observed. 'You won't tell, will you? Anyone?'

'No, of course not.'

I left the radio silent on the way home from Warwick. There seemed to be much thinking to be dealt with. Was I complicit in the murder of one of my grandchildren?

No, I didn't think so. It was still an embryo, not even a foetus, much less a child. There was no way it could have survived on its own. Did an embryo have a right to survive at the expense of the woman who did not want it?

But suppose it was destined to be prime minister, a great movie star or a billionaire?

But, perhaps, a junkie, a thief or a murderer.

Life is a lottery.

Elizabeth's pregnancy and its resolution were certainly a major event, and they seemed to merit a classification of 'bad'. What was the ultimate cause? It wasn't the misuse of birth control pills; that was proximate. Ultimately, it was the duplicitous lust of a 'friend'; and, taking the matter out of human hands? If there's a god, it wasn't He – more like the devil to wheedle and coax the kind of behaviour that causes chaos.

But I want to know – if I may – what is the position of God, if He is there, on this abrasive subject: abortion? Would He be the author of the Church's position that it is a cardinal sin? (Although I noticed that the Church in Ireland did not take a public position on the referendum there). Or would She give women the right to choose? Though perhaps there is an important rider on that statutory choice: that She has the final judgement in each case.

Jo was tossing the sautéed potatoes in a pan for our late supper. 'How is Elizabeth?'

'She's relieved and recovering. She'll be fine. She wants no external discussion of the subject—even with her brothers.'

'I know.' She took my hands and looked into my face. 'Thank you, Bertie.'"

"How does Elizabeth feel about it now, Uncle Bertie?"

"I don't know, Sarah; she's never mentioned it since."

"Do you suppose there are moments when she wonders what that child would have been like?"

"Possibly, but I feel sure she believes she made the right choice at the time." He pauses for a moment gazing into the distance. "Now that she's married and has two daughters, perhaps she does reflect on the child that wasn't – much as she would if there were a miscarriage."

"Do you want me to leave this episode in your memoir, Uncle Bertie?"

"Yes, leave it in for now, Sarah."

Chapter 7
Children's Books

"Uncle Bertie, I remember one Sunday, before we started our partnership, you were complaining about how hard it was to write children's books. You had a copy of a book you had written, and you weren't happy."

There is a sour expression on his face. "Yeah. I had two hundred of the darn things printed. Cost me nine hundred and thirty-six pounds. I sold seven on Amazon, gave away about two dozen, and none of the local bookstores wanted it. I was going to be a J K Rowling, except for younger kids. My plan was to have a beach house in Barbados, and I was going to take one family in a weekly rotation along with Jo and me all winter. Seven copies! Do you know what my royalties were on those seven copies?" I shake my head. "Eighty-seven pence each, which totals six pounds nine. I mean, how humiliating is that?" He glares at the floor and rubs the back of his neck. "W W Smith and Waterfields said they buy only as directed by head office. There was one independent in the area – Jonathan Mason's – up on King's Road. It was quite a big shop, and their website said they carry some books by local authors. I thought *if I could get this big one to buy, maybe the other independents in London would follow.* So, I went there on a Tuesday afternoon, and asked to see Mr Mason. He was a scholarly looking fellow, older than me, with a halo of grey hair, and half-moon reading glasses. He looked me over, took my book – I had a dozen copies with me – and started reading it, page by page for five minutes. He looked at the back cover for a while and then at me. 'Nice little book, Mr Smithson,' he said, 'but it's nothing special.'

I bit my lip to cover up my hurt feelings. 'What do you mean?'

'Have you looked at the books on my children's shelves?'

'No, but I've looked at most of the children's books at the Wandsworth Library.'

He probably read my defensiveness, because he said, 'Let me be specific…if I may?'

I swallowed hard and nodded.

'The best children's books have two elements. They start out with a problem or something that's bad, or threatens to be bad, and they end with something good or much better than it was. And, in between, the hero or the heroine does something magic or wonderful to make it happen. Your book is an inventory of interesting animals. Nothing really happens. The pictures are well enough. Bright colours, smiling animals, but children want to know something about the character's personality. Is your giraffe clever or sneaky? I can't tell.'

So, when you saw me that Sunday, Sarah, I was pretty crushed."

"I remember. But you've never told me why you decided to try children's books. If I'd had to guess, I'd have said you would start up a recruitment firm for the construction industry, or you'd be a sales agent for some whizzy new construction tool. I know you were unhappy with your job at the big AtoZ superstore, but was it the boss, or your hours, or what?"

He leans back, contemplating the ceiling. "After a while at AtoZ, the work was no longer challenging. I thought I'd be advising craftsmen about creative approaches to interesting projects, but ninety percent of my clients were dummies with questions like, 'Where can I find a screwdriver for a screw that has a funny cross in the top?'"

I laugh. "Even I know that's a Phillips head in the hand tools aisle."

"Exactly, and I must have sold two hundred of them. At the same time, I was contemplating my death in gloomy, nihilistic terms: the absolute end of my existence. This threw gloom over what were already boring work hours. Convinced that I needed an important, challenging 'project' which make enjoyable use of the few talents I have, I was struggling to identify the opportunity. So, what are my talents?" He pauses to consider.

I respond. "Well, you like making things from model airplanes to high-rise apartment buildings. I think you're good at practical, rather than theoretical undertakings. You tend to like and trust people, without being an extravert."

"Thank you, Sarah, and taking a couple of English courses on the Open University, at Jo's urging, had convinced me that I can express myself. My kids had their endeavours, but neither politics, nor selling real estate, nor becoming a news presenter would suit me. My siblings are (or were) artistically inclined: Carol-Ann toward music and drama and Jason loved art. But as a practical man,

I knew that the performing arts weren't for me. Jo had an inclination toward art in her modelling, but at age fifty-eight, she has lost interest, even though there is a demand for a woman who looks a very desirable fifty. She has focused on literary editing, has written a book on the subject, and has managed to attract some bestselling authors. Lately, she has become a ghost writer for famous people with a story to tell.

When we talked about my dilemma, she said perhaps I should consider writing. 'No,' I said, 'I don't think I have the patience to write a couple of hundred pages.'

'How about children's books, they're shorter? Besides you're very good with kids and you have a prolific imagination.'

So, I spent hours in the children's section of the Wandsworth Public Library, which offered a vast cornucopia of tots to teens' literature. Some of the books were so captivating that, involuntarily, I started again at the beginning. Some I set aside before I got halfway through. I began to realise that the ones with the gold award stickers in the covers had some characteristics in common. The text was magical: hovering just beyond the edge of reality while being assertively real; exciting the imagination while appealing to the ordinary; full of change and action without losing focus; presenting adult ideas in ways that were comfortable, yet stretch young inquiring minds. *This is wonderful, just up my street, I can do this!* When I got home, I wrote a story, which I thought was quite fetching, about a little girl who went to the zoo for the first time and how she got home that night and dreamt that the animals all tell her secrets. I thought about the illustrations: in vivid primary colours, lacking the details that adults would want but allowing the childish mind space to complete the mental picture; suggesting a particular feeling; and somehow totally congruent with the sense of the text. I began to search the internet, looking at the work of many illustrators. How to find my Leonardo?"

I convulse with laughter. "You didn't think of me, Uncle Bertie?"

"No, Sarah, I was fixated on finding a practising, professional artist."

"But I am a practising, professional artist. I get paid a few quid now and then for something I do."

He holds up his hands in surrender. "So, I found this artist, Dominic Caruso, based in Los Angeles. He was about thirty, probably a hippy type, specialising in child portraits, dogs and cats—not too expensive—and I liked his style, mostly acrylic paintings, but some pastels. I worked out a deal that he would get a lump sum of one thousand dollars for ten paintings of Cathy with her animals."

I wince at the price of one hundred dollars per painting. *No wonder the animals are expressionless, poor beasts!*

"Then I did a mock-up on my PC and sent it out to seventeen children's book publishers." He sighs heavily and continues, "I got four *No Thank Yous*, but I heard nothing from most of them. Then one day, I noticed a pop-up advert for a co-operative publishing company, which said, 'Authors wanted. We will publish your book.' So, I sent them my mock-up and they sent me a contract – for nine hundred and thirty-six pounds. But that wasn't all. I had to pay for the editing – three hundred and seventh-five pounds. The very picky editor who worked on my manuscript said that I should have a comprehensive edit to improve the book's sales. The comprehensive edit was going to cost me eight hundred and fifty pounds and premium press release to everybody that mattered would cost another three fifty. I said 'No' to both." He folds his arms and stares dolefully at the carpet. "So that's where I was when you saw me that Sunday. Defeated and dejected."

"You had a dream that wasn't coming true, and I was completing a master's degree in fine arts at Coventry. I had been studying and dabbling in art since I was a toddler. I had a lot of dreams of what I would do after I graduated – doing family portraits in charcoal, being elected to the Royal Society, moving to Nepal, taking a native lover and producing breath-taking watercolours, being recognised for my sombre portraits of famous people. But I never dreamt of being an illustrator of children's books. If I had, I would have thought *poor Sarah! She'll jump over a very low hurdle and look at her bank account. Almost empty.* What I didn't realise when I was dreaming up dreams is that illustrating books for children isn't really about painting, it's about children – their imagination, their innocence, their playfulness. When I'd somehow produced a painting that captures those dimensions, I, too, began to feel like a child, and to be on the same wavelength as children was so much better than being an adult – I can't tell you how good it feels."

Uncle Bertie looks at me thoughtfully. "Is that because you missed out on some of your childhood?"

I take a deep breath. "Probably. As you know, I'm the oldest child, and as such, was expected to grow up quickly. My parents are both emotionally repressive, in the sense that of course they have emotions, but they grew up thinking it's a weakness to display them…and I had my own emotional turmoil. So now, when we were on an event with children and there was a flock of them around me behaving as if I'm Superchild, I just want to scoop them up and hug them all."

"I know what you mean, and I like children – particularly girls – Elizabeth, you, JoJo and especially Heather. You don't have some of the faults that boys and I have – being aggressive and impatient, being thoughtless. How does the rhyme go? 'Sugar and spice and everything nice. That's what little girls are made of.'"

"Don't count on it in my case, Uncle Bertie."

"And that was the end of our conversation that Sunday," he says.

"No, it wasn't. I said, 'I think you need another illustrator.'"

"I don't remember that. On Monday, Jo said that you wanted to speak to me on the phone and I thought *I'm fond of this kooky, diminutive, just-turned-twenty-three grandniece, but I'm afraid this may have something to do with her father's rumoured affair*."

"I asked if you had forgotten me, and you said, 'You're the crazy Monopoly player who always wins at Seaford.' So, I asked what else I did."

"I remembered you did a wonderful charcoal portrait of your mother. Then, suddenly, I recalled: *you're the one who's getting her master's degree in art at Coventry*."

"So, we talked about the uncertainty that both of us had about working together and I said, 'The thing about me, Uncle Bertie, is that I'm very flexible. I'd like to be a painter, but you have to live in a garret on bread and water, painting twenty-three and half hours a day for five years, before you make enough for your first Big Mac. As a teacher, I can share a two-room flat, work twelve hours, six days, and live on spaghetti and meatballs. But as a children's book illustrator, I can have a flat in Mayfair, a chauffeured Rolls and dinner at Scotts.' I was exaggerating a bit to cheer you up."

He laughs at the recollection of it. "I liked your enthusiasm, Sarah, but I thought *it's probably more like the garret scenario*. Then, you suggested, 'Let's try it for a while. I'll finish my studies at Coventry, and you keep telling single women how to fix their toilet, but on the QT, we'll be working on that blockbuster first book.'"

"I think Jo interceded at that point," he says. "She told me, 'Look, Bertie, if you and Sarah are going to work together, it ought to be on an equal basis.'

'Of course,' I said, not having the least idea what she had in mind.

'You ought to take a good course in creative writing,' she said.

'Aw, come on, Jo. That'll just slow things down. Besides, I've taken that big course in English Literature on the Open University.'

'Not good enough,' she commanded, accompanied by head thrown back and set jaw. 'Sarah has been studying art since she was three. She has real artistic skill. You can read and write the Queen's English well. That's not good enough. You've got to learn the craft of writing literature.'

So, somewhat reluctantly, I trudged off to my first class at the City Academy, beginning at six-thirty pm and finishing at nine, and running twice a week for twelve weeks. I thought *I don't really need this.* The small classroom was on the first floor of an Academy building with a view of the back of a large high-rise. There was a table with eight chairs, and six other students, one other man and five women, ranging in age from late teens to early forties. Even the instructor, Jon Baker, who turned out to be a freelance drama scriptwriter for the BBC, lanky as a pole vaulter, blonde with a ponytail, was my sons' age. Jon took firm command, using the whiteboard to outline or demonstrate a particular skill or issue. Then he assigned a piece of writing to the class: 'Describe a particular argument with your best friend from both points of view. Twenty minutes.' We each read aloud what we had written, and each piece was discussed, with suggestions and praise from Jon. 'Bertie, you've said that Richard was *frustrated.* Think how you can show that he was frustrated, rather than telling us.' At first, it was hard work, but by week four, I was starting to enjoy it, and I was absolutely beaming when I showed my certificate, signed by Jon, to Jo and you."

"I was sitting cross-legged on the library floor, piles of children's books strewn randomly about me, while I teetered uncomfortably on a child's chair, my knees bumped up against my chin. Nearby, a small group of children – probably classmates – tried to make sense of the two of us. Why was this old man reading our books? He didn't have any kids with him – just this girl wearing torn jeans and a faded college sweatshirt, and she was also too old for our books. *Maybe one of them has learning disabilities.*

I turned to one of the curious spectators. 'Hi, what's your name?'

'Sam.'

'Sam, my name is Sarah, and I'm an artist. Could you come over here a minute? I have a question for you.' Sam, who must be about eight, trotted over and stood obediently by my shoulder. 'Now, don't bother to read the words, just look at this picture. What does the picture tell you about what's happening in the story?'

Sam tilted his head from side to side. 'It's about dragons. There's a good dragon and a bad dragon, and a little boy who's trying to ride the good dragon.'

'Would you like to be the little boy in the picture, riding the dragon?'

Sam shook his head. 'No. I don't like the good dragon. He's too sneaky.'

'So, you don't trust the good dragon?'

I turned to you, Uncle Bertie. 'I think Sam is right. The expression on the face of this dragon is a bit sneaky: slit eyes, forked tongue out the side of his mouth. The text is fine, but it's undone by the dragon's face.'

I tossed the book to you. 'But I think there is a problem with the text, Sarah. The good and bad dragons are introduced together. It should have started with the good, allow him to build his credentials, and then introduce the bad.'

We spent most of the next hour with critics Sam, Lily, Christy and Rob learning what works, or not, with young readers.

As we left the library, I asked, 'What are you considering for our first story, Uncle Bertie?'

You took a deep breath and said, 'I am thinking of a little boy about eight who has a magic blankie—you know, one of those nearly worn-out cotton crib blankets—that he takes to bed with him every night. What's magic about this blankie is that during the night, it will carry him anywhere he wants to go at any point in the past. Then, one night, he wants to go and find out where and how vaccines were first made. He has just had a smallpox vaccination. He finds himself in the Gloucestershire home of Edward Jenner, the English doctor who is considered the inventor of modern immunisation, in 1794. It tells the story of using cowpox in a vaccine against deadly smallpox. And when he gets to Jenner's House, Jenner explains, in simple terms, what he did. There is some urgency and tension at the beginning about finding a weapon against smallpox, and then triumph when Jennings succeeds, and lots of other vaccines are developed.'

'It occurred to me, Uncle Bertie,' I say, 'that this could be the first in a series of great inventions.'"

"A day of two later, there was an email attachment from you, Sarah, a water colour painting of a little boy in his blue and white pyjamas, with a blissful expression, partially wrapped in a green blankie, flying through the clouds with a sliver of moon in the background. In fact, I have it framed over there. Enchanting!

It took me three months to write about three thousand words of text which had survived many editorial passes through you and Jo and several critical readings with Abigale and her children.

You produced a dozen captivating water colours, which, if laid out on a table in order, bring the story to life almost on their own: Jenner's home in Berkeley, Gloucestershire; Jenner with a patient; Robbie, the hero, talking to Jenner; the milkmaid having her hand scraped; James being inoculated, Blossom the cow, and modern inoculations.

I was absolutely hooked in spite of having no hint that this venture would please anyone but you, our families and me; in fact, it may attract the scorn of critics, and be counted as a waste of our time and expense. But I remember that beautiful fighter-bomber, and this is a far more valuable creation. I put in my notice at AtoZ; the work there has become a distraction.

You sent the illustrated manuscript to your instructor, Jon, to be edited. He suggested some sequence changes, additional showing of emotion, language changes ('remember: this book is for eight to twelve-year-olds'), corrections of punctuation errors, and the addition of two more illustrations."

Uncle Bertie sighs and shakes his head at this point in our recollections. I remind him of his assertion that women are less impatient than men and that this trait will pay off.

Corrections and changes made; we send querying emails off to fifteen literary agents in the UK who handle children's books. Jon helped us write a tempting email to which we attach a synopsis, our bios and a sample illustration.

Chapter 8
Coming Out

"Uncle Bertie, could you tell me now how you found out that I'm gay?"

"Well, I came home from work late one afternoon, and Jo said, 'Sit down, Bertie.' She handed me a rather substantial whiskey on the rocks, and her face showed a preview of unwelcome news. She waited until I had taken my first sip. 'Sarah is gay.'

'What? She's gay? Who told you that? I don't believe it!'

'Her mum told me that Sarah is living with a woman.'

'Well, they're probably just sharing an apartment.'

Jo regarded me patiently. 'To be interested and polite, I asked Anne about the woman. She's a senior nurse—a ward sister—at St. George's. She's in her mid-thirties—Sarah's a young twenty-three, and I said, She's quite a bit older than Sarah; how did they meet? Anne said, Sarah was a bit evasive about that, and I gather that they're more than just friends.'

'That's hardly convincing proof, Jo.'

'Perhaps not, but do you expect Anne to make a public announcement: *My daughter is gay?* Besides, I thought you ought to know.'

'You're right. Thanks, Jo.'

I decided to finish the whiskey, not because I was in shock, as Jo might have expected, but because I was thrown off course and needed to analyse the situation. It's not that I tend to think of gay people as lesser human beings: they're just different and I don't understand what makes them different. For me, you are one hundred percent normal female – a little crazy perhaps, but bright, creative and confident. I had no notions about your sex life: it was decidedly none of my business, but nonetheless I felt confident that you were being pursued by one or more young men, and I had a vague expectation that you would suddenly announce an engagement to a man I would eventually meet. Those assumptions were now shattered.

It's not that I blame you, Sarah, for my dashed assumptions. You are what you are. OK, maybe you could have given me a hint, but how would that have worked? You may be facing many dimensions of uncertainty: of your own identity and intentions, of me and my reactions, of the affections of this senior nurse, of your family and friends, and the world at large.

In the current situation, with both of us on tenterhooks, you and I cannot communicate as freely and spontaneously as we have in the past. There will be this little ice island between us, a massive berg below.

I decided that I must talk with you."

"I'm glad you did, Uncle Bertie. It's true that I had a lot of things on my mind, and I was very worried it could end up spoiling what was otherwise an excellent chemistry between us that dates back to when I was three.

So, there we were in the library to do some research, and you suddenly said, 'Sarah, is there something personal you've been meaning to tell me?'

I remember that moment so well, Uncle Bertie. I felt like I had turned to frozen stone. *What if he decides he can't work with a gay woman? What will happen to our lovely project?* I managed to stammer, 'What do you mean, Uncle Bertie?'

I'm sure you realised that I was petrified, because you smiled, patted my knee and said, 'Do you suppose that Mexican place across the street can make a cup of tea?'

'I don't know. I've never been in there.'

'Neither has anyone else. Let's give it a try.'

The Guaca Mole smelt of chilli peppers and garlic. There was one waitress in jeans and a dirty apron arranging napkins stuffed with utensils. A cook, singing a romantic Latin song along with the radio, was stirring what must be a pot of chilli con carne. We ordered tea from the disappointed waitress, but how could she expect us to order Mexican cerveza and nachos at ten thirty in the morning?

I sat on the edge of my chair, head bowed over, took frequent sips of tea, put the cup down, picked it up again. I was afraid the tea would make my nerves even more electrified.

Your voice was soothing. 'It's OK, Sarah, don't worry. I just thought we ought to talk.'

I looked at you for the first time and I could see no judgement, only concern – for me! 'I'm so sorry, Uncle Bertie. I just didn't know how you would take it.'

'Tell me about her, Sarah. What would I particularly like about her?'

At that moment, I felt my rock turn to jelly, and my eyes overflowed with tears of relief. My shoulders relaxed, and I took a deep breath. I told you she's a wise person – especially about people and that you'd like her. 'She can talk to anyone and make them feel comfortable.'

'A bit like the Queen,' you said.

'Yes, but she's not regal at all, she's very casual, but organised.'

'One has to be organised to be a ward sister.'

'Unlike artists,' I said, 'I'm a terrible housekeeper. She's also a good cook.'

You took a moment to reflect. 'It seems to me that you complement each other's approach to humanity in different ways: you with your art, appealing to the aesthetic sense and emotions; and…what's her name?'

'Jenny.'

'Jenny appeals through her physical and psychological care. You know, Sarah, it occurred to me at that moment that you, for all your brashness, feel the need for tender, loving care—perhaps because your mother, Anne, tends to be rather distant emotionally.'

I tilted my head to one side. 'She just makes me feel good about myself—something that's sometimes hard for me.'

'How did you meet her?'

I considered this question and chewed my cheek. 'We met at a speed dating event for women put on by a pub on the south bank.'

'A gay pub?'

'Yes.'

'Forgive my curiosity, Sarah, but I could never have guessed that you are gay.'

I gave a rueful chuckle. 'I did a good job of hiding it, even from myself.'

'It must be very difficult to come out.'

'Oh, Uncle Bertie, it's absolute torture! You feel so vulnerable and you're terrified of being rejected by your family and childhood friends. There's something inside you that keeps saying *No, don't admit it!* In Jenny's case, she actually lived with a man for several months.'

'When did you realise that you're gay?'

'I don't think there's ever a *when*, Uncle Bertie. It's like a butterfly coming out of its cocoon in very slow, painful motion. When I was about eleven, I noticed that I wasn't as interested in boys as other girls were, but I thought *it'll probably happen later.* When I was fourteen, I had some boyfriends, but I didn't want to kiss any of them, and I thought *well, they're just not attractive enough.* Then, when I was seventeen, I kissed one of my girlfriends, who was repulsed, and I vowed to myself never to do that again. At university, I fell in with some girls, who, I'm pretty sure were gay, but they never pushed me, and I kept my distance.'

'But something must have happened that destroyed the uncertainty.'

I hesitated. 'Do you really want to know, Uncle Bertie?'

He paused for a moment. 'I would like to understand what you've been through: it's all unfamiliar territory for me. But only if you're comfortable in telling me, with the understanding that I'm not a gossip.'

'Well, there was one girl in that university group that I really liked. She's very bright, cheerful, and an excellent tennis player. There was a party at her place. I had way too much to drink, and I woke up in bed with her. We spent two days together, mostly talking, and she convinced me; but by that time, I didn't need much convincing.'

'What happened?'

'She broke my heart.'

We gazed at each other.

'Thank you, Sarah, for being so honest with me. I feel now that I know a very special Sarah, and I hope you'll continue to be my business partner.'

I shook my head in wonder. 'I love you, Uncle Bertie.' I folded and unfolded my hands. 'Jenny is my lover, but you're still my mate and business partner.'

I feel the tears well up in my eyes. "That was such a good conversation, Uncle Bertie. It means so much to me! It just vaporised my terror of coming out."

"We still had another hurdle to get over: the rest of the family."

"When Jo and I were having a beer and a glass of wine before dinner, I mentioned, in generalities, my conversation with you.

Jo said: 'I think you're to be congratulated for taking the situation so constructively. I was afraid you'd disapprove.'

'If it weren't for the high regard I have for Sarah, I might have been. What I still don't understand, though, is why it happens to some people, but not to others.

The church, for example, doesn't approve of homosexuality, which implies that God doesn't approve, but as an all-powerful God, how can He let it happen?'

Jo said: 'The church used to believe that people had a choice, but I think they're beginning to give that idea up.'

'I'm starting to think it's not a choice people have,' I said."

"I can confirm to you, Uncle Bertie, it's not a choice I've made."

He says, "For me, it's become one of God's mysteries.'

I gaze out the window for a moment. "If you're right that God has the eventual ownership, therefore He must approve, and it would be unwise for us humans to disapprove."

He smiles. "I agree."

"To continue the thought about the rest of the family," he says, "I was sitting in the kitchen talking to Carol-Ann. I was trying to figure out how much she knows about you, not wanting to blurt out anything that might give Santa Claus away. Carol-Ann started creeping up on the subject, slowly, eyes averted, by bringing up you and Jenny and your household, and how it was arranged, etcetera. I started nodding as if I knew all that and more. Our eyes met. 'I know,' I said. 'We had a talk.'

'Oh, good. Have you met Jenny?'

'No, I haven't. Have you?' I said.

'No. Anne has. Says she's very nice.'

I said, 'Should we invite her to Sunday lunch?' The onus was on Carol-Ann and me to formalise a decision about Sarah: should she be added into the Smithson family roster, and be included in the Sunday lunches and the Seaford holidays? You hadn't approached your mother, Anne, about the possibility of inclusion, nor was there a hint of marriage, but you two were living together. Since Sarah is Carol-Ann's granddaughter's partner, I thought Carol-Ann should have a say.

'No, not yet, Bertie.'

I paused for a moment, considering. 'No. Carol-Ann, I think, in fairness, Jenny should be included. After all, Jason and Gerri weren't married, and it seems to me we should have an enlightened view of homosexuality. I think it's best for all concerned if we include her in the family as soon as possible.'

No announcement had been made that Sarah was gay and had a female partner, but that information had seeped out, perhaps through osmosis, and the family was ready to assess this woman: was she worthy of you, our Sarah?"

"Oh my God, I was so nervous about this, when Mum told me that Jenny was invited next Sunday. I kept thinking *what if somebody says something awful?* And I had trouble sleeping. Jenny, bless her heart, kept saying, 'Don't worry, Sarah, I'm sure it'll be fine.'"

"On Sunday, as it turns out," Uncle Bertie continues, "there was no evidence of homophobia in the family, but a considerable level of curiosity about this different woman, Jenny.

Jenny presented herself very nicely in a white cashmere sweater, a black pearl necklace, ankle-length, navy-blue skirt, and brown, patent-leather pumps with black satin bows: she is most certainly a reserved lady, who has prematurely greying hair, and an attractive, gentle smile. Her body language suggested she was open to the possibilities arising in this chaotic family. You, by contrast, were a bundle of jangling nerves. I took you aside, with a hug around the shoulders, before I even had a chance to speak with Jenny. 'It's absolutely fine, Sarah. Jenny is already a big hit. You don't have to worry. Look, even your father (James, who we suppose had an affair) is trying it on with her!'

You dissolved into tears and laughter.

Later, I had the opportunity to ask Jenny about her nursing career, and she told me she has worked in A&E and as a nurse in theatre, before becoming a ward sister. I said, 'It sounds like you've seen more than your share of human trauma and drama, Jenny.'

She smiled. 'Well, Bertie—may I call you Bertie?'

'That's me.'

'I've seen a lot of self-protection fade as patients face the reality of their situation, and that process can be more traumatic for some patients than the disease or the physical injury.' She smiled at my puzzled look. 'Some people can't take responsibility for their conditions which could have been avoided by attentive self-care. They protect their self-esteem by blaming it on bad luck, or God, or their partner, or whatever...'

'It sounds like you sometimes help patients in this self-discovery.'

'Bertie, we try to avoid making it a harsh process, like tearing off a particularly sticky plaster. It should be more like gently shaking a spouse who has overslept. In A&E and in theatre, I saw too many cases of personal carelessness or neglect. In the general wards at St George's, most of the patients we see will recover, and I don't want them to make the same mistake again, so the staff and I spend time with some of the patients, exploring how the accident

71

happened, how it could have been prevented, or, when symptoms first appeared. What might they have done then? What we try to do is elicit a commitment to a change in behaviour.'

'Sounds like mostly carrot-dangling; do you ever use a stick, like the fear of death?'

She compressed her lips. 'Never explicitly, Bertie. It's almost always there, just underneath the mask. Once the self-protective veneer slips, the fear is visible.'

I took a sip of my wine. 'I have the impression, Jenny, that you're a psychologist as well as a nurse.'

She laughed. 'I've read some, and I tend to be an introspective person, thinking much of the time about what I could do better.' She looked around the room. 'I feel comfortable here, Bertie.'

Thinking about you and Jenny, Sarah, my theory is that you two are like the poles of a magnet: you offer that spontaneous joyful approach to life, and Jenny has a serious, thoughtful orientation. You need each other."

I feel the tears welling up from a lump in my chest. "Uncle Bertie, I can't describe how much it means to Jenny and me to be included in the family as a couple. It's just so important. Jenny told me, 'I finally feel that I belong in a family. It's so good, Sarah!' And now I know who I am: a gay woman, a successful artist with a wonderful partner – life is delicious!"

He gives a shrug. "You know the family loves both of you."

Chapter 9
Vocations

We wait and we wait, and we wait. Uncle Bertie takes two or three long walks a day with Leo, his golden retriever, to relieve his stress. But finally, an agent sends an email asking to see the manuscript. We respond and inform all the others of this potential interest. Three agents have the manuscript and wish to represent us. We arrange meetings with all three and select Conrad Morgan as our agent; he seems to have the best contacts with decision-making editors at the international publishing houses. Conrad loves *The Flying Blankie,* but he suggests that the creators be listed as 'Grandpa & Sarah', rather than 'By Albert Smithson with Illustrations by Sarah Wentworth'.

He says: "You'll want a brand name, a name that kids can recognise, so they'll ask the librarian for 'more books by Grandpa & Sarah'."

Uncle Bertie wants me to admire his new outfit: navy blue corduroys with the tag still on the back and a polo shirt with a tiger logo. He stretches his legs out and glances at me. "You look very sharp this morning, Uncle Bertie. Any special occasion?"

"I'm feeling pretty good now that Conrad's found a publisher for us."

"Let's not forget," I say, "that we have another round of editing to go through. There's also the front and back cover and the press release. The watchword will have to be 'patience'." *He'll need to understand that the publication date is still months away.*

"I'm OK with that, Sarah. At least I'll know that I've made it as an author."

"So, you think that having a contract with a top five publisher is a badge of honour?"

"Yes, exactly. It's been, what, two and a half years since I decided to be an author. Thirty months of failure and frustration, a huge amount of time and money wasted. Before you joined me, I was beginning to think I just didn't have it in me. I was failing, sinking in what I thought would be an easy swim. So, I was not only a poor swimmer, but I had no other sport that I liked and in which I could perform well. I wasn't happy at Zeus Construction, which I thought would be my job for life. Then there was AtoZ, a job with no challenge. So, I was depending on writing to be my lifesaver. I very nearly drowned…"

I interrupt. "Did you feel that the devil was trying to push you under?"

He gives a sheepish chuckle. "It did occur to me…I guess what I'm trying to say, Sarah, is that finding, getting into, and performing well in a vocation that is both challenging and emotionally rewarding is essential in life. I never realised that until now." He looks at me and frowns. "What are you grinning about?"

"I'm just remembering what Gerri told you at your mother's funeral."

He looks at me quizzically. "Oh! The three things, one of which was having a challenging, satisfying vocation." I nod. "Yeah, well, she was probably right. The funny thing is my three kids. Michael and Elizabeth had no trouble, but Jeff, like me, really struggled."

"Tell me about Jeff."

"Since he was a child, Jeff had been keen on politics. Elections to student council always attracted him like a bear to honey. It wasn't power, per se, that he was after. His thrill was finding and implementing solutions to problems that people care about. Listening to people, building coalitions, and finding solutions defined Jeff's vital identity. Without them, he was merely working.

He studied business at University College London. He started out as a floor manager with Woolworth's before they went bust. He got a job at Boots; that at least was in healthcare. He moved to BetterU Fitness as an assistant manager, where he clearly felt hemmed in by corporate management, unappreciated and unhappy despite a decent salary. He lamented the high turnover in membership, which means he is constantly inventing new member recruitment schemes. I pointed out that there was a plus side to this problem: that he has a continuing opportunity to meet voters and impress them with his superior management and interpersonal skills. This led into a discussion of local English politics, which favoured the incumbent. To get your feet on the first rung of the ladder, one has to cultivate the local Labour big wigs and have a high civic profile. 'I sometimes feel that I ought to hire a PR agency—not that I could afford one,' he said.

He decided to give politics a try, and, on his second attempt, he was elected to Wandsworth council, a part-time post that allowed him to build his network and gain political experience. He wanted to be a professional politician, with his eye on a run for a seat in parliament at the next election, and he knew that there are a host of hurdles to be cleared.

The general election was only weeks away, Jeff, having won selection as the Labour candidate for parliament, representing Tooting (our district), was in the trial of his life: did he have the genuine commitment to a political career? Did he present himself, his vision and his party skilfully enough to gain sufficient votes to best a Conservative incumbent who is also a serving minister? And could he survive the character slurs, the setbacks and the exhaustion while retaining his own ability to find and exploit weaknesses in his opponent? Initially, the bookmakers had given Daniel Weybridge, his opponent, favourable odds based on his incumbency, his margin of over seven thousand votes in the last election, and the strong backing of the Conservative Party. But Weybridge had severable vulnerabilities: he had been officially reprimanded for declaring personal expenses on a block of flats which he owned and rented; as minister for schools, he approved the sale of six local school properties which had been used for recreation; and his public appearances suggested a person of entitlement – a member of the upper class, educated at Eton and Oxford, who jolly well knows what's best for the rest of us.

Jo, Carol-Ann, Jason, Michael and I had been pressed into campaign service, initially as leaflet distributors, but, more recently, we had been drafted into the legion of persuaders. We knocked on doors, hoping to get the promise of a vote for Jeffrey by focusing on known Labour voters, and those who weren't declared Conservatives, but sometimes we accidently get argumentative Conservatives, who tried to convince me to vote for Weybridge. It was a good night when most of my contacts said they'd vote for Jeffrey.

The election odds had narrowed, and Weybridge had issued a challenge in the interest of strengthening his lead. As debater in parliament with years of argumentation experience at Oxford and Eton, he had proposed to dispute novice Smithson in front of a live audience in the Tooting bingo hall. Coverage to be provided by the local press and London Radio.

The challenge had placed Jeffrey's team in a quandary: to decline will make the Labour candidate seem weak, if not frightened of the Conservative; to accept risks a humiliating defeat at the hands of an older and more experienced MP.

Jeffrey himself had no doubts. 'I can beat him by doing two things: first, by coming across as an ordinary person who truly understands what most people expect from their government, as opposed to an elitist who thinks he knows what's best for the people; and two, by presenting more of a centrist agenda, moving away from Labour's hard left agenda. He won't expect that, and he'll be primed to mock Labour's approach.'

'But, Jeffrey, Labour headquarters won't like it when they hear that you've deviated.'

'What are they going to do?' Jeff said. 'Disown me, and draft in a last-minute, desperation candidate?'

So, the challenge is accepted with several conditions: initially, each candidate would have fifteen minutes to present his policies in government, with Weybridge to start; this would be followed by one hour of questions from the floor, moderated by a London Radio newsreader. The program would conclude with a ten-minute summary by each candidate in the same order as the opening.

The program began with an overtime pontification at the lectern from Weybridge, dressed in a five-hundred-pound suit, starched white shirt, and silk club tie, on the Conservative gospel: tax little, spend less and be happy. When the moderator switched off his microphone in the seventeenth minute and he was forced to take his seat, he was angry and embarrassed.

Jeffrey, dressed in tan chinos, and a white, long-sleeve polo shirt with the Wandsworth Council coat of arms, stood at the edge of the stage, microphone in hand. 'How many of you contacted your MP during the last five years?' About half the audience raised their hands. 'And how many of you who contacted your MP in the last five years were fully satisfied with the response you got?' About ten percent of the audience responded. 'OK. One of the promises I make to you tonight is that I'm going to ask the same questions at the next general election in five years' time, and if I don't have a larger positive response to both questions, I will immediately stop my campaign, because I believe my number one job is not to represent the Labour Party, it is to represent the interests each of you have in government.' There was an unexpected applause.

Jeffrey went on to talk, without notes, about his job managing the health and fitness club, and he drew parallels between a health and fitness club and parliament: they both existed for the benefit of the public: efficient, affordable and free of corruption and special interests. He outlined his approach to some of the principal issues facing the UK: more money for the NHS and elderly care via a modest, graduated insurance scheme that would make prompt, quality care more readily available. Clear, simple and no-nonsense rules for immigrants that focused on filling vacancies in the workforce. More generous and prompt processing of valid asylum seekers, with money to come from a reduction in wasted overseas aid.

At the end of his talk – which lasted fourteen minutes – there was an applause.

'How are you going to pay for all the goodies you're promising?' was the first question from the audience directed at Jeffrey. His response was that the insurance scheme he proposed will be directed to the NHS and to social services for care of the elderly. There would be no new taxes. Yes, there would be a cost for this insurance, but it would be modest and there would be clear, long-needed benefits. 'It's well past time for us, as a country, to address this problem. If we don't, it will only get worse.'

When asked for his position on underfunded health service, Weybridge said that a commission would be appointed to study it.

'What you mean is it will be kicked into the long grass!' someone shouted from the audience.

Weybridge's face was flushed with anger. 'We cannot throw money at every problem we have.'

Thereafter, the audience's sentiment turned largely hostile toward Weybridge, and some people wearing blue Conservative hats, badges and ribbons departed.

The Conservative MP used his summary speech to attack Labour's history of profligacy in government. He closed with: 'Please don't make the same mistake again!'

Jeffrey asked his family, Cathy, JoJo (thirteen) and Willie (eleven), to stand up in the audience. 'I am a family man. We live on a modest income. My wife, Cathy is a paramedic with London Ambulance. Our kids, JoJo and Willie, go to Thames Brook school. We don't have fancy holidays. Every year, we go to a rented house in Seaford on the south coast with the rest of our family. We have a mortgage and car payments—no other debts. We're saving for the kids' university fees. That tells you a little more about me, and how we believe finances should be managed. Thank you for listening.'

The event had attracted wider than expected publicity, particularly on social media, but also by *The Guardian*, which made much of Jeffrey's 'deviation' from Labour's hard left party line. Current polls suggested that the election of the MP for Tooting was too close to call.

The official announcement was made in the early morning: Jeffrey Smithson was declared winner of the parliamentary seat for Tooting by a margin of three thousand and twelve votes."

"I remember that well, Uncle Bertie. I was fifteen at the time," I say. "There was a celebratory early breakfast, featuring real English sparkling wine, orange juice, eggs Benedict, coffee and more wine hastily arranged by Aunt Jo and my nan at your house. Nobody was paying much attention to what the kids were doing. The adults were hugging each other and Uncle Jeff. None of us could quite believe that a Smithson has been elected a member of the Parliament of the United Kingdom. I decided to join the adult celebration and had five or six glasses of wine. I was drunk by six am."

"Yes, you were! I remember that. Your mother was really annoyed. She said you were to be grounded for a week."

"Yeah, probably." I give a shrug. "I knew you were happy, Uncle Bertie."

He takes a deep breath and looks out the window. When he looks back, there is a shadow of disappointment on his face. "Of course, I was proud of Jeffrey, and very happy for him. After over twenty years of planning, preparing, failing and trying again, he had achieved the role he coveted. But I was also jealous: still stuck in the thankless foreman's job at Zeus Construction, no real challenge, nothing to learn, and no way to move up the ladder to something interesting."

When we return from lunch – Aunt Jo made a wonderful fish chowder and cheddar on toast – he says, "We were talking earlier about our books, and how much better I felt about myself to be creating something that people enjoyed. I was just thinking *It's not a matter of you've done it and it's done.*" He makes a gesture of wiping his hands. "You have to keep doing it. You've got to show the people who like you that you like them, and that you're still doing it."

Knowing what's coming, I say, "But that isn't hard, is it?"

"No, I've learnt to loosen up, go with the flow and enjoy it."

"You? Go with the flow – never."

He laughs. "You and I were taking turns reading from our first two books, about a year and a half after the first one was published. We were sitting on folding chairs on the auditorium stage of the Wilbur Whitworth Primary School in Derby. Just behind us was the purple, floor-to-ceiling curtain and front of us were ninety-six children, sitting attentively, but with some squirming and whispering.

I closed the book and glanced at the screen behind me where the image of Robbie was waving goodbye from his flying blankie. You switched off the remote projector, and we both turned toward Mrs Shuttleworth, the head teacher. 'Can we have a round of applause for our readers?' There was a brief, but enthusiastic burst of applause. 'Now you can ask some questions of the authors, but first, let me ask you a question: what did you get out of these stories?'

There was a large show of hands. Some of the respondents were called on.

'I learnt how a vaccine works.'

'When you read, you can discover a lot of things.'

'I found out about smallpox.'

'Reading stories helps your imagination.'

'Pictures can show you a lot about the world.'

'OK, children, now we have some time when you can ask questions of the authors. Remember, please, to stand up and say your name.'

Hands shot up, and the headteacher called on one of them. A girl of about eight, like the others, in her school blazer and plaid skirt, stood up. 'My name is Louise. How do you know what to write about?'

You said, 'We don't really <u>know</u> what to write about. We both have ideas, and we ask lots of people like you, and then we pick the idea we like best.'

'Where did Robbie get his magic blankie?'

'We think he got it in his dreams.'

'Do cows still get cowpox?'

I said, 'No, I think cows get vaccinated now.'

'Is he really your grandpa?'

'No, not really. He's my great uncle. That means my grandma is his sister.'

'How did you learn to paint so well?'

'I probably learnt the way you do—experimenting in school, but after a while I took some lessons.'

Our move to the entrance hall coincided with the end of the school day and the arrival of mothers, with purses, who could purchase the autographed books their children were anxious to take home.

For you and me, Sarah, it felt like a special day which went well beyond seeing proof that our creations are valued by the best judges. It's feeling the enthusiastic involvement of young readers in the processes of reading, learning and thinking with <u>our books</u>."

"It was super, Uncle Bertie. We even sold over a hundred books."

"A year later, after two more books, many reviews, remote interviews and a blizzard of publicity, we were in the States. I could never have undertaken that trip without you, Sarah: twelve cities in America in two weeks! Yes, the publisher had arranged all our events, our transport and hotels, but I've never been outside the UK, not even to Scotland, or Northern Ireland. And America? It's absolutely huge! Yes, they speak the same language – in theory – but they don't really. The anxiety exploding in my brain from the challenge of getting from spot A in New York City to spot B in Philadelphia by myself, on time, with my suitcase and my satchel would have made me a gibbering idiot for the interview in spot B. But you looked on the whole trip as a great adventure, and when something invariably went wrong, you would laugh, take counsel with the natives, and invent a timely solution.

After our second train ride, from New York to Philadelphia, following our first train ride from Boston to New York, and having become lost and disoriented in sprawling Pennsylvania Station, with its trains running north, south, east and west, I decided to adopt the persona of a kindly old gentleman with amnesia whom you could lead around. Seriously, Pennsylvania Station is a world class maze: two dozen tracks on two different levels, a big sports arena above and more underground tracks below, three different arrival and departure areas, endless shops, bars, and restaurants and over one million people every day.

You would stop someone and ask, 'Where can we find the trains to Philadelphia?'"

Uncle Bertie adopts that harsh New York accent. "'That would be Amtrak, honey. Go down that corridor there and bend around to your right.'

But all of your sleuthing skills were required to find the exact track from which the 18:10 express would be departing. And much of America is like that. It's not like Waterloo Station with one open, airy waiting area, a single row of train tracks and one big electronic train departure board. Americans seem to like things to be disorderly. Maybe it's their frontier spirit or the rapid growth which means that things just get bolted on.

But having said that, once I became a slightly demented traveller, I enjoyed the trip.

We were usually booked into three events per day, per city. For example, we might have a nine o'clock interview with a newspaper, on radio or TV. Then there would be a reading, or perhaps two, at a school, and in the afternoon, we would do book signings at a large bookstore where the event was pre-publicised.

The most difficult events for me were the TV interviews, which we did in Charlotte, Atlanta, Birmingham, and Detroit, with local stations – no *Good Morning, America!*, fortunately, but retrospectively, unfortunately.

After the Charlotte interview, you said, 'Uncle Bertie, I could see you were a little nervous.'

'I know. I felt like an idiot. Did I look like one?'

'No. You just didn't look relaxed.'

'I felt like I was walking on coals.'

You giggled. 'You know what I do, Uncle Bertie? I pretend I'm a celebrated artist like Jenny Saville, and, employing my usual kookiness, I just lead the prying interviewer on a merry chase.'

'Yes, I saw that. Perhaps I should pretend I'm Bill Bryson: a laid-back writer who has extensive experience of everything.'

'Bill Bryson and Jenny Saville will make an interesting couple.'"

"After that trip, Uncle Bertie, I have a real appreciation of what a budding music singer goes through to build a career on the road: you don't remember much about the cities you've visited because you're already off to the next one. But I particularly liked Boston – perhaps because it's part of New England and acts like it. There was also that wonderful seafood restaurant on the waterfront. New York was, as expected, teaming with people and steaming with energy. We saw the (cracked) Liberty Bell and the Declaration of Independence in Philadelphia; if there'd been no revolution, what would the world be like? Miami was a rich tropical paradise with a long beach and very expensive shops. New Orleans had that wonderful French quarter with creole cooking and splendid jazz. Detroit looked all right; so did Pittsburgh. They were both supposed to be part of the Great Rust Belt, but they both looked prosperous, particularly Pittsburgh with its collection of skyscrapers at the junction of three rivers."

I take a minute to look through my notes. "Uncle Bertie, you mentioned that JoJo and Heather were two of your favourite granddaughters. In the morning, I'd like to hear more about Heather, in view of what happened."

Chapter 10
Heather

"I know that Heather's memory is very important to you," I say. We haven't talked about her yet and I want to be sure we include her."

He takes a deep breath, releasing it slowly, and looks toward the ceiling. "I mentioned the first time I held Heather. It was when Jo and I bought this house twenty years ago and I had gone to Michael's estate agency. She was only two months old, but she would look at me with those big dark eyes of hers, and she would hold my gaze as if to say, 'I know you're my grandpa. You and I are going to be very good friends.' I remember a Sunday she had got down from her highchair. I lost track of her. Then a felt a gentle nudge against my leg. I looked down and there was Heather, arms raised in surrender. I took the hint, picked her up and she settled comfortably in my lap, falling asleep. Most Sundays, she would bring me a story she'd written or a piece of art she'd created for me. At Seaford I had an annual obligation to build a sandcastle and to complete a jigsaw puzzle with Heather while we talked about worldly issues that concerned her.

At the age of seven, Heather was still my youngest grandchild. A bright, sociable second grader, she had won two prizes in Sunday school: perfect attendance (thanks to her mother Abigale) and best oral story about Jesus (apparently, she recited a dream in which she spoke with Him). But, more importantly, her affability had captured my heart.

She'd been tired, pale and short of breath. I thought it might be one of those many childhood diseases that children get. The GP had been treating her for anaemia with iron and B12 supplements. Her condition didn't improve. She was referred to a paediatric consultant, who ordered extensive blood tests. The diagnosis: acute myelogenous leukaemia.

We were all ravaged with fear and barely controlled grief. My son, Michael, was terrified and could barely look at his daughter without crying. Abigale was called upon to be a bulwark against a family epidemic of despair.

'Mummy told me I have leukaemia,' Heather said to me in a confidential tone on Sunday. Not knowing which direction this disclosure was going to take, I leant forward and took her hands. 'It's quite a serious disease, Grandpa.' She pushed a strand of her light brown hair away from her eyes and chewed the inside of her cheek.

'Yes, I know, Heather.' I was trying desperately to think of the right assurance.

'But Mummy says that I'm going to have some treatments to make the disease go away. I can still go to school and I can still see my friends.'

'That's very good, Heather, and you know that everybody will be cheering for you.'

She cocked her head to one side, and looked at me, chewing her lip. She squeezed my hands, released them and flung herself into my arms. For a long moment, I embraced her. There was a trace scent of jasmine in her hair. I must have made a slight snuffling sound trying to forestall tears. She pushed herself to arms-length to look at me.

'Don't cry, Grandpa. I'm going to be all right.'

'I know you will be, sweetheart.'

I took Heather a small brown rabbit with white fluffy ears and tail. She smiled, looked at it thoughtfully and hugged it to her with her left arm while she drank juice with her right. 'Thank you, Grandpa. She's quite a happy rabbit, so she'll be my friend.' Heather set her juice glass on the table and looked up at me. 'You know, Grandpa, with leukaemia I can't make enough blood.'

'Yes, I know that.'

'Last week I got some more blood.' She paused, looking wistful. 'I don't know whose it was.'

'Maybe it was mine. Does it seem all right?'

'Yours, Grandpa?' This was an amusing puzzle.

'Maybe. Lots of people have given blood for kids like you.'

'Thank you, Grandpa.'

I had difficulty restraining myself from snatching her up from her chair and enveloping her in the safety of my embrace.

The doctors had decided that Heather's blood count was now good enough that she could begin chemotherapy. Abigale had become an expert in the various chemicals, their dosages, durations, efficacies and side effects, to the extent that I wondered whether she or the renowned Professor Abraham Wiseman was the clinician in charge of Heather's care. For three days running, Heather went to the nearby St George's Hospital where the chemotherapy was administered, usually through a vein in her arm, but sometimes through a spinal tap to prevent the disease relapsing in her brain or spinal cord. With breaks of two weeks, these cycles were repeated for three months.

Heather had lost all her beautiful brown, curly hair which cascaded down over her shoulders. This loss, more than exhaustion, frequent nose bleeds, bruising and headaches, was Heather's overriding sense of injury. Abigale could hardly hold back her own tears as Heather brushed away great handfuls of fine hair. A custom-made wig was offered, but Heather, petulant and aggrieved, would have none of it, until one Saturday afternoon she was watching a women's field hockey match: England vs USA, and she noticed that a favourite English player was wearing some sort of red bandana over her head – perhaps to keep her hair under control or to absorb perspiration. The game was frozen, and her mother was summoned. 'Mummy, can I have one like Nancy Stewart's?' she asked, pointing.

She had two fitted red bandanas; one was the laundry backup.

The blood tests showed that Heather's disease was in remission, and Professor Wiseman had recommended, if she remained in remission for six months, a stem cell transplant. Family members were surveyed for a close match with Heather's human leukocyte antigens (the measure of immune system compatibility); the expectation was that Heather's brother, Thomas, eleven years old would be the best fit. But we were startled to learn that the best match in the family was Michael. He would have some of his bone marrow transplanted to his daughter.

Two weeks later, Michael called me in the evening. 'Dad, Heather's had a relapse,' he sobbed. 'The cancer's back.' All I could hear was a long moan.

I sat down hurriedly, afraid that blackness would overwhelm me. 'Oh, my heavens, Michael. That's terrible. What can they do?'

There was sobbing and snuffling on the phone. 'Professor Wiseman is talking more chemo at a higher dosage that he's hoping will kill the cancer. But he admits there's a risk that will kill her blood-making cells.'

My brain had gone numb, but I could feel my heart racing. "How do they deal with the risk?'

'He wants to inject my stem cells right after the chemo. He's hoping they'll quickly become blood-making cells.'

I tried to search for something positive in this flood of horror. All I could think of was: 'Does Heather know?'

'Abby told her today, trying to make it just another necessary step.'

'What was Heather's reaction?'

'She said, *Oh, Mummy do I have to?*'

Jo and I went to see her a couple of hours before she was due to go to the St George's for a treatment, to ease the anxiety she felt about the needles and the bags of poison which made her feel so unwell. On our way, we stopped at a neighbourhood toy shop in search of a pleasant distraction.

Heather was not herself. She was sitting on the living room sofa glancing at a Tom & Jerry cartoon on TV, and scanning a Frozen story book, but paying no attention to either diversion. Her weight loss was obvious in the angularity of her face: prominent cheek bones, brow and chin, which had only been the invisible structure of a delicious cherub look.

Jo said, 'That's a pretty dress you're wearing, Heather.'

The little girl looked down at her pink and white striped frock, gave a slight shrug, and said, 'I like it.' She looked around the room. 'But I don't like going to St Georges.' Jo was about to say something when Heather continued, 'I know I have to do it, but I don't understand why I'm the only one who has to do it.'

Abigale explained that there are lots of people all over the world who are having treatment for cancer right now.

'Yes, I know, Mummy, but I'm the only one of my friends who's having treatment.'

By way of a hoped-for distraction, Abigale said, 'And your friends have brought you lots of presents, Heather.'

'Yes, I know, Mummy, and they're very kind, but it doesn't answer my question.'

Abigale shot us a look of desperation. Jo moved to sit next to her granddaughter. 'I don't know, Heather, and I don't think anybody in the world knows why somebody gets cancer and other people don't.'

'Does Jesus know, Grandma?'

Jo looked up at the ceiling to hide her eyes full of tears. 'Well, we can ask Him, Heather.' A moment's pause. 'Actually, it would probably be better if we all sent a prayer to Jesus asking Him to make you well. What do you think, Heather?'

'Yes, let's do that!'

Jo began the prayer, which started as a simple supplication and went on to mention special attention which Heather deserved. Abigale picked up the thread and I even find myself adding a small prayer asking Jesus to help her with the discomfort of the chemo. Heather broke the silence that followed: "Jesus, please make me well like You did for that woman who touched Your robe.'

Heather closed the Frozen book with a look of satisfaction. 'What's that you brought me, Grandpa?'

'It's a book of origami. It shows you how to make things out of paper.'

I sat next to Heather who watched intently as, following the illustration, I began folding a sheet of blue paper until I held up a finished creation.

'Is that a bird?'

'Yes, it's a bird. See: you can make it flap its wings.'

'Oh, Grandpa, that's really cool!'

Heather was on a children's oncology ward at St George's. She would have her last series of chemo here, recognising her extreme vulnerability to infection, and general weakness, which left her breathless and dozing most of the day. She was a clear favourite with the nurses, who had put her on a drip of antibiotics, pain killers, and goodness knows what else, but during my short visits with her, she seemed in good, if dreamy, spirits.

'Grandpa, can you download some more of Adele's albums?'

'Sure, sweetheart.' I picked up the iPad, which I had given her.

'What's the name of that famous choir, Grandpa?'

'The Mormon Tabernacle Choir?'

'They live in Salt Lake City, America, right?'

'That's right. Shall I find some of their music?'

'Yes, please.'

On a Thursday, Michael sat next Heather on her bed, and he said he was going to give her some of the 'inside of his bones'.

She looked at him searchingly. 'Will that make me very strong, Daddy?'

'<u>Very</u> strong, I hope,' he said.

A day later, her temperature had risen rapidly to one hundred and one; she was being given new and more powerful immuno-suppressant drugs.

Michael, Abigale, Jo and I sat with Professor Wiseman in a small room off the ward. 'I'm afraid that Heather's high temperature is an indication of graft-versus-host disease. Blood tests have confirmed this. It means that Heather's immune system has wrongly recognised your cells, Michael, as invaders and there is a savage, unnecessary battle going on in her bloodstream.'

'What can be done, Professor?' Abigale asked.

'It's very important we keep her temperature down, and we'll keep up the immuno-suppressant drugs.'

I saw Heather when her temperature was one hundred and two; she was wrapped in ice blankets which had brought her temperature down from one hundred and four. She was flushed and dreamlike, floating on the edge of consciousness. 'Grandpa, do you think that Jesus has a white beard now?'

I adjusted my position to hear her better. 'Why do you think Jesus has a white beard, Heather?'

'He always had a brown beard, but He's much older now. So, I think He's more like God. He has a white beard, you know.'

She drifted off to sleep.

Heather was in a coma, in intensive care. The doctors tried everything they could think of. Her blood pressure was down to seventy-eight over forty.

She had suffered a cardiac arrest, and the doctors were unable to restart her heart.

It was without a doubt the worst day of my life. Never have I suffered a tragedy approaching the overwhelming loss of Heather. Much as I am fearful of the prospect of my own death, I would have willingly gone to my grave in her place. Had I suddenly lost voice, sight and hearing, I would have felt no more crippled than by this black pool of grief from which there seems no escape. As bleak as life seems for me, I can't imagine the suffering of Michael and Abigale – all I can do is hug them and weep with them over the loss of a supremely lovely creature, whose beauty was not solely physical; she had a wise and patient appreciation of the people around her and a loving curiosity about the world and life itself.

I am angry at the injustice of life snatched away from one who should have been first in the queue to explore and savour, with her enchanting smile. How could it be? How could a loving God permit it to happen?

I haven't spoken with anyone about it, and I'm sure many of us noticed it, but I couldn't understand Heather's apparent placement of her own fate in Jesus' hands. I don't mean that she gave up. On the contrary, she put up with one painful treatment after another in the brave knowledge that it was necessary. But when confronted with an overpowering adversary that no human could master, she placed her faith in a greater power – one that she had learnt about in Sunday school. God bless her! She has left me standing far behind her. I have been exposed to religious education off and on for nearly sixty years, but I have no faith. She, in two or three years of Sunday lessons, had an extraordinary faith.

Women continue to amaze me. Sometimes, they can retreat into bitter seclusion after a careless slight by a close friend when all could be put right by a straightforward discussion, and yet when there is a major accident they can rush in, providing emotional comfort without sinking into incapacitating grief. It seems they can be overwhelmed by small bothers, but unaffected by grand tragedies.

Jo is like that. For a full day after Heather's death, she wept. There were teardrops in her cereal, on the sheets as she made the bed, on the manuscript she was editing, on her sandwich, her computer keyboard, in her Chablis and on her pillow. The next day, there was always a packet of tissues in her hand for mopping threatened tears and clearing her nose. And today she is with Abigale and Father Anthony to arrange the funeral.

'Michael is taking it very hard,' she said on her return.

'I'm not surprised. She was his precious little girl.'

'Yes, but it's more than that. He's blaming himself for Heather's death.'

I held up my hands. 'For goodness sake! It makes no sense. He was selected as the best match, and he responded generously.'

'I know, but he's convinced that umbilical cord cells from a random stranger would have saved her life, whereas, his cells killed her.'

'Well, that's Michael. Not thinking straight can be his speciality. How is Abigale?'

'That woman is a damn saint! She sent Michael to the office—Lord knows what good he'll do there—at least he's not underfoot. She's had a long talk with Thomas, who was coming off the rails with grief. He seems to be OK now, very sad, but able to go to school.'

'What did Abigale tell him?'

Jo considered me for a long moment. 'Thomas is a lot like you, Bertie. He needed the wisdom of a sensible adult that he respects.'

'You're not going to tell me? I am interested.'

'I know you are, but I'm not the right person to talk to you about this.'

'Who is?'

'Father Anthony.' I groaned with preordained disappointment. 'Sorry, Bertie, but it's like our conversation about faith. I won't be helping you if I put my particular spin on things.'

By this time, I had met with Father Anthony a number of times for theological-philosophical discussions and it's fair to say that he was anticipating my call.

His study was a cosy room looking out on a garden at the back of the rectory. One wall had floor-to-ceiling shelves crammed with what must be serious books – at least their white or tan spines give no hint of humour or entertainment. In addition to an old, dark wood desk strewn with books and papers, there were four stuffed easy chairs.

'I'm very sorry, Bertie, that we lost Heather,' Father Anthony said. 'She was a truly special young person.'

'Yes, and what I don't understand is how could a loving God permit her to die so young?'

The priest steepled his hands. 'Bertie, I'm going to talk to you man-to-man, and I'm going to leave the Church out of this discussion. Is that all right?'

'Yes, of course.'

'Embedded in your question is the assumption that God is all powerful: correct?'

'Yes.'

'Do you think it's possible that *all powerful* might be too strong a description for God?'

'Perhaps, but doesn't that put you into trouble if there's someone or something more powerful than God?'

'It would, but suppose that God is very powerful and that there is no one and nothing more powerful?'

'You're proposing that power is shared in something like the Trinity?'

'Possibly, but speaking generally, God may have delegated some of his power. For example, there are scores of equations—like $E = MC^2$—that control how the universe works, and if He invented them and put them in place, He can't very well go about contradicting them when He feels like it. God's role in the universe may be self-limited. For example, if God is not matter, or radiation, or energy, He is something else, not everything, and perhaps his role—perhaps the largest role, is not everything.'

'I think I see your point: that in Heather's case, she contracted leukaemia through the working of various laws that God put in place to control the universe, and therefore God may have unintentionally but necessarily allowed Heather to fall ill.'

'Possibly.'

There was a long pause while I tried to process all of this. 'Father, do you believe in miracles?'

'Yes, I do.'

'Why didn't He work a miracle in Heather's case?'

'I don't know, Bertie. There were certainly enough prayers for a dozen miracles, if that is a criterion for a miracle, and there are many miraculous recoveries of dying believers, which could have included Heather; also, numerous instances of believers seeing the same heavenly scene, which is called a miracle. Perhaps, the Lord had need of Heather closer to him. She surely captured his attention.'

'So, you believe in an afterlife, Father.'

'Yes, but I know nothing of its form or purpose.'

'You know that Michael, her father, is blaming himself for her death in that his cells triggered the disease that killed her?

The priest looked out the window of his office with a sad expression on his face. 'I am sorry to hear it.' He turned and looked at me. 'You know, Bertie, some within the Church would say that it is a test from God, and I believe that sometimes God does put us to the test so that we learn and grow, but not in this case.' He placed his hands on the desk in front of him. 'We spoke before about Satan and at the time, you had no awareness of him.'

'I have no personal awareness of him now, but having examined some major events, as you suggested, I am beginning to see his fingerprints here and there, as my wife would say.'

He gave a wry smile. 'Josephine is a wise woman, and she may see Satan's fingerprints on her son.'

I was amazed at what seems a huge leap in logic. 'But Father Anthony…how…could it be possible…for the devil…to…'

'…to influence someone's thinking?' He looked up at his bookshelves. 'There is a book in Spanish written by a priest who is also a psychiatrist, and who dealt with many cases of so-called *possession*. He says that our unconscious is accessible. We have all heard of cases of mind reading; the New Testament is full of examples of Jesus reading the thoughts and even understanding the character of those he met. Well, this psychiatric priest says that God and Satan (and perhaps some saints) can readily read our minds—but also that God and Satan can plant thoughts, or enhance an awareness, if one is tuned in, so to speak.'

'But why would the devil want to pick on Michael?'

'I don't know, and I don't want to speculate.'

When I got home, I gave Jo, who was ironing but listening, a brief account of my discussion with Father Anthony. When I started to mention Michael, she stood the iron up on its heel and focused her attention on me, nodding at certain points as if to lodge something in her memory.

'What I don't understand, Jo, is why he refused to speculate about Michael, when much of our earlier conversation seemed like speculation. After all, he knows Michael reasonably well, though he doesn't often come to mass.'

'He knows that Michael is somewhat like you, as concerns faith.'

I paused to consider. 'So, are you suggesting, that I need to be careful of the devil?'

'You are, Bertie, and I very much appreciate it, but posting an extra sentry or two could be a good idea.'

Chapter 11
Michael

"Uncle Bertie," I say, "I remember Heater's funeral. It was other-worldly – a funeral mass that is not funereal. The pews in church were full-to-capacity with children from secular and church schools, their parents, neighbours, friends, family, and unknown mourners. One sensed a mood of blithe expectation, rather than sadness, an anticipation of the elevation of a small, beloved soul to somewhere much deserved. Yes, there were wet cheeks and handkerchiefs, and even a few bent over in grief, unable to face the altar, but most were dry-eyed, thoughtful, even hopeful.

Heather's white casket lay before the altar and was almost invisible in the surrounding spectral avalanche of floral bouquets of every description: daisies, marigolds, roses, lilies, peonies, carnations, lilacs, poppies, chrysanthemums, dahlias, and even some hastily gathered dandelions, goldenrod and queen Anne's lace. Their origins were as varied as their forms and colours: florists, supermarkets, and the vacant fields of Wandsworth; wrapped in floral paper, tissue paper, cling film or nothing at all, sprinkled with hand-written notes in childish script, and mingled with occasional teddy bears and stuffed toys. It was as if the children of Wandsworth expected that their tide of floral tribute would carry their friend's spirit to that uncharted, but glorious place.

No one sat at the organ bench. The choir of the Thames Brook School, of which Heather was a member, was singing their repertoire of chirpy childhood songs, accompanied by the music teacher at her piano.

Father Anthony appeared in red and white vestments. 'Good afternoon, at the request of Heather's family (I suppose he meant Abigale), the mass has been altered to make this a service of love and remembrance.' He continued with a tribute to Heather, and an expectation that she 'now knows that Jesus' beard is still brown. She thought that after all these years it might have become white.'

The choir sang *I Love to Tell the Story*, followed by a recitation of the 23rd Psalm by a classmate.

Then my cousin, Thomas, got up from his seat next to Abigale and walked to the lectern. Deliberately, he set his notes down and faced the congregation for a moment. One could almost feel his determination to carry on with the assignment he had given himself, in spite of his aura of sadness and doubts of his abilities at the age of eleven to address nearly two hundred strangers. 'My sister didn't want to go to heaven. She wanted to stay here with all of you and me, but now that she's there ahead of us, we should be very happy for her.' He paused to look around. Someone in the audience began to applaud; it is taken up by the entire congregation. Encouraged by all the beaming faces, he smiled and continued, telling two stories 'about my sister that I'll always remember'. One, about last summer at the seashore, how she spent several hours comforting a distraught toddler whose lost parents could not be found, and when the parents reappeared, the toddler wanted to take her with him. The other about how she had won the five-pound prize in the age seven spelling bee, and on her way home, gave the money to a crippled beggar who is usually outside the post office."

"That's a very good description, Sarah, and just as I remember it. I'd like to pick it up from there.

Father Anthony conducted a service of remembrance, interspaced with more singing by the choir, more children reading scripture, and he explained the liturgy as it progressed.

I looked over at Michael. He seemed oblivious to what is going on, head down, supported by one arm, his other hand clutching a sodden handkerchief. I felt sorry for him, and yet, at the same time, I was angry that he was making no attempt to join his family in a ceremony of hopeful remembrance of his daughter.

I knew that Jo was involved in some discussions with Michael and Abigale about interment vs cremation. Michael was very much opposed to cremation, and Jo's impression was that Michael could not tolerate the thought of his little girl being reduced to ashes, but equally Michael seemed to want to have a permanent monument to Heather, one which he could visit and where he could lay flowers from time to time. Jo sensed Abigale's view that Heather would not have wanted a monument, that Heather would have liked to be remembered through the preparation of a digital slideshow and a compilation of videos that could be distributed to those who wanted it. In the end, it was decided that Heather would be interred, though no monument would be created. Friends and family would be asked to send digital photos and videos involving Heather to Abigale, who would pass them on to a company in London that creates memorial files for families, with the help of interested family members. My suspicion was that not being content with a bland, disjointed compilation, considerable help would be required from Abigale.

The actual interment took place on a Wednesday afternoon with only the family and Father Antony present. Michael, it seemed, wanted to monopolise, privately, the expression of his grief. He wanted to limit attendance to the three members of his immediate family, for which he was publicly chastised by Jo: 'What's the hell's the matter with you, Michael? You're not the only one who's lost someone he loved. There are plenty of cousins, aunts, uncles, grand aunts, uncles and parents who lost someone they loved. What's happened to your sense of family?'

Heather was interred next to her great-grandparents, Sarah and Jeffrey, in Wandsworth cemetery near an old weeping cherry tree. In about a month, there would be a small bronze marker recording her dates of birth, death, and her parents.

The Heather's Digital Compilation turned out to be a large but cathartic project for Abigale. Having received several hundred photos and videos, she had to winnow wheat from the chaff, put them in chronological order and weave a storyline through them. Only a few of the videos had a useable soundtrack. Who was to narrate the story? Abigale's answer: the family, so nearly all of us were summoned to a multimedia studio on Union Street in East London on a Saturday morning to record dozens of bits of narration. Watching the screen and reading from a script that Abigale distributed before the recording, we each stepped up to the microphone, to be replayed often on rainy days at Seaford and on the Sunday nearest to Heather's anniversary.

I stopped by the Smithson Estate Agency to find out, first-hand, how things were going. The premises were larger now. There was an open area with four desks, two of which were occupied by agents I didn't know, and there was one large cubicle at the back occupied by Michael and Abigale, who was working at her computer, uploading premise photos to a website, copying and pasting text. Since Michael had a client with him, I sat with Abigale, watching her work and listening to her report about Thomas at school: he's doing OK. I told her that I liked the bronze plaque and loved the digital compilation. She was only half attending to me, rather her attention seemed to be more focused on Michael, who at this point, seemed to be engaged in a heated argument with the customer. As I tuned in, I recognised that the discussion was about a commission due on a sale, with Michael insisting it was five percent and the customer equally certain it was four. Abigale was shaking her head; she whispered, 'There's no written contract.'

'Why not?' I asked.

She inclined her head sadly. I waited for an answer. 'He doesn't pay attention to the details.'

I frowned, puzzled. Another whisper, 'He hasn't gotten over it. Drinking way too much.'

I was suddenly reminded of Michael, the out-of-control, sixteen-year-old tear-away.

The client, red in the face, got up and dropped a piece of paper on Michael's desk. 'Here's four percent. You can sue me for the rest!' He turned on his heel and stormed out.

'Good riddance!' Michael shouted after him, got up, and, pushing past me, bailed out of the office.

I was about to follow him when something told me *Wait!* When I glanced at Abigale, she was biting her lip in frustration. We sat in silence for a time; the rest of the office seemed to have recovered and was busy. 'Where did he go?'

'To the pub.' She grasped her mouse and gave her attention to the screen.

'At eleven o'clock in the morning?'

'At three in the afternoon. Whenever.'

'Well, I'll go and speak with him, Abby.'

She reached out and touched my sleeve. 'With all due respect, Bertie, the only one he ever listened to when he gets like this was your mother.'

'If not my mother, you, or me, who then? Father Anthony?'

She closed her eyes, lips compressed. 'He blames the Church almost as much as himself.' She paused and looks around the office wistfully. 'If he doesn't get control of himself soon, he'll be an alcoholic with no employees, no customers and no family.'

'How about Jo?'

She was pensive for a moment. 'The thing about Mike is: he respects real authority. Jo doesn't come across as authoritarian, but she has authority as his mother, and he respects her.'

I was amused. 'So, you and I lack the necessary authoritarian credentials.'

'Yeah, I'm afraid so.'

When I reported my sortie to Jo, she became flushed. 'Not authoritarian, eh? Well, maybe not, but I am pissed! Michael is an absolute idiot! I picked Thomas up at school yesterday, and I usually take him home, but he said, Grandma, can I stay at your house for a while? When I wanted to know why, he said, Mum and Dad are always fighting. I've had quite enough of Michael being depressed and sorry for himself!'

After dinner, I heard Jo on the phone. 'Michael, this is your mother. I want to see you here at my house tomorrow at three o'clock, sober…You'll have to cancel it. I said three o'clock and I mean three, exactly, sober! Do you understand me?…No, your father will be working then, but he's expecting a full report when he gets home…The subject is your stupid and self-destructive behaviour.' I heard her physically slam the phone down.

Jo's mental comportment struck me as being like that of a wrestler who has finished a long, hard match, who is sore all over, but has unanimously been awarded the win.

'I don't know what gets into Michael. He can be so stubborn and illogical.'

'You got him to shape up?'

'I'm not sure; we'll have to see.'

'What happened, Jo?'

'He was sitting in the armchair over there, and I was standing here. I said, "I'm ashamed of you, and the whole family is embarrassed by your behaviour. You seem to think you're the only one who has lost Heather, blaming yourself, drinking too much."

'He started to cry. "I can't help it, Mum. I loved Heather so much and I killed her.'

'Let me make one thing clear to you, Michael, you did not kill Heather. You did not kill that child! You made a personal sacrifice to provide her with your bone marrow in the interests of saving her life.'

'But Mum, she would have had a much better chance if they had taken frozen umbilical cells.'

'Show me your certificate of membership in the Royal Academy of Immunologists!' He looked away sheepishly and said nothing. 'Listen, Michael, I have had a long conversation with Professor Wiseman, and with Dr Franklin, who is the medical director at St Georges. They basically said three things. First, that the conclusions of the HLA analysis were correct. You were clearly a better choice than Abigale or Thomas, and they were pleased that you were willing to donate. Second, that a live stem cell transplant is always favoured over a frozen transplant. Frozen cells would be a last resort. And, third immunology is not an exact science.' I let that sink in. Then I said, 'Even if an HLA mistake were made, would it be your mistake? What good would it do for anyone, absolutely anyone, for you to lament about it?'

'He slumped down in the chair and began to weep. 'I have lost my only daughter. She was so lovely!'

'Michael, I want you to stop it. Man up!…Do you remember when Grandma Sarah's much-loved husband died?' He nodded. 'Did she become disabled with grief?' He shook his head. 'My conclusion is that your grandmother had more balls than you.' He cringed as if I had struck him with a whip. 'What I want to know, Michael, is who the hell promised you a rose garden?'

'No one,' he said very softly.

'I asked, 'And who promised Jeffrey he'd win the election?' He shrugged. 'Nobody!' I shouted. 'Your brother has balls. At the moment you are a complete wimp!' He was biting his lip bitterly. Maybe it was unfair, but I took advantage of that old sibling rivalry.'

'Was that it?' I asked.

'Not quite. I told him, Now get your arse out of here! Stop behaving like a spoilt, petulant brat! Man up, and I don't want to hear any more complaints about you.'

'Jo,' I asked, 'when did you have that long conversation with the doctors?'

She gave me a feigned cherubic smile. 'I didn't.'

I guess – and I hadn't realised this before about my wife – she is capable of being an actress. Years and years of conveying a mood to the camera had trained her to harness and amplify her emotions.

The three on them were here for the family lunch. Michael had one beer with lunch, and he was teasing his brother about his vote with the Tories in Parliament. 'You better be careful, Jeff! Labour is going to send its goon squad after you.'

Abigale was relaxed – and very pretty – said the business was doing OK. And Thomas was playing a noisy video game with his male cousins.

Chapter 12
Jo and Jason

I turn the pages of my notes. "Uncle Bertie, we haven't really talked about your wife or your brother, except incidentally."

"OK, let's start with Jo." He looks out the window for a moment. "Perhaps, I'll just start at the beginning…Jo's mother, Maisy, had two children: Josephine and Herbert, two years older. The father of the children, Conrad, whom Maisy never married, had been in and out of prison for assault and burglary convictions; he would come home drunk with a wad of cash and slap Maisy around. According to Jo's aunt Mildred, Conrad was 'the devil's spawn', but there was a weird love-hate relationship between him and Maisy. He used to take her to a two-star casino on the Isle of Man. Terrible place, but she loved it.

When the children were about eight and six, Maisy fled with them to Mildred after a particularly destructive homecoming by Conrad. 'He came here looking for 'em,' Mildred told me, 'and he started slappin' and punchin' me until Gerald called the cops. He left and never came back, but Maisy went lookin' for him. She was in no shape to find her own belly button.'

I asked Mildred, 'Did Conway ever abuse the children?'

'Abuse? I don't know for sure, but he didn't hesitate to swat 'em around. They wasn't worth tuppence to him.'

Maisy's search became more futile, distant and desperate, culminating in a month-long, non-stop, drinking bender that resulted in her death, at which point Mildred and Gerald took the children into their official care and later adopted them.

It must have been a major transition for childless Mildred and Gerald to suddenly face the task of rearing two abandoned orphans. More importantly for Jo and Herbert was the abrupt upheaval from a chaotic, love-starved, alcohol-saturated environment to an orderly, caring home where Jesus was King.

On reflection, I asked Mildred, 'Why were you and your sister so different?'

'Maisy was twelve years younger than me, Bertie, and you might think that as the late addition, she would be the family pet. But somehow Maisy got it into her head that she was a mistake, and she became extremely rebellious. She refused the rules of our father, and as a result their relationship became impatient love-hate. In acting out her imagined identity as an unwanted rebel, she trashed the family values.'

Gerald and Mildred had a corner florist shop on Garratt Lane, with tiers of blossoming plants outside. There were stacked buckets of flowers from roses to carnations in the humid, sweet-scented interior. A large refrigerated storeroom with foggy, glass doors stood behind the busy counter. Mildred and Gerald have long since passed away, but their florist shop is still there under new ownership.

When Jo was about fourteen, Gerald and Herbert drove out to Reading (where Gerald came from) to watch the Reading Royals play football at Madejski Stadium. They were both killed in a motorway accident on the way home.

Mildred told me that, for Jo, this terrible accident represented a severe metamorphosis, far more significant than the trauma of adoption, and likely comparable to Paul's experience at Damascus. Jo would wail, 'How can God kill two of the dearest people in my life, after snatching away my father and allowing my mother to kill herself?'

Mildred was due much of the credit for Jo's transition to sainthood, stifling her own grief to help her adopted daughter deal with hers. There must have been countless hours of grief-stricken embraces, assurances of condolence and love, but there were many days that they spent in the solitude of St Christopher's Church, during which Mildred transferred to the young Josephine her absolute belief in a loving God and the hateful other.

Jo doesn't talk about her metamorphosis. I only know that Mildred told her to reach out to God in prayer. If Jo did this, Mildred insisted that God would respond to her.

I first met Jo when she was twenty, working part-time as a sales assistant at Debenhams while she was living with Mildred and studying for a degree in English literature. I went into Debenhams, Southside, to look for a birthday gift for my mother, and I was browsing aimlessly around the ground floor. There was this pretty, young woman gazing out wistfully from behind the perfume counter, as if the world was passing her by. There was something lonely and sweet about her. Tentatively encountering me at the far end of her counter, she asked if she could help. When I told her I was looking for a birthday gift for my mother, she considered me as if my appearance in blue dress shirt and jeans would help her divine my mother's the character. I was impressed when she selected six gaudily packaged products and proceeded to describe the scent of each and the personality of the woman who would treasure it. To prolong the transaction, I asked her about her hours of work, what else she was doing, and her ambitions for the future. She told me about her studies at UCL and her ambition to 'eventually' become a fashion model.

I said, 'You should be a fashion model now.' She blushed and said her aunt didn't consider it a suitable occupation.

I formed the impression that she hadn't the time or the freedom under the guidance of a strict aunt to take on a boyfriend. I bought a perfume, and mentioned, casually, that I would see her again.

A day or two later, I asked her what was her favourite perfume. She said, 'Chanel No. 5.' I asked if she had any; she said, 'No,' in a tone which meant, *I'm not entitled to it*. I bought a small vial of the *eau de'cologne*, asked her to wrap it, and gave it to her: 'When you're wearing this, believe that your dream of being a fashion model will come true.'

On Friday, near the end of her shift, I asked her if she would like to have a cup of tea. For a long moment, she hesitated and then nodded. Over an hour and a half, we had three cups of tea and rambled through our personal histories and hopes. At the half hour mark, she called her aunt to say that she was having tea with a friend from work. Finally, I said, 'I'd be very pleased if you and your aunt could have dinner with me any night you choose.'

I had a lot of respect and fondness for Aunt Mildred, and I'd like to believe she was my secret admirer. As for Jo, there was so much to admire in her. She has a sweet naiveté moderated by gutsy endurance, and a formidable mixture of intelligence, common sense and kindness. I was impressed by her longing to be in a 'real family', and her unshakable faith. She was also, far and away, the best-looking young woman who ever gave me the time of day.

We were married six months after we first met."

"Do you want to talk about Uncle Jason?" I ask.

"Yes, OK." My granduncle sits silently in his chair, looking into the distance, sad memories flickering across his face. He takes a deep breath. "When we were kids, his bipolar wasn't so severe. He was four years younger, which is a pretty big age gap, but we used to play together – football and rugby – with a bunch of kids, or just the two of us in the back garden. When we were bored, we'd get up to mischief. I'd find an old tin can, and we'd tie it to the back of somebody's car. Usually, I'd think of the mischief, and I'd urge Jason on to do the dirty work. I guess he thought he'd impress me.

For Jason, education was usually either a great adventure into the unknown or the torture of being dragged to school in chains. Subjects with strict rules like science and mathematics were an anathema, but freewheeling topics, like art, were a treat. His receipt of a high school diploma (a year late and with much help from his friends) was an event worthy of several bottles of Scotch whiskey purloined from our father's raided cabinet.

I remember that as an adolescent, he flirted with the idea of being a stand-up comedian. 'It's so cool to make people laugh, and it's easy for me to think up lots of jokes.' The viability of this option eroded over time with the onslaught of repeated depressive phases.

On the pretext of becoming an art teacher, he signed up for a two-year degree in art, but never obtained the expected teaching certificate.

How he got his job was a mystery. His explanation was simple: 'They hired me!' His hiring predated Jeffrey's election to the council, and it seemed doubtful that Brucie – the road works scheduler – could have been an influence. His job title was something like arts co-ordinator for the council, but to hear him describe his role, it was only a notch or two below the Prime Minister. We know that he dreamt up, arranged and delivered all kinds of art-related, free events for the citizens of Wandsworth. He had a cadre of rabid, art-freak volunteers, mostly women, who provided much of the manual labour involved in publicising these events and bringing them to fruition, and he had infiltrated the various venues around the district with offers of free publicity and customer footfall in exchange for hosting his events: malls, pubs, bingo halls, health clubs, church halls and libraries had welcomed artistic citizens.

For visual art lovers, there were brief classes in painting of all kinds, and for all ages, but mostly beginners, taught by competent volunteers; there were photography workshops where amateurs shared their pictures and experiences. Depending on the kind of music one likes, on Friday and Saturday nights, pubs may feature a local rock group, a guitarist, a singer or singing group, or the Wandle String Quartet. The performers were rewarded with applause and free beer. For the literary set, local published authors gave readings, lectures and book signings, and for aspiring writers, there were self-managed workshops where attendees shared problems, ideas and their work.

Jason's enthusiasm for these creative events, and his vociferous participation in them, had led to a degree of local recognition which had swung his bi-polar balance more toward the manic end of the scale. Nonetheless, if asked what he would like to be doing in ten years' time, his answer was: 'Exactly what I'm doing now.'

When Carol-Ann called to tell me that the council had made Jason redundant, I thought *Oh, dear, that's very bad news!*

I didn't have much chance to spend time with Jason one-on-one, or, as they put it nowadays: 'quality time'. We both worked irregular hours, seven days a week. Of course, I see him on Sundays during the family lunch, but that just amounts to brief brotherly banter. I saw first-hand the effect the redundancy had on Jason one Sunday when Carol-Ann took me aside. 'Bertie, I'm concerned about Jason. Look at him over there. Sitting all by himself and staring at the floor as if he doesn't have a friend in the world. It's not like him, Bertie. He's usually singing and joking by the piano with a bottle of beer in his hand. See that empty glass on the table beside him? That was two-thirds full of whiskey half an hour ago.'

'Have you spoken to him?'

'Yes. He claims he's coming down with the flu—doesn't feel too well—I shouldn't get too close to him—slow to respond to my questions—didn't look me in the eye.' Carol-Ann moved so that I could not avoid her penetrating eye contact. 'I don't think he's sick, Bertie. I think he's very depressed.'

'Have you talked to Gerri about him?'

'Yes. She says he's upset about losing his job. She says he'll get over it. But you know Gerri: she's a chronic optimist who hasn't had more than fifteen minutes of feeling blue in her entire life. I like Gerri a lot, and I'm sure she's very good for Jason, but does she have any idea what real depression is? Could she be empathetic about it? Besides, Bertie, she's a cheerful barmaid. If she got fired tomorrow, how long would it take her to find a new job? Tuesday afternoon she'd be pulling pints somewhere else. Does she really appreciate how rare Jason's job was and how perfectly it fit him?'

I called Jason the next morning. I was worried and not prepared to be fobbed off. 'Jace, are you available for lunch on Wednesday?'

'Naw, Bertie. Haven't been feeling too good lately. Think I'm coming down with a flu.'

'I've already had this year's flu,' I lied, 'so you're safe with me. I'll pick you up with the car and some of my prescription flu medicine at twelve-fifteen.'

'Naw, Bertie. I don't feel like goin' out for lunch. Not usually very hungry.'

'Look, Jace, I'm your brother, remember? And I don't really want to listen to excuses. I want to talk with you. OK? I'm comin' to pick you up on Tuesday at twelve-fifteen!'

We were seated in the lonely far corner of the dining area at The Happy Gardeners, my local, patronised by only three male benefits winos at this hour on a Tuesday. Jason was cradling his double neat whiskey protectively, his eyes fastened to the paper placemat.

'I know it must be very difficult,' I began, 'losing your job.'

A long silence followed in which he seemed to be alone, wondering perhaps how he got here. 'Yeah.'

'What are your plans for the future, Jace?'

He breathed a long sigh. 'Nothin'.'

'Aw, come on, Jace. It isn't the end of the world.'

His head jerked up and for the first time, his eyes met mine. 'How do you know, big brother?' His lips were curled in savage anger.

We stared, confronting each other, for a long time, and were interrupted by the waitress standing next to us. 'What are you going to have, Jason?'

'Another whiskey.'

'To eat?' I asked.

'Nothin'.'

I turned to the waitress. 'We'll have two burgers, medium rare, with chips, and I'll have another ale.'

Bertie swallowed the last of his first whiskey and resumed his sour contemplation of the place mat.

'Jason, I'd like to understand. Tell me why this is so hard for you.'

He gave me a long look of contempt. 'You forget, big brother, how hard I had to fight to get this job. Council didn't want me. I persuaded 'em to give me a one-month trial without pay. Then they paid me five pounds an hour. After nearly thirty years, they paid me twenty pounds, but only because so many people liked the Arts Forum and complained for me.' He took a drink from the new whiskey. 'I'm not like you, Prince Albert. I've got some handicaps. Can't just take whatever comes along. But I loved the arts, and I used to get people excited.'

'I know that, and I think you can still get people excited about the arts.'

'Not anymore, big brother. I've been looking…looking for thirty years for something that pays better. There is nothing…absolutely nothing.' He took another drink. 'So, I'm done.'

I had seen my bipolar brother in plenty of downs, but nothing quite like this. 'I feel sure there are charities out there—arts charities—that would love to have somebody doing what you can do.'

'No!' He slammed his fist down on the table causing his fork to bound to the floor. 'I am fifty-two years old, Albert! I don't have a pension! I can't afford to work for free!'

I paused to let him take another drink. 'Charities have paid staff, and I was…'

'Yeah but,' he interrupted angrily, 'none of 'em has the balls to start a paid Arts Forum like I do.'

'Maybe it could be a little different…'

'Bollocks!' he shouted. 'What really pisses me off is that the council didn't give a rat's arse about all I've done for them. They just see me as some sort of weird person who does stuff they don't give a shit about and who takes money away from their housing budget!'

'The mayor certainly wouldn't say anything like that, neither would all the people who've worked with you over the years, nor would the Professor.' The last bit was me clutching at straws.

'The Professor was the one who got me the job in the first place, and he told me he can't fight city hall nowadays. The mayor doesn't call any shots—it's the suits in the middle—and much as I know you love our great democracy, the voters have no say. They're told, "We have to keep our costs down, madam. Would you rather have your weekly dance session or a care home for your aged mother?"'

Our hamburgers arrived. Jason pushed his away and ordered another whiskey.

'Jason, you know that alcohol is a depressant; when you're in a down mood, it's just going to make things worse for you.'

'Can't make it any worse than it is already,' he snarled. 'Besides, it makes me feel like I'm somebody for an hour or two.'

'I hope you're still taking your medicine.'

'No! I'm sick of that medication!' He banged his fist on the table again, causing the catsup bottle to tip over. 'That medication is just a proof of my handicap. I'm a cripple!'

'You're not a cripple, Jace—or handicapped. You have a condition that can be treated if you take your medication,' I said evenly.

'That is such a load of bollocks!" he shouted. "Do you have any idea, big brother, what it's like to live inside my skin for fifty-two years? A good-for-nothing charity case! If you had been born as me, you would have died of liver failure before you were twenty-five!'

I paused while he rubbed his fist and took another gulp of whiskey. It suddenly occurred to me that my brother was suicidal.

'Jason, have you talked to Samaritans?'

'Yeah.'

'And?'

'I asked them what's better: to go under a train or jump off a cliff.'

I took a long breath. 'For heaven's sake, don't even consider it.'

'Why not?'

'Because all your family—Gerri, me, Carol-Ann and all the others—and all the people you've helped in Arts Forum would be devastated and, in a few months, when you've got a new Arts Forum, you'll be glad you stayed around.'

'I want to tell you two things. First, if you add up all the sadness you mention, it would be a lot less than the sadness I'm feeling right now, and second, there can't be any new Arts Forum—ever. Besides, people will get over their sadness. Hell, Gerri will be married within a year. Take me home, Bertie. Sorry about the hamburger.'

As I look back on it, Sarah, there was nothing we could do. Carol-Ann went to see him a couple of times, and of course, Gerri was with him much of the day. He stopped coming to the Sunday lunches; when I asked Gerri about him the following Sunday, she was irritated and somewhat impatient. 'He's just the same, Bertie—maybe somewhat more mulish.'

'What can we do?'

She pressed her fists together under her chin. 'I got the GP and a psychiatrist to come 'round. He threw them both out. They won't section him—he's no harm to others. All we can do is hope he pulls out of it.' She stared fixedly in the distance. 'Meanwhile, he has no income and all of our savings is going on booze.'

'Shall we take him off your hands for a while?'

'Nice of you, Bertie, but he wouldn't go.' She looked at me briefly. 'You're part of his problem, Bertie, not that it's your fault.'

I was suddenly feeling sick with horror. 'What do you mean, Gerri?'

She waved a hand in dismissal. 'It's the usual story: younger brother idolises older brother and can't live up to the icon.'

I protested, 'But I'm no icon; I, too, have feet of clay.'

Gerri shrugged. 'He was unable to see any clay, as you put it. Only a statue of purest silver.'

'Oh, my God! I wish you'd told me sooner, Gerri. Maybe I could have made you an indecent proposition in front of him.'

She laughed. 'He would have concluded that it was only fair that he should share me.'

Gerri's voice was choked and almost unrecognisable. 'He's done it, Bertie.'

'Oh, my God! What happened?' I glanced at the mobile phone screen, hoping it's a dream, but it's six fifty-five in the morning.

'Beachy Head. Sometime during the night.'

The image of the great, white, looming cliff, topped with lush grass, not far from Seaford flashed into my consciousness.

'There's usually a patrol there, but in the darkness, fog and heavy rain, he wasn't spotted, or they couldn't stop him. He must have been running, because his body landed in the sea, not on the beach, and washed ashore. He was found this morning.'

There was silence between us. I was short of breath with a chest ache. When it receded, there was loneliness, abandonment.

I said, "If he was running, he must have been very determined.'

'Yes.' There was a snuffle. 'I feel I've let the family down.'

'No, Gerri. You've been saving his life for twenty-five years, and we did all we could.'

'I just hope he's in a happier place.' She blew her nose. 'But he didn't believe in any happier places.'

My brother, an atheist? 'I didn't know that.'

'You assume, Bertie, that everyone else has religion, and that you're the odd man out.'

I felt a sudden surge of guilt. 'I hope he didn't take after me.'

'Hard to say. It wouldn't have made any difference either way. Even saints kill themselves.'"

I feel the tears welling up in my eyes. "I really liked Uncle Jason a lot; he could be side-splitting funny and frequently, an absolute whirling dervish. I know sometimes he was down, but he kept pretty much to himself then. Did you know he wrote a recommendation to uni for me?"

"No, I didn't know that."

"He said that he works with lots of artists every day, and I'm 'in the top two percent—for creativity, execution, kookiness and good looks.'"

Uncle Bertie laughs. "Didn't that put some of the admissions officers off?"

"On the contrary. I got two interviews I never expected to get."

He shakes his head sadly. "For me, it's a terrible tragedy that he ended his life."

"I don't agree, Uncle Bertie. He knew that what he came into the world to do so well was over."

"Are you saying that suicide is OK?"

"No, I'm saying that he should be remembered for all the things he did for so many people and not for his suicide."

"OK, I get that, but you said, 'what he came into the world to do.'" He looks puzzled.

"Yes, I did."

"I never thought of that. Very interesting." He is stroking the back of his head. "Do you suppose that you and I came here to produce children's books?"

I just smile at him.

"Carol-Ann," he continues, "found that the blonde vicar was distinctly cool, under the circumstances, to conducting a funeral service, and did not 'encourage the family to be thinking in terms of a memorial at St Bartholomew's'.

Carol-Ann protested that this did not 'seem very Christian, particularly in terms of providing some comfort to a mourning family'.

Reportedly, the response was, 'Only God can end a life, Carol-Ann, and the church must make clear the importance of this belief.'

Carol-Ann told me she was tempted to point out to the vicar that Jesus, as ultimate dispenser of compassion, would surely have found a way to both disapprove the act of suicide and comfort the grieving. 'But I felt that, barring a doctorate in theology, I would be pushing it,' she said.

At Gerri's suggestion, she, Carol-Ann and I were repeating the boat trip out into the English Channel from Newhaven, this time with my brother's ashes. 'Jason would never have wanted a headstone in Wandsworth—or any other cemetery,' Gerri said, 'not even one next to his mother.'

Released downwind, the ashes swirled and drifted, skimming across the waves before being captured in the seafoam. Yes, this was the way Jason would have liked it: being re-united with cosmos earth. He wouldn't have liked any sort of formal remembrance service, with long-faced, weepy relatives standing about, sipping red wine to warm their spirits. But, he would have liked the free-for-all remembrance we had last Sunday, at which only funny Jason skits were permitted, and involved even his grandnephews and grandnieces, including thirteen-year-old Willie, Jeff and Cathy's younger son, who gave an uproarious imitation of Jason singing and playing the guitar with no attention to the music.

I remember encountering the Professor not long after Jason's death. He said he tried to get the council to re-hire Jason, and I thanked him for his efforts.

The Professor looked up at the sky and a smile slowly slid across his face. 'When he was down—I could tell when he was down: it was written all over him—I used to say to him, Jason, go home, take your medicine, go and sit on the embankment. Notice how everything moves on: the river flows to the sea; the clouds keep passing overhead; and people are always hurrying somewhere. The world isn't going to stop for you or your illness, because it, too, is going to pass. And when he was up, I would say to him, Jason, I want you to do me a favour: I want you to remember—really remember—how the world is for you today!'

I smiled and patted the Professor's shoulder. 'What I'm having trouble understanding is why Jason rejected all the help that was available to him, and why he saw himself as a complete failure, because he wasn't a failure.'

The Professor considered me for a long moment. 'I'll tell you why, Bertie: because the devil got involved.'

I could see that the Professor was completely serious. Doubtful, I leant back in my chair. 'How, exactly, did the devil get involved?'

He took a deep breath before responding. 'You know about the devil, Bertie?'

'Well, sort of. Father is trying to convince me that the devil is the author of all the bad things that happen in the world.'

'Father who?'

'Father Anthony.'

The Professor chuckled. 'The old exorcist. Well, he should know.' He breathed a long sigh. 'I don't know exactly how the devil does it, Bertie, but, trust me, he does it. We can't see him, but he can see us. He can hear us, but most of us—except people like Father Anthony – can't hear him. We can try to talk to him—I don't recommend it—but we don't know what he hears—pretty much everything, I reckon. It seems to me that he can talk to us without us hearing him—like directly into our subconscious. And, with somebody like Jason, he'd be telling him over and over, You are a failure. You ought to kill yourself! He keeps it up, using his honey-coated tongue, until the person believes.'

'But why would he pick on Jason?'

The Professor was apologetic. 'Well, the devil may be lazy but he's not stupid. He'll pick out the most vulnerable people—the people without faith—to do his dirty work.'

'And why does the devil do all this dirty work?'

'It's his job, Bertie.'

I couldn't resist telling Jo about my conversation with the Professor. Initially, she made no comment, but I decided not to let her get away with that. 'Come on, Jo, so you believe the devil is like that?"

Her enigmatic smile appeared. 'Something like that, but the Professor seems to have worked it out in some detail.'"

Chapter 13
Carol-Ann and Raymond

Uncle Bertie seems distressed this morning. He looks like he hasn't slept or shaved; when he sits down, he fidgets and sighs. I am about to ask him about my grandmother, but I decide to ask, "Uncle Bertie, are you all right?"

He bites his lip, looks at me and then away. I wait for a while.

"No, I'm not all right."

"What is it?"

"Do you remember my nightmare about the doctor with the grey crew cut?"

"Yes." There is a sinking feeling in my stomach as I wait for what I fear is coming.

"Well, he came back last night."

"Oh, dear!"

There is a long silence.

"What did he say?"

"He kept pointing at this computer screen and shouting, 'It's malignant! Inoperable! You have six months.' I must have been shouting, too, because I woke Jo up.

'It's just a dream, Bertie. A very bad dream,' Jo said."

"Let's take a walk around King George's Park. Maybe there's a morning football match at the Academy."

We go out into the park and walk for about half an hour. Boys are practising football, but no game; there are lots of dogs, some sunshine and a pleasant breeze. The crocuses are blooming, and the daffodils are starting to open in large clumps. We sit on a bench and he says, "Yesterday we talked about my wife and my brother. Shall we talk about my sister and her husband?"

"That's fine." I open my notebook and press the button on the recorder.

"Did you ever see your grandmother at work?" he asks.

"No."

"Well, she operated in the eye of a tornado at work. Somehow, she managed to appear calm while there was chaos all around her. My impression was that inflated egos of the people she served put unreasonable and conflicting cost, schedule and content demands on her. She was the stage manager of a local theatre, presenting art films, live music from rock to classic, operatic excerpts, corporate presentations, political events, snooker, bridge, beauty and darts contests, and plays of every sort from wildly alternative to traditional favourites. The sets, the lighting, audio, video, props, pianos, on-stage seating, backstage and dressing rooms, and so on are all her responsibility. There was a part-time, semi-reliable crew of six, and several dozen outside suppliers on whom she depended.

I remember when Jo and I had tickets to a *Classics of Opera Night*, and we were invited to come by on Saturday morning to see the preparations. There was a melee of people on the stage, loud voices and plenty of gesticulation.

'The backdrop is completely wrong!' a fat man with his white hair slicked back into a ponytail was shouting.

Carol-Ann turned to look at it briefly. 'It's the same one we used last year.'

'But...' The man took hold of Carol-Ann's shoulder. 'We have a different opera this year. Different singers, different music, completely different programme!'

'So.' Carol-Ann swung to face him. 'You want a different background, Mr Kleinfeld.' A statement, not a question. 'Norman, would you take Mr Kleinfeld to see the backdrop curtains we have? You can have whichever one you like, Mr Kleinfeld'. We later learnt that Mr Kleinfeld was the 'empresario' responsible for taking the four hapless singers from one enthusiastic venue to the next.

The orchestra was beginning to rehearse, and there was an issue with the grand piano. 'There is no piano solo so it doesn't need to be in the front. Put it in the back out of the way.' This was the directive of a spindly legged man with a walrus moustache, whom I assumed to be the concertmaster. Unsurprisingly, the pianist was having none of it. 'I can't see the conductor from back there. It's all very well for you, sitting right next to him, to relegate me to the rear.' The conductor, head down in his sheet music, was studiously ignoring this spat until Carol-Ann accosted him. 'This is not my problem. You sort it out and tell Norman where the piano goes.'

One of the luckless singers, an overweight alto made up to take a good thirty-years off her six decades, announced, 'There is no refrigerator in my dressing room. Would you please have one installed?'

'Madam,' Carol-Ann responded, 'this, unfortunately, is not La Scala. If you want to chill your gin, you'll have to use the fridge in the lunchroom."

The singer feigned great offense. 'I have no use for gin. It's my special mineral water from the Alps I'm worried about.'

'Sorry, madam, but I can assure you that none of the staff drink water.'

Carol-Ann had reported to the same director of operations for twenty years, moving up to the position from being senior stagehand at a West End theatre. It was in the West End that her dream faded. She had graduated with a degree in music, and an advanced level of proficiency in the violin, soon to be translated into a seat in a chamber orchestra, part time. Then she met Kevin, her first husband, became pregnant, and the music faded, but when Anne, your mother, went to nursery, she found a seat in the West End Theatre Orchestra. This was fine when a musical was running, but when a drama was booked and without other connections, there was nothing. Perhaps she felt the need to be absent from new husband, Raymond, during the day. In any event, she took a full-time position as stagehand at the theatre.

I knew she would feel as if she were on board a rocket at lift-off if she could sit in the violin section of the London Philharmonic. But unfortunately, there was no fuel in the rocket: she has no compelling credentials, and her old skills, good as they are, would not propel her to succeed in an audition.

She was philosophical about it. 'I have a good boss who lets me run my show, which is always busy, often with idiots, but sometimes with heroes, and it's nice to have money of my own.'

I wondered who these heroes were: good looking actors, robust trumpet players, or maybe Latin conductors?"

"Uncle Bertie, do you think that my nan is happy in her work? I mean she never got to be a violinist in a top orchestra."

"I think so, Sarah. Without her job at the theatre, how could she satisfy her repressed need to command? Raymond would never put up with it, but he's useful in other ways, if you know what I mean. She is an icon in the family, a saint in her church, The boss at the theatre, and she can have that violin cradled at her chin on a whim."

He continues, "After Brucie's death at Seaford, Carol-Ann told me that Raymond, Brucie's father, had an MRI that showed that his aorta also had a dangerous aneurism. The cardiologist recommended that he consult with a specialist surgeon immediately to arrange for corrective surgery. Carol-Ann said, 'Raymond has learnt that the mortality rate in surgery for someone of his age and condition is about seven percent, that recovery takes six months, and can be painful for the first couple of months. I'm afraid he's trying to rationalise putting off the surgery.'

'He can't do that,' I said. 'Didn't the cardiologist tell him there is a high probability of the aneurism rupturing soon?'

'No. In fact, risk probabilities weren't discussed. I suppose the cardiologists don't want to terrorise their patients with statistics. Raymond says that an internet site mentions some patients end up dying of other causes.'

'Oh, for goodness' sake. We've got to keep working on him, Carol-Ann!'

Raymond was in a red plaid bathrobe, laying on the bed propped up on a pile of pillows. His eyes were closed, there was a surly expression on his face, and his hands were laced across his ample waist.

This was the first time I'd seen him since he came home from the hospital, having received a call from Carol-Ann: 'Ray is suffering from flaccid upper lip. A little male company may encourage him to give up being a wimp.'

'You look pretty well, Ray. How are you feeling?'

'Terrible,' he said, opening one eye.

'I understand the surgeon says you're doing very well.'

'What does he know? He cut me from here to here! Just like a damn chicken!' He pulled open the lapels of the bathrobe, revealing a bright pink line extending from his collar bone to his upper belly. Small pink dots on either side of the line marked where the staples were. It was a pretty impressive scar.

'I suppose it hurts a bit when you cough, Ray.'

Then I realised my blunder. He squeezed his eyes shut and lamented, 'Oh, Bertie, you don't know the half of it. I can't get comfortable at night. Sometimes I get terrible heart burn, and I'm sure the implant has come loose.' He looked up at the ceiling morosely.

'Well, you'll soon be feeling better, Ray.'

Carol-Ann came in with a small tray with tea and ginger snaps and set it down next to him on the bed.

'Soon be better. Ha! I have another five months of this to endure, not counting all the physiotherapy I have to go through, and the long walks, and not being able to lift anything or to drive. I was doing just fine before the operation.'

Carol-Ann, fists on hips, glared at her husband. 'Don't forget what happened to Brucie!'

'Yeah, Brucie! It's because of him that I have to go through all this.'

My mouth was just open to respond, but my sister gave me a wave off. 'Raymond!' Her voice was probably loud enough to reach the street. 'You started this. He inherited the aneurism from you.'

'Yeah, and I probably got it from my grandfather.'

'Wherever you got it, you're lucky to be alive, Raymond.'

'Well, I don't feel so damn lucky,' he pouted.

'You should feel thankful, Raymond,' Carol-Ann said. 'You should be thankful to the women's prayer group—fourteen women—prayed for you, beginning weeks before your operation, and some of them are probably still praying for you.'

Raymond's mouth was open, but silent. 'The prayer group?' he finally inquired, 'But, I don't know about that.'

'No, you don't. But they all know you.'

He coughed unnecessarily. 'So, what did they pray for?'

'They prayed that your operation would be successful and that you would recover quickly.'

'And what do I have to do now? Give money?'

'That would be nice. Better yet, you can pray for them.'

On the way out, I asked Carol-Ann about how often—in her experience—prayers were successful. She looked at me sceptically, knowing my religious history. 'You expect me to tell you they work every time?'

'No, I honestly want to know what you can tell me.'

'Well, I haven't any statistics, but if you go to Lourdes, they'd probably quote you a high number, and an atheist would probably say, "But how much of that good result is due to the patient, himself, believing that he had been cured?" The plain fact, Bertie, is that if prayer were statically proven, we would be spending half our time on our knees, and atheists would be out of business. But, nonetheless, I think prayer is effective.'

'In what way?'

'Several ways. It's a means of caring for someone else that makes us feel a little better about ourselves. It brings the carer into direct communication with God; that's good. The person for whom the prayer is said will feel more optimistic about a positive outcome: also good. And, who knows, maybe the prayer is heard and there is a positive outcome. Call that a miracle, if you wish.'"

"What's your view on prayer, Uncle Bertie?"

He takes a deep breath and looks past me. "Well, at the time, I thought perhaps I should give it a try. But you know, Sarah, when most of your life you've told yourself that prayer is a self-indulgent waste of time, you don't know how to start. You tell yourself *I should,* but then you don't know how. It's like trying to learn a new language in your sixties."

"So, were you a hopeless case?"

"I got quite a lot of help from Father Anthony."

He stands up to stretch and sits down. "You know, Sarah, when I reflect on Carol-Ann and Raymond as a couple, I am amazed at the choice of spouses that people make. I find myself thinking: why <u>him</u>? Or why <u>her</u>? For example, why did Jo choose me? She's a beautiful, intelligent, successful, kind woman. What would she want with the likes of me? OK, she is a little stubborn, a bit too idealistic, doesn't like sports or dirty jokes. She can't sing or play music, or sew, but she's a good mother, friend and lover: just what I need.

In my sister's case, it's more difficult: Raymond is a pain in the arse. Why did she go for him? The easy answer is he has money, but Carol-Ann has a decent job, and Raymond is hardly a tycoon. When they were dating, and she was in a frenetic hunt for a new mate, she said, 'he's very bright' – a trait she clearly admires, but she's no myopic in need of a seeing-eye dog. In fact, when it comes to empathy and tact, he's like one of those blind skiers: without her, he'd be hitting every tree on the slope. OK, he's not bad looking and there are reports (none from me) that he can be quite charming. As for his kids: Brucie – rest his soul – was not a great reference for skilful parenting. Your mother, Anne, Carol-Ann's daughter by her first husband, Kevin, avoids outright hostility by smiling a lot. And Albert, Carol-Ann's son by Raymond, sidesteps disagreements via adroit political manoeuvring.

Could it be sex? Jo doesn't think so, and I can only extrapolate old data on Carol-Ann. Maybe it's shared values? The only one I can think of that they both think that family is important."

"I think that's it, Uncle Bertie: family," I say, "Mom told me that Poppa Ray had no family at all when he met my nan; it was just him, Brucie and Margaret. His first wife, Miriam, had a large, interactive family, and Poppa Ray was kind of a king pin. So, when he was divorced by Miriam, her family shunned him and he was an outcast. He became a stray dog with two puppies, who found our handsome pack of show dogs and was invited in, for which he is very grateful."

"Maybe that's why he has trouble getting along with me: he thinks he should be top dog."

"Maybe subconsciously," I say, "but I'm sure he knows that could never have been possible. Besides, he has a grudging admiration for you." I take a moment to look at my notes. "And I think my nan always wants to have a man around. In my opinion, it isn't just about sex, it's to satisfy the feeling that she isn't complete without a mate."

Uncle Bertie laughs. "As far as I know, my lovely sister hasn't been without a man for more than a month since puberty."

I close my eyes and shake my head, refusing to be drawn further on the subject. "Let me ask you, Uncle Bertie, did you sympathise with Poppa Ray when he tried to postpone his operation?"

"If I'm truthful, Sarah, Ray would look like a stoic hero compared to me. I would be a craven coward, hiding in my closet unable to even think about open-heart surgery. I still have nocturnal, quarterly visits from that same neurologist with the grey crew cut, from which I wake up in a cold sweat. And good old Doctor Ramsden, who's aware of my fear, thinks he's being helpful by mollycoddling me every time I have a sniffle, but actually he's just amplifying my paranoia."

"Were you involved," I ask, "when Poppa Ray was diagnosed with cancer?"

"Yes, it started with a request from Carol-Ann as she cornered me in the kitchen on Sunday afternoon and said confidentially, 'Bertie, I need your help on a particular issue with Raymond.'

My suspicious curiosity was immediately aroused, but I put on a neutral face. 'What is it, Carol-Ann?'

'Well, in the last year, he's been quite tired. He puts it down to growing older, but I felt it was more than that, and I insisted he see the GP. You know how he hates anything to do with doctors, but I finally dragged him to the surgery, and I have to say that the GP listened to me, asked Raymond a lot of questions, examined him and ordered some blood tests. Of course, Raymond procrastinated for weeks before he finally had the blood test. The surgery called and said the doctor wanted to see him about the results of the blood test.'

'Oh, dear.'

'It turned out that Raymond has pretty severe anaemia. That startled him a bit. The doctor then said she wanted him to do a faecal blood screening – you know: one of those tests where you take a sample once a week for three weeks.' Carol-Ann grimaced and took a deep breath. 'I had to take the samples and send in the envelope.' She looked down at her clasped hands. 'The surgery called again, and when we went to see the doctor, she said that the results were positive, and she recommended that Raymond have a colonoscopy.' A long sigh of resignation. 'When Raymond heard what a colonoscopy is, I could almost hear him thinking to himself *I'm not having that!*'

Carol-Ann paused and looked pleadingly at me.

'So,' I said, 'you want me to talk him into it.'

'Please, Bertie.'

I thought for a moment. 'I've never had a colonoscopy; I've had a flexible sigmoidoscopy about five years ago, but that doesn't cover the whole colon. It wasn't too bad.'

'Well, tell him that, and tell him that he can have a sedative. I'm afraid this is much more serious that he thinks.'

'You can tell him that.'

'Come on, Bertie! This is a man thing. He thinks he's tough and doesn't need all these silly medical treatments. You remember how he was with the aorta problem. The only thing that scared him into having that surgery was his son's death.'

'OK, Carol-Ann, I'll give it a try.'

I found Raymond in his local, sitting with some friends, on a Tuesday evening. So as not to create an urgent situation, I leant over and said softly, 'Can I have a word with you Raymond when you have a chance?' I ordered a pint of best bitter and sat at the bar.

Raymond sat next to me and said, 'What is it, Bertie?'

I got up and moved to a booth in the back. 'How are you, Raymond?'

'I'm doing just great.'

I looked around as if something had eluded me. 'Carol-Ann says you have a health issue."

'Don't believe everything she tells you, Bertie. I'm doing fine.'

'How can you say that you're doing fine when your red blood cell count is two point nine when the minimum is four point seven?' (I have no idea what his RBC is, but 30% below the minimum sounds scary to me.)

For a moment, he looked confused. 'Well, I do get a little sleepy in the afternoon.'

'Of course! And that's because of all the blood you're losing.'

'What are you talking about, Bertie?'

'I'm talking about all the blood that you're flushing down the loo.'

'Oh, come on, Bertie. Just a spot now and then.'

'You think that a spot now and then is causing you to be sleepy in the afternoon? No way!'

"OK, Doctor Smithson, what's causing it?"

'Thank you, Raymond, but you know I'm not a doctor. What did the GP tell you?'

'She said that I should have a colonoscopy, but you know how these female doctors are. They send you to have all sorts of useless tests.'

'Why do you think it's a useless test?'

He frowned and looked towards the barman as if <u>he</u> knew the answer to this question. 'Well…I've never heard of anyone having test like that.'

'I had a proctoscopy about four years ago, and they found a polyp which they removed.'

He sat forward in his chair. 'Was it malignant?'

'No, fortunately, it wasn't, and it was a simple procedure—just half an hour, during which I was awake.'

He adjusted his position as if it was causing discomfort. 'It must have been pretty painful to have that great probe shoved up your bum!'

'You know, it's amazing, Raymond. The scope, complete with light and camera is only one centimetre in diameter.' I held up my separated thumb and forefinger. 'Actually,' I continued, 'it's always possible to have a sedative to relieve some to the tension.'

'Are you getting a commission from the doctor?'

'I can tell you one thing, so it doesn't take you by surprise.'

'What's that?'

'The doctor explained to me that the colon is like an accordion—with pleats in its circumference—and to open the pleats, to look inside, the doctor will release a little air into the colon.'

Raymond smiled. 'So, you feel you have to fart.'

'Exactly, and it's all gone ten minutes later.'

'Well, I don't know, Bertie. I'm not very keen on it.'

'The way I look at it, you invest half an hour of inconvenience to find out that the problem's not very serious, and if it is serious, they'll soon have a plan to really fix it. It may be a situation like your aorta, where the fix has added many years to your life.'

Ray agreed to have procedure done, but Carol-Ann had to make the arrangements. The result was not good; there was a major tumour near the beginning of his colon. MRI scans revealed that part of the liver was involved. With this complication in mind, the doctors had recommended that the colon cancer tumour be removed surgically, followed immediately by direct liver chemotherapy.

The surgeon reported that the surgery had gone well, with a section of the colon removed and a cannula inserted into the hepatic artery to be supplied by an external pump feeding chemicals continuously. I gathered that the success of this strategy depended on the assumption that the malignancy had not spread further.

Raymond was not taking the chemotherapy well, either physically or psychologically. He had lost weight (not a bad development, actually), he was tired, without appetite, feeling sick and his lower digestive tract was functioning erratically. Carol-Ann said that he was complaining constantly, and when I visited him, he had no interest in talking about anything except the horrors of his treatment. I suggested television, a book, a podcast, a Fulham game in a wheelchair, anywhere in a wheelchair. No, No, NO!

I was wondering whether he would really prefer to be dead.

But how could that be: at least he had a chance of coming out the other side of this alive. *If only he would accept that distracting himself would both make it more bearable and give his body a chance to heal.* But then I recognised that this was me thinking and not at all what I would be feeling if I were in Raymond's shoes: illogical terror.

Chapter 14
Zeus Construction

"Uncle Bertie, you've mentioned Zeus Construction a couple of times. You worked for them for quite a long time, but then you left. Why did you leave?"

"To help you understand, Sarah. It's probably best if I go back to the Franklin Building job…Pouring concrete is a tricky business. If it's not done efficiently, a batch can begin to set, before the next pour is added. This can lead to 'cold joints' which are horizontal planes in the finished concrete. A cold joint in a vertical column constitutes a major strength reduction.

On a large job like Franklin, there is a concrete truck scheduled to arrive every fifteen minutes, and everyone associated with the pour must be focused and effective. There's no time for daydreaming or breaks. As construction foreman on a crew of six men (no women on this crew) during a concrete pour, I have everyone assigned to specific duties. Brad was at the truck with the driver, making sure that the concrete flowed steadily to the pumper. The two Poles were at the pumper. Frankie and Mort were the delivery team: Frankie directed the boom operator to the column and Mort monitored the in-column fill. Then I had the new guy, Faheed, standing by ready to make slump tests, in case the mix started to harden too soon, and water needed to be added.

I'm not superstitious, but I was apprehensive then. I was short two guys: both the Poles had called in sick, so I transferred Brad to boom operator, and Faheed to monitor the pumper and engine. I was usually on the delivery floor, observing the process, and shouting directions.

We were at a point where a delivery truck, and the queue behind it, were half an hour late with traffic problems. We had to wash out the pump and shut it down while we waited. The delivery team had come down out of the structure to take a break.

Finally, and even later than forecasted, a truck arrived, but there was trouble getting the pump started.

Everything ran smoothly through another four trucks. At the start of the fifth delivery, Frankie directed the boom to a column, and as the fill was about to begin, Mort suddenly yelled out: 'Stop! This column is already half full!'

I investigated and found that Frankie, during the break in filling, lost track of which column was next. As a result, the half-full column had been neglected for several hours. The site manager was advised, and he directed that the column be isolated to deal with a probable cold joint. This was serious. The half-full column had to be stripped of its forms, a structural expert from head office was called out to direct repairs, and the site manager was mad. Angry, because there was more expense on an already tight budget, and because concrete fill was on the project critical path, meaning that the entire project could be delayed. Mad, also, because he was one of the most critical and short-tempered bosses I ever worked for – successful, yes, but a son-of-a-bitch to work for.

'Bertie, explain to me how this happened!' He was standing in my personal space, nearly shouting.

I took half a step back. 'It seems that Frankie lost track of the columns during all the waiting.'

'For Christ's sake, Bertie, has he got anything better to do? I've been watching him, Bertie. He's always joking around—no wonder he wasn't paying attention. We don't need comedians on this job; I think he needs a P45 (the final payslip on termination of employment).'

I felt the heat of resentment swell up in me for the boss' easy fault-finding. 'Frankie's been with the company a long time, Conrad. He's also black. So, he could fight us twice for discrimination at employment tribunal.'

'Nobody's calling him a lazy old n-----, but if that's what he is, he ought to go. Let me remind you, Bertie, that it's <u>your</u> job to monitor the performance of your team. And, I should ask why <u>you</u> didn't keep track of the columns.'

'That's a task I delegate, Conrad, and I have other things on my mind.'

'Like what? Like whether you're being kind enough to your boys?'

'Like how I'm going to run my crew with a third of them absent.'

Conrad turned away in disgust. Over his shoulder, he said, 'We haven't heard the last of this, Bertie!'

When I talked to Frankie about it, he said, 'Sorry, boss, I screwed up. Lately, I have a lot of stuff on my mind.'

I could imagine. He was in his late fifties, younger than me, and he had refused to take the slightly enhanced early retirement package. His wife had cancer; she was unable to work. His son, daughter and three grandchildren lived with them on a council estate. The son – mid-thirties – had severe MS but helped out at home. The daughter – a single mother – worked as checkout staff at Poundland. I thought it was amazing that Frankie had any sense of humour at all, and I was sure he absolutely needed his salary.

There was that unsubtle criticism from Conrad that I was too soft on my crew. Probably, I was softer on them than a lot of other foremen. Oh, I talked tough with them, but they knew that was expected, and down deep it was not me. They tended to share their personal problems with me – particularly the problems that may affect their work. For example, Dawidek, the younger Pole and Erni, his cousin, had a wedding to go to somewhere in Poland that weekend, and they had to drive. They already had their vacation time planned, and time off without pay was awkward. They'd call in sick and get the right paperwork from a Polish GP.

Construction had a pretty hard culture – near zero empathy. It was hard work for hard men. Who needs the warm, friendly, social courtesies? They just get in the way.

I didn't know it's like this when I first signed on. You had to adapt if you were going to survive. Would I sign on again, if I had to start over again? Probably not. Make that <u>certainly</u> not, if I knew then what I know now. Back then, I had a place at South London Polytechnic, and my father was urging me to 'Study something technical. The future will be technical, Bertie'. There were courses in electrical and mechanical technology, and something called construction management that led to a three-year degree. Electrical and mechanical sounded more difficult, while construction sounded practical: lots of building was underway, and I liked making things. My first three of thirty-seven years with Zeus Construction, I worked as an apprentice in the logistics department. Then, I was assigned to a big rail project. But most of my career had been in the head office in half a dozen, first-level management positions, shuffled from one to the next when I was desperate for change. Several times I tried to change companies, and once, I got to the interview stage, where my prospective boss asked me which was more important: output or morale. I said something like, 'They're interrelated, so it depends on the situation.'

I'm just not a tough guy, and I concluded that my only chance to get some kind of promotion is to do a good job on this Franklin Project: it's important and it's in the field where careers are made or broken.

So here I am, in a job for which I'm not well suited and which I don't really enjoy, nearing retirement. I feel very torn: I could have been happier – and more successful – in some other vocation, but I'd never been on the dole. I have some good friends and a great family, we'd been OK financially, and this, after all, is what life is: you don't get to choose everything.

Conrad Morgan had sent for me. This was unexpected. He usually finds me on the site, or calls his directions via the mobile radio network. When I entered the site office portacabin, Conrad was sitting at his desk, alone. No one else was there, though five other managers shared the three remaining desks. There were battered steel filing cabinets, including a large drawing file topped with a pile of drawings, clothing lockers, and dozens of safety-related postings taped to the walls. External construction noise was muffled to permit the use of telephones. Nearly everything was covered in a veneer of ochre dust.

'There you are, Smithson,' he said, swivelling his chair around toward me. Not 'Bertie', as normal, but 'Smithson'. At my core, there was a sudden vacuous feeling. "I've decided to change you out. You're not cut out for construction management. Johnny Priorfield is coming in to take your place.'

'But, Conrad, I've been doing construction management work for over thirty years.'

'Not very well, I'm afraid, as you'll recall from my last review of your performance.'

What was he talking about? The review lasted all of five minutes and all he focused on was my 'hands-off management' and the need to 'ride herd on your people'.

My brain was chaotic; a bitter surge of anger rose in me. I couldn't think of anything to say except, 'So, after over thirty-five years of working for Zeus on dozens of projects, mostly on time and within budget, I'm out of a job?'

He said nothing. I turned and headed for the door without a word.

He called out, 'Talk to HR. They may have something for you.'

I turned around, strode to my locker, opened it, and changed slowly and methodically into my street clothes, keeping him always to my back. No word was spoken. I could sense his uncertainty and discomfort, as he shuffled papers on the desk. He got up and left.

I departed the site and walked aimlessly. What should I do? *You should go home. Yes, I know, but I need to think first.* Gradually, I became aware that I was ashamed to confess to my family, but particularly to Jo, that I'd been fired. There was a self-critical bias within me that was saying, 'you didn't measure up as a manager, Bertie.' It was unthinkable that Zeus – third largest in the industry and my working home for thirty-seven years – could have erred in its decision to let Morgan fire me. Therefore, I was guilty of the cardinal sin of management malfeasance. *You didn't measure up, Bertie. You may have tried, but your incompetence gradually caught up with you.* I felt physically sick.

I walked through Holborn, busy with thousands of people whom I do not see, filled with traffic that made no impression, a beehive of active shops and offices, noisy, odoriferous with fast food. An assault on my senses that I barely recognised.

What to do?

Perhaps don't admit to being fired. Say that I quit. They would believe me – even Jo. I could do that. After a while, though, Jo would know. I couldn't lie to her forever. So, I'd tell her. What to do with the others? I don't know, but Jo would know.

I had to make sure I got paid for my unused holidays. Make sure my pension pot was correct, and that they had the right figure for my employee shares. I'd call Jim Westcot. Maybe he knows of an opening I could fill.

As I dialled the number, I felt the grey shroud lift from my shoulders. I could see a faint glimmer of hope. The call went to voice mail. I left a message.

What else? What could I do to that bastard? Hire a hit man? *Come on, Bertie, be sensible.* Anybody else I should contact? Friends? Old bosses? Would anybody be surprised? Would anyone be angry on my behalf? The grey shroud settled itself once again.

I was at my front door. Looking around, I found there was no one to observe me entering at 11:13 am.

I called out, 'Jo?'

No reply.

Footsteps on the upper stairs. 'Bertie?…Bertie, is that you?'

'Yes.'

She paused to look at me. 'What happened?'

'I've been fired.'

'Oh.' There was no shock, just apprehension. Her hands reached out to me. There was her arm around my shoulder. 'Come to the kitchen. Let's get a cup of tea.'

I looked across the table at her, and I could feel her focus entirely on me. 'Tell me, Bertie.'

She listened, tea mug in hand. She put it down. 'They don't deserve you, Bertie.'

I gave a snort. 'They think they deserve better.'

'Of course, but they won't find it. What are you thinking?'

'I've got a call in for Jim Westcot; maybe he has something for me.'

She pursed her mouth as if encountering a disagreeable taste. 'Bertie, I think you ought to get shot of that outfit. Take your pension and run.'

If I had really thought about it, I would have known that's what she would say. 'What should I tell the family—neighbours, etcetera?'

She gave a shrug. 'Not important. Tell them that by mutual consent, you've decided to take an early retirement package. Anybody who knows you knows you weren't happy there.'

Jim Westcot always wore a rumpled white shirt and striped tie with a shiny, soiled knot. He was a thin, nervous fellow, whose leathery face was much as it was when he hired me and who still had an officious nameplate informing all visitors: James E Westcot, Personnel Manager. Perhaps that nameplate and his intimate knowledge of the peccadillos of every senior manager had kept him here forty years.

'Hmm, bit of a pickle, eh, Bertie?' He paused to look at the ceiling. 'Ever see him drinking on the job?'

'Who?'

'Conrad.'

'No.'

'Rumour has it that he does.' Jim said. I gave a shrug. 'Well, about the only thing I've got is for a QC specialist on a small job we have in Manchester. It's a grade nine, represented. Interest you?'

Grade nine: five grades below me, and Manchester? Forget it! 'I don't think so. What's early retirement look like?'

'I thought so.' He reached for a manila folder and perused its contents until he found the sheet he was looking for. 'Age sixty, grade fourteen manager, thirty-seven years' service: sixty-four-point seven percent of final salary, plus optional health insurance—family coverage—comes to one ninety-eight-fifty a month.' He looked up at me.

'I'll take it.'

'You don't want to think about it?'

'What's to think about?'

He put on a coy expression. 'Well, I could give you, say, three months, with pay, to think about it, and then the two-point-seven percent cost of living kicks in, which would mean nearly two percent extra in your pension.'

He really was a pretty good guy, and I guess he did like me after all these years. 'Thanks, Jim, thanks a lot!'

'Anything you can tell me about Conrad?'

'Rumour has it that he has a collection of porn.'

'On the corporate laptop?'

'Yeah.'

'Thanks, Bertie and good luck!"'

"I can remember, Uncle Bertie, that was a pretty rough time for you."

"You know, Sarah, it's like the death of a friend: someone who was important in your life is gone, permanently. OK, I wasn't happy working construction, but after thirty-seven years, you depend on it – it's part of who you are, or at least who you think you are, and when that friend suddenly and completely rejects you, you feel betrayed.

I just had to get out of the house. Finding a job is like being cooped up like a battery chicken for six months trying to lay an ordinary egg. One would think that at four-point-eight percent unemployment, there would be plenty of choices, but I don't fancy stuffing shelves in Sainsbury's, driving for Uber, sorting potatoes in Sussex, filling potholes for the council, security guarding at the mall, reading metres for Thames Water, caring for the elderly at Primrose House, or teaching assistance role in school. So far, I've sent out responses to seventy-three advertised professional positions – jobs I felt were interesting and work that I could do – like logistics supervisor at a freight company, sales engineer for a roofing supplier, environmental technician with a refuse company, and maintenance supervisor on a large private estate. There were sixteen replies informing me that my application was unsuccessful, four of which indicated that 'more qualified' candidates had been selected. I've had two interviews. The freight company had interviews over three days, and on the day I was there, there must have been ten other candidates. After a brief discussion, I was informed that I didn't have sufficient logistics experience. Similarly, the roofing company told me I lacked a sales track record. It was always what I didn't have and never about what I possess: maturity, dependability, honesty, trustworthiness, people skills, and an eagerness for work.

It is downright depressing to continually feel like a loser!

Chapter 15
A to Z

"It must have hard on you and Aunt Jo for you to be without a job," I say.

He scoffs. "It may have actually been harder on <u>her</u> having a sourball of a husband under foot all day, and I'm sure she was looking for other remedies besides sending me out to do the shopping or offering my DIY expertise on projects that other Smithson families were undertaking. One night at dinner, she suggested, 'Bertie, I think we ought to get a dog.'

I thought about it for a moment and recognised what she was really saying: *Bertie, you need a dog.*

Excellent idea!

Much as I was eager to demonstrate my resilience in the face of adversity, I could see the benefit to my mood in having a loyal companion, unconditionally devoted, available twenty-four-seven. Besides, some walking exercise would do me good physically and mentally.

I searched the Internet and after examining the pros and cons of various breeds, I decided that a golden retriever was my kind of dog. Mature dog or puppy? Looking at pictures, I was captivated by adventurous, cuddly, roly poly puppies. Besides, I liked the idea of establishing a relationship from the beginning. What if an older dog decided that after a week or two s/he doesn't like me? There are plenty of puppies from which to choose. There was one advert which had a video of a litter of eight puppies cavorting around their mum. Not registered…a little less money…four still available…location: St Albans. I made an appointment and hurried off to see.

I found three females and one male. They were all delightful as I sat on the floor with their mother, getting acquainted. But the male won my heart when he bounced over, looked up at me, took my trouser leg in his teeth, pulled, gave up and climbed into my lap, from which vantage point he surveyed the activities of his sisters.

I was reminded of my father's dog when I was growing up: a shaggy, mid-size mongrel named Jake who was devoted to my father. At the time, I had a hankering for the companionship of my own dog, but it was not permitted, and gradually the desire faded. Now it was back, irresistibly.

He was going to look like a grand and golden domesticated lion, and my birth date is in August, so he would be Leo. He was curious about his new home, which featured his own bed and some chewy toys (he preferred Jo's shoes). His first night in the kitchen was punctuated by several 'woofs' at two-ten in the morning, representing, perhaps a soulful farewell to his birth family. Thereafter he was peaceful, except for some dedicated chewing on a doorstopper. He and I would certainly be best of friends.

So, there I was in the semi-deserted café on Garratt Lane, Leo lying next to me, nursing my psychological wounds, at eleven on a Wednesday morning, and trying – unsuccessfully – to develop an action plan over my second cup of cappuccino, when I felt the presence of a figure. It was the Black Philosopher. 'Good morning, Bertie, mind of I join you?'

'No, not at all, Professor; would you like a cup of coffee?'

He seated himself. 'Don't mind if I do.'

I signalled the barista, and I noticed that the Professor was regarding me expectantly. 'You ever been out of work, Professor?'

He surveyed the café as if expecting an acquaintance. 'No, Bertie, I've always got something keeps me busy.'

I unburdened myself of my firing from Zeus and my search for a new position.

He sat, unmoved, looking out the window. 'Well, looks like you've got to start over.'

I was hurt. Wasn't I at least due some sympathy? 'Start over?' I asked rather sharply.

'Yeah.' He looked around the vacant café with a sweeping gesture. 'Getting fired happens to thousands—maybe millions—of people every day. It's not exactly a near-death experience.'

'Well, it certainly feels like it,' I said petulantly.

He raised the palm of one hand. 'If it is, Bertie, you're a cat with another eight to go.'

I began to reiterate the litany of my job search failures. He held up both hands in surrender. 'Bertie, let me ask you: how do you want to be seen in the world? Never mind the flowery adjectives and the wild daydreams. What could the <u>real</u> <u>you</u> be doing?'

This was a question nobody had ever asked me before – nor had I ever thought to ask it of myself. Pushing my chair back from the table, I made space to reflect. 'Well, I like to show other people how to succeed in their work, using my professional skills and experience.'

'So, you'd like to be known as a very good teacher.'

'Yes, but not in the classroom.' I paused and added: 'But, Professor, I really don't want to go back to school to get my teaching certificate.'

'Hmmm. You want to use the skills you have, which are related to construction, building things.' He looked at his hands. 'And where would you be doing this teaching?'

'Preferably not in a classroom. I prefer the work environment.'

He took a deep breath, looked at the ceiling and exhaled. 'You know the big AtoZ store down near the station?'

'Yes.'

'I suggest you have a chat with the store manager. He's a fellow named Griskowski.'

'I'd like to see Mr Griskowski, please."

The clerk at the information desk looked at me through narrowed eyes. 'You have an appointment?'

Side-step the question, Bertie. 'You know...' I lowered my voice to a confidential tone. 'I have been referred to Mr Griskowski by the Professor.' I put on a slight smile. 'Just over an hour ago.'

'Oh, I see.' She didn't at all. 'His office is on the upper level, in the far corner.'

I entered a door that read: *Staff Only*. Inside were several cluttered desks, two were occupied, one by a man in AtoZ coveralls on the phone; the other by a severe looking woman with the air of a guard dog. I approached her with an endearing smile. She frowned. 'Yes?' she demanded.

I explained that I worked for Zeus Construction, and that I had been referred to Mr Griskowski for possible employment.

'If you want to send in your CV, we can put it on file.'

'But, ma'am, I was referred to Mr Griskowski by the Professor.'

'Who?'

'You know: Mr Jenkins, the Professor.'

She picked up her telephone. 'There's a man here to see you. Claims Professor Jenkins sent him.'

She hung up the telephone, picked up a paper and perused it. 'You can go in.'

Griskowski was a very large, pro-wrestler of a man, with a shaved head, overpowering his undersized desk. He looked up, wondering, perhaps, what hold would be best in the next bout. 'Who is this Professor Jenkins?'

'He is well-known in Wandsworth and a friend of mine. He suggested specifically that I should speak to you.'

Griskowski looked doubtful. 'And who are you?'

After a couple of sentences about my unemployment, I had a sudden inspiration. 'To tell you the truth, I didn't really know why the Professor sent me here, but when I got here, it made sense. I come to AtoZ a couple of times a month to pick up stuff I need for a home project. I have a complete tool kit, but there's always some little extra I need. I love this place, and I usually leave with more than I really have to have. There is something comforting about knowing that everything you could possibly need is available here.'

'You say you worked in construction. What kind of construction?'

'You know that high rise over there?' I indicated the direction. 'That was my project. I supervised everything: pouring the concrete, laying the bricks, wiring it, plumbing it and painting it.'

He considered me for some moments. 'You know what an awl is?'

'Yeah. You have various sizes in the hand-tools aisle. It's for starting holes in wood or leather.'

He pushed his chair back and raised his feet to his desk so that he could consider me at his leisure. 'Do you like spending time with people?'

'Mostly, yes. The professor says I ought to be a teacher. I don't particularly like self-centred dictators like my ex-boss.'

'You have references from Zeus?'

'Yes, I can get you a letter from the personnel manager, Jim Wescot.'

'How much sick time do you take off?'

I looked out the unwashed window, thinking. 'I believe the last time I was off sick was about fifteen years ago. My wife and I went to a new restaurant—

131

it's closed since then. I had their fish pie, and I got food poisoning. I was off work two days.'

'You ever a union member?'

'No.'

He laced his fingers across his waist and looked at the far wall. 'Well, here we have three employees who don't fill shelves, don't work at the tills, and don't have a sales quota. They move around the store looking for puzzled customers, and they help them. They listen to what the customer wants to do, they explain what will solve that problem, and they help the customer pick out the right tools and supplies. One of those positions is currently vacant. Four days a week, ten hours, plus eight to ten voluntary overtimes. It pays twelve pounds an hour; overtime is time and a half. Interest you?'

So, with overtime, it paid over six hundred a week. Forty-five weeks would be about twenty-seven K. With my pension, it was better than working for Zeus!

'Yes, I'm interested!'

The store manager picked up his phone. 'Brian, this is Griskowski at Wandsworth. I've got a candidate for our open consultant position. If I send him over to see you, will you check him out and put him through the training?' He looked up at me. 'Your name and contact details?'

Jo was pleased when I told her about my 'interview' at AtoZ. 'I hope you get the job, Bertie. It's right up your street.'

'But what am I to do about Leo? He can't come to work with me.'

'When I'm home, I can take him to Wandsworth Common for a run. If I'm not home, we'll have to get a dog walker.'

'You don't mind?'

'Not at all. We're pretty good friends. I just have to make sure I don't leave my shoes around.'

A day or two later, I received a phone call from Brian Czarnecki – has AtoZ been taken over by the Poles? He called me in for an interview during which he read Jim Wescot's letter and made a note of each of my assignments mentioned in the letter, together with a summary of what each assignment involved. Why did he need this information? I didn't dare ask. He then referred me to Louise who spent twenty minutes filling my personal information into a form on her PC. 'We'll be in touch, Mr Smithson.'

As I made my way home on the bus, the impersonal approach of both Czarnecki and Louise left me with a queasy feeling in my stomach. *What if they turn me down?*

Three days later, I received a large envelope from AtoZ in the morning post. In it were a four-page contract for me to sign, a Welcome to AtoZ, and an Employee Handbook. I was asked to join a new employee orientation course."

"Uncle Bertie, with the benefit of hindsight, should you have taken the AtoZ assignment?"

He frowns and scratches his chin. "It's easy to say that I should have held out for something more challenging and interesting. But, you know, Sarah, I was feeling pretty desperate when I met the Professor. I mean we still had some savings in the bank, and Jo was still making some money, so, while I tend to worry about money, I knew we would be OK for a while. The trouble is your state of mind when you've been out of work for six months. You become more and more convinced that you're a failure with each rejection you get, and you keep lowering your expectations of the job you'll take. Besides…" There is a grin creeping across his face. "If I had held out and gotten a real whiz-bang job, would I have been tempted to write books with you?"

I laugh. "Uncle Bertie, your mention of the Professor reminds me that I was asking my nan about him, because it does seem strange that a bus driver would have a PhD. My nan said that she never knew this Professor, but that her mother talked about him occasionally, and Nan thinks he must have passed away some time ago."

Uncle Bertie rubs his jaw. "Well, he referred me to AtoZ about ten years ago, and I believe he died around two years ago."

Chapter 16
Infidelity

"You said there was an introduction to AtoZ seminar for new employees, Uncle Bertie. Where was that?"

He looks away and folds his arms. "It was at a Happy Holiday Hotel in Birmingham."

"Were there many attendees?"

"Yes." I look at him expectantly. "I was probably the oldest attendee. Most were in their twenties, but there were a few – mostly guys and one woman – in their forties. Guys, who were going to be product advisers, shelf fillers, or consultants, like me, outnumber the women, who'd be going on to cashier training." He pauses and sighs. "The one woman in her forties is an attention-getter: blonde, good-looking, socialiser, wearing skirts and tops designed to 'show you at your best'. Perhaps she was going to be a back-office manager.

Classes ran eight to one and two 'til six-thirty; dinner was at seven-thirty with free seating to encourage interaction and a sense of belonging to the 'AtoZ family'. There was plenty of activity at the Happy Holidays bar between six-thirty and seven-thirty, and then after dinner until the bar closed at eleven.

I was ignorant about how the twenty-somethings conducted their social lives. Jeffrey and Michael had been married for over a decade and then we pretty much gave Elizabeth free rein, unfortunately. My impression from Happy Holidays was that they didn't waste any time; two or three beers with an attractive member of the opposite gender and the hormones took over. How did I know? It was the groans of ecstasy from the adjoining rooms, which had been assigned as singles. And it was possible for me to pick out the exhausted, adventurous ones in class the next morning.

I was sitting at one of the tables for two at lunchtime, along one wall of the dining room. I was about to tuck into my chicken curry when the mysterious forty-something blonde plunked her tray down opposite me. 'Hi, mind if I join you?'

My spirits lifted in the presence of an engaging female who might not consider me over the hill.

'You're very welcome. My name is Bertie.'

She scrutinised my name tag. 'I'm Gloria—Gloria Honeyfield.' For a moment, she fiddled with the top button of her scalloped satin blouse. 'I thought you might be kind of lonely, sitting here all by yourself.'

I smiled. 'Introverts are seldom lonely, but we almost always welcome company.'

She cocked her head to one side. 'So, what is your role at AtoZ?'

'I'm to be a consultant. One of those guys who help you find what you're looking for.'

'And what are you looking for, Bertie?'

Ignoring the come-on, I said, 'I was looking for a worthwhile job to help supplement my pension.'

'So, you're a pensioner already?'

There was a welcome comment! 'Yes. I retired a little early from Zeus Construction.'

She picked up her knife and fork to take a cut of her chicken. The ring finger of her tanned left hand had a white band under what must have been a ring. 'You weren't one of those guys who whistled at me from the second floor of a construction site?'

'No, I don't think so. If I had seen you, I certainly would have taken off my hard hat.'

She giggled. 'Well said, Bertie!' She glanced at my name tag again. 'Bertie Smithson. Is your wife, by any chance, Jo Smithson?'

'Yes, Jo is my wife. How do you know her?'

'My ex-husband is a fashion photographer. I'm sure he's taken her pictures a few times.'

'Small world.' I said.

Ex-husband, no ring. It must have been a recent split. 'What will you be doing at AtoZ, Gloria?'

'Oh, I'm going to be a cashier. I'd like to be a cashier on the builders' tills. That pays a little better, and they say they like to have outgoing personalities there—chatting up the best customers.'

'I'm sure you can do that pretty well.'

There was a shrug and a big smile. 'Yeah, it comes naturally.'

'What did you do before you got this job, Gloria?'

'Oh, I worked as the cashier for one of the better Saville Row tailors—chatting up the customers, processing their credit cards.'

'How come you're not still there?'

She turned reflective and pushed the lima beans around her plate sourly. 'Let's just say there was a falling out with the boss.'

There was a droopy-eyed smile as she looked at me. 'You going to be around after dinner?'

'I expect so.'

'Good. I'll see you then. I'm skipping happy hour. Got to work out in the gym. Keep my figure, you know.'

Gloria certainly was entertaining. I wondered where she was planning to take this – if anywhere – not that I'd go there if it were offered.

I decided to give Jo a call – mainly to bolster my anti-Gloria defences. 'There's an attendee here who says she knows you.'

'Oh, who's that?'

'Gloria Honeyfield.'

There was a long pause. 'I don't know her. I have worked with her husband. He's a photographer—not a particularly good one.' She sounded defensive. 'What's she doing there?'

'She's going to be a cashier.' I told Jo my suspicion that Gloria was fired from a Saville Row tailor.

Jo raised her voice. 'I'll bet she was fired for theft or fraud. I wouldn't believe a word she says, Bertie.'

After I hung up, I wondered why Jo was so negative about a woman she didn't know.

After dinner, I was having a chat with a pretty black woman – aged early thirties – a successful asylum-seeker from Somalia, who would be starting as a cashier, and who hoped to become a product advisor.

'Hi, Bertie, are you going to buy me a drink?' It was Gloria dressed in a frilly, white blouse, immodest scoop-neck, and flouncy short skirt in which she should not decently bend over.

'Of course, what are you having?'

'A margarita, please.'

As a beer and ale man, I knew nothing about margaritas, except that they are Mexican, strong and expensive, and never before had I bought one for an on-the-make woman whom I barely knew. Well, there's a first time for everything.

'Thank you, Bertie. Let's sit over here so we can have a nice chat.' She gestured toward two remote chairs. To my amazement, she could sit without being arrested.

I took my pint of Guildford Pale Ale over to the appointed location, where in the subsequent conversation I learnt that she was scheduled to join the Hounslow store as she lived in Hounslow, 'but more toward the Chiswick (fashionable) end'.

There was a pause in the conversation. She leant forward, and with an effort, I kept my eyes on her face.

'Bertie, I'm going to tell you a little secret that I learnt from Belinda, an old friend of mine. We went to school together in Uxbridge, she now lives in Chiswick, and she's a fashion model like your wife. My ex, Dave, Belinda and your Jo were on a shoot together when it happened.'

I sat back, crossed my arms and frowned. 'What happened?'

'As I say, Belinda is a friend of mine, and she thought I should know.'

'Know what?'

'Come with me, Bertie. This is too private to discuss in public.'

I hesitated. I could feel the heat rising in the back of my neck, aware that I was being led on – to what?

I had to know this secret which apparently involved my wife – but is Gloria trustworthy? Maybe I should have insisted that she tell me here. She was already crossing the room, turning and beckoning me. I followed her. She closed her door behind us. 'I'll be just a minute, Bertie.'

Moments later, she re-emerged from the bathroom. 'Just had to make myself a little more comfortable.'

She was wearing a white, terry-cloth hotel bathrobe which must have shrunk in the laundry, and she carelessly flopped herself down in the one upholstered armchair. Gloria was pretty obviously wearing nothing – or very little – under the robe. Her smile suggested that I was an old friend. Warily, I sat on the edge of the bed facing her. The heat in my upper back had been replaced by a tight chill. 'What is this secret, Gloria?'

Negligently, she crossed her legs. 'Your Jo had a roll in the hay with my Dave on that assignment. In fact, Belinda said it went on all weekend.'

I recoiled, as if a bucket of ice water had been dumped on me. Gloria offered me an indulgent, slightly sympathetic smile.

I clenched my fists, and I could feel the heat returning. 'I don't believe you, Gloria.'

She paused. 'When I confronted Dave about this, I got him to confess. He told me that Jo has a semi-inverted left nipple which he said was *cute*.' She spat the last word. 'I have no such problem.' She uncovered her breasts.

It felt as if some large, soft-footed creature was crawling up my back inside my shirt. A spider! I reached around to swat my back. There was nothing. *The spider is in front of you, idiot!* shot through my mind."

"Hold on, Uncle Bertie, I'm not sure I want to hear the rest of this."

He pauses, considering me as if to measure my disquiet. "You'll see in a few minutes, Sarah, why you, as my biographer, need to hear the rest of this."

I grit my teeth and draw a black spiral in my notebook.

"I said, 'What is it you want, Gloria?'

'The question is: what do you want, Bertie? I have a simple solution to several problems, all at once. I can get even with Dave; you can get even with Jo, you and I can have a splendid time and no one need be the wiser.'

For a moment, the two of us were frozen between doubt and temptation.

There was a flicker of acidity in Gloria's face that undermined her apparent friendliness. I turned away. 'No, Gloria, I have to speak with Jo.'

'Suit yourself, Bertie, you know where to find me when you have Jo's confession and you're ready to even the score.'

I was able to avoid Gloria for the rest of the week. On Friday afternoon, she passed me a slip of paper without comment. It had an address and mobile phone number on it.

'How was the seminar, Bertie?' Nervously, Jo switched off the BBC news. I'd never seen her watch daytime news.

I, with my heart racing, sat on the couch, facing her. 'Gloria says you had an affair with her husband.'

Jo trembled with bitterness. 'So that's why she introduced herself: to tell you stories about me.'

'Is there any truth in the story, Jo?'

She crumpled upon herself, racked with sobs, hands covering her face. 'It wasn't really an affair, Bertie. More like a one-nighter.'

'Belinda told Gloria it was more than that, and Dave confessed.'

'Oh, God, Bertie!' Her face was still hidden in her hands, her voice almost unintelligible with grief. 'Saturday. It started on a Saturday. Over on Sunday morning.'

'And what since?'

She sat up, facing me, her face wet with tears. 'Nothing. I swear to God! Absolutely nothing!'

'Why, Jo?'

'Oh, God, I don't know. A moment of madness. Too many margaritas by the pool. It started to rain. Belinda and I were sharing a room. We moved in to get out of the rain: Will, the lighting guy, Belinda, Dave and I. The guys were ordering pitchers of margaritas. There were silly games. Losers had to take something off. Belinda was making out with the lighting guy. Dave was coming on to me. All of a sudden, I...I lost my mind.' She was shaking her head, her whole body, as if to dislodge a demon.

'Were there drugs?'

'I didn't think so, but I don't know. Maybe in the margaritas. They just kept coming. The rain postponed the photoshoot. It's a blur...I can't explain it.' Her hands were raised to the ceiling in supplication. 'I have no excuse, and sometimes I wish I were dead.'

'Have you ever cheated with anyone else?'

'No!'

'Was there anything about me that was bothering you?'

'No. No. OK, we have fights sometimes, but there was nothing then. I would never try to hurt you that way, Bertie, believe me.'

My impassive questions – I wanted the unembroidered truth – may have suggested to Jo that I was prepared to talk.

'What else did Gloria say?'

'Not much. She propositioned me in a half-open bathrobe in her room.'

'Oh, my God! Did you...?'

'No. I said I wanted to talk to you. She gave me her contact details in case I'm in need of revenge.'

Jo collapsed, like a puppet whose strings had been cut, onto the sofa, defeated, moaning, shaking with sobs, agonisingly alone, as my grandfather's clock ticked away the minutes on the mantlepiece.

She sat up and faced me, almost unrecognisable, her eyes red, cheeks pale and streaked with charcoal, lips lifeless, her brow corrugated with deep lines. She was not my Jo, and I was torn by her agony. 'I…I guess I had it coming. It's my payback.'

She looked hopelessly around the room. 'Oh, Bertie, I'm so sorry for what I've done. I love you and I didn't mean to hurt you, but I know I have hurt you terribly to sin so casually, so thoughtlessly. OK. OK, Bertie.' She took a deep breath and looked for a Kleenex; I gave her my handkerchief. 'I just wish it weren't Gloria.'

'Why?'

'She showed up with Dave at a meeting; she's beautiful. Her figure is better than mine. If you go to her, she'll want to prove that she's much better than I am.' She wiped her face with the handkerchief and grimaced at the black smudges, then matter-of-factly: 'I'm afraid I'll lose you Bertie.'

'To Gloria?'

'Yes.'

'Not a chance, Jo.'

'Why not?'

'I don't like the woman. She's an unforgiving, scheming, egotist.'

She took a deep breath. 'Well, go ahead then.' I shook my head. 'Why not?'

'Because, regardless of what we've said, it would hurt you, you'd remember it and assume the worst.'

She gritted her teeth. 'But that's what it takes to make things even.'

'Talking about it can make things even. Besides, I'd rather do it with you.'

She was incredulous. 'You would? Really?'

'Yes.'

'Let me go wash my face.'"

"You must have been very hurt, Uncle Bertie."

"Yes, it hurt my pride. But Jo did everything she could to make me feel good about myself; she's wonderfully loyal and contrite. After all, she's still my Jo, my imperfect and essential lover and best friend."

"Did you ever think twice about taking Gloria up on her offer?"

"When I was in a cynical mood, I'd think: *wouldn't it have been interesting to take Gloria up on her offer and say nothing to Jo*? That way we would have been even. Gloria would have her revenge and Dave would have been punished.

What would Gloria have been like? Fantastic? Frigid? An average woman – whatever that is?

But Jo would still be living in purgatory unless she found out, in which case I would have three strikes against me: one for cheating, two for not confessing, and three for not confronting her. As for me, I'd be living in double purgatory (pretty close to hell): once for my guilt and twice for constant doubt about Jo's fidelity.

When I try to put the whole messy business on Father Anthony's Good vs. Bad scales, it seems that the bad outweighs the good, so that if there was a satanic spirit involved, it has to be counted as one of his masterpieces from the first sip of Jo's margarita until I crumpled Gloria's note and tossed it in the bin."

We reach simultaneously for our teacups. Eying each other silently, we sip our tea. My pulse is returning to normal. "Uncle Bertie, you don't want all this in your memoir."

He looks at me blankly. "Why not?"

"It's very personal," I protest.

He looks away, considering. "I don't mind; Gloria might object." He gives an exaggerated shrug.

"But, how about Aunt Jo? She won't want people reading about her."

"You can check with her, but I think she'll say, 'Go ahead'. I have long since forgiven Jo. She confessed to Father Anthony, who told her that God has forgiven her. I don't think she would care about somebody who reads her story with an unforgiving mind."

There is a picture of my grandaunt in my mind: trim figure, fashionable, cloche-cut grey hair, alert brown eyes and a ready smile. "She's an amazing woman." My granduncle just smiles. "Have you encountered Gloria since then?"

"No, and Jo won't go on a shoot with him. She says a lot of agencies won't use him, so they may be hurting financially."

"I'm curious about the spider that was crawling up your back. Where did it come from?"

"Goodness knows, but I'm glad it showed up."

"Do you suppose it fell out of your mailbox?" I ask.

He pauses, recollecting, and then laughs. "You mean as a message from God?"

"Yeah."

"I suppose that's a possibility."

Chapter 17
Friends

Uncle Bertie leans back in his chair as if to re-create a memory. "I was still working for Zeus and I was sitting comfortably in one of those folding canvass chairs with an excellent perspective of the village cricket pitch, with a slight chance of having to leap to my feet should a batsman hit for six in our direction. There was a can of Eagle bitter in my hand and a friend on either side of me.

'This guy is definitely one of our best batters,' Geoff, our host, announced. On weekends, during the season, Geoff, who managed a sporting goods store in Aylesbury, was out and about watching his local team.

Richard, a Jewish solicitor living in Amersham, asked, 'How does he do against spinners?'

'Usually OK. I think he should be good for at least sixty runs today.'

I sipped my bitter and watched the cricketers in the company of these two old mates who dated back to high school in Wandsworth. We had each gone our separate paths, but we'd always managed to get together for an afternoon or a dinner; sometimes with wives, three or four times a year.

'You know,' I said, 'this village green looks just the same as when you and Martha moved here—what is it now? Thirty years ago?'

'Thirty-two years. We had our thirty-third anniversary in April. But, no, Bertie, there's much that's changed here. There used to be three beautiful, old oak trees there by the road. They went in that hurricane a few years back. That line of elms as replacements still have plenty of growing to do. And the inn over there has changed hands.'

'Wasn't it called *The Black Swan* before?' Richard asked.

'Yeah. It's been bought and sold twice since we moved here. Now it's *The Queen of Hearts*. That's the owner standing over there.'

I followed Geoff's gesture and my eyes encountered a tall woman with Lady Godiva blonde hair wearing a short, low-cut sundress and sandals.

'My goodness! Is that all her?' Richard asked.

'I don't know; you'd have to ask the experienced few.' Geoff gestured toward the home team bench.

We watched the runs roll up and engaged in idle conversation for a while.

'I've been approached again about taking early retirement.' Geoff said. 'They want to promote some of their young bucks—an objective with which I have some sympathy, in principle, but not in practice.'

Richard was nodding his agreement. 'I have the same problem. They want to promote an associate to partner, but since nobody wants to get a smaller piece of the same pie, the number of pie-eating partners has to be reduced. It seems there is this widely held sentiment that our generation is blocking opportunities for our kids—not only at work, by refusing to retire, but by refusing to move out of the houses we bought thirty years ago for less than ten percent of what they're worth today.'

'As for me,' I said, 'I'd be happy to take early retirement if I could afford it.'

Geoff smirked. 'What would you do with yourself, Bertie?'

I said, 'That's a good question. I don't know, but it should be something that's interesting and challenging.'

'That sounds like more work,' Richard said.

Geoff said, 'I'm going to retire in five or six years, play a lot more golf, spend some time with my grandchildren, and maybe go on a cruise with Martha.'

'My problem feels a little different,' I said. 'I've been working at Zeus for thirty-five years now, but the job isn't doing anything for me except providing a pay-check.'

Geoff laughed. 'That's important.'

'So, what's missing for you, Bertie?' Richard asked.

'I guess what's missing is that I'm beginning to feel like I've missed out on something that is really me.'

'Have you got a bucket list?' Geoff asked.

'But, you see, it's not really a bucket list, Geoff. It's feeling that I've done something really useful, something challenging and memorable, before I depart this earth.'

'How about all the buildings you've constructed?' Richard asked.

'Who's going to remember that I did all the steel work in the Peabody Tower? And, more importantly, do I care?'

'So, you want something that will have your signature on it, so that people will say, "I remember Bertie Smithson. He did this!"' Richard suggests.

'No, Richard, it's not about other people, it's about me, but you're right about the signature. I'd like to be able to say, *I did this. It was challenging, and it represents the best of me.*'

'Oh, come on, Bertie, we can't all be Leonardos,' Geoff protested.

'I don't think he's talking about being a Leonardo,' Richard said. 'I think he's talking about a unique accomplishment from his perspective before he dies. It's really about making peace with yourself before you go.'

'You guys are getting pretty morbid,' Geoff said. 'When you go, you go.'

Richard leant across me to face Geoff. 'I think you're missing my point. I remember when my mother was dying of cancer. She was in denial that it was terminal, and she went about her business as usual until she had to be hospitalised. She suddenly realised that her life was about to end. She was filled with anger and bitterness, and that's the way she died. It was very sad.'

'Why was she angry and bitter?' Geoff asked.

'I believe she felt her life had suddenly been cut short. It represented the sudden, unexpected termination of everything she knew.'

Geoff raised a palm dolefully. 'Unless one believes in an afterlife.'

'Do you, Geoff?' Richard asked.

'Not really.' He scanned the pitch as if he would find a prompt of what to add. 'But it seems rather morbid to dwell on the topic.'

'But here's the crucial point, Geoff,' Richard said, gesturing with both hands. 'There will come a moment for all of us when we know we're about to die. At that moment, I believe we all want to think, *I've done some good things and a few not-so-good things, but very few useless things.* And, if we can feel that way, I think we can step out of the way of terror, anger and bitterness.'

Geoff was biting his lap. 'That sounds like a terse obituary, Richard.'

Richard took in the action on the pitch for a moment before responding. 'In Judaism, there is the concept of *emunah* which is usually translated as *faith*, but it is deeper and broader than faith, so that *emunah* becomes a definition of oneself, a part of one's identity. It is profound faith in God, faith in his teaching, and faith in oneself to live in accordance with his teaching. My challenge, similar to Bertie's, is that I am trying to achieve *emunah.*'

'OK,' Geoff said, 'but do you believe in an afterlife?'

'Judaism has the concept of *Olam Habah*, which translates as *the world to come*.' Richard paused for a moment. 'Individual Jews hold various beliefs about an afterlife, ranging from its non-existence to faith in a heaven and a hell. I am ambivalent. In any case, it's irrelevant to my argument, which is that if one is about to die, one would like to feel that not a moment of his life was wasted.'

'Well,' Geoff said, his voice raised, 'I don't think I've wasted any of my life.'

'That's excellent,' I said. 'My concern is: am I going to make the best use of the life I have been given? When I was younger, it was a distant concern, and, anyway, I was doing the best I could. I was tactically, rather than strategically oriented. For me, it would be easy, now, to drift along, but I have a real fear of facing my end with not enough feeling that I'm leaving the game a winner.'

Geoff smiled and patted me insincerely on the shoulder. 'What's it going to take for you to feel like a winner, Bertie?'

'I don't know, Geoff, but if I can feel that I've made full, constructive use of the talents I've been given and I haven't seriously disappointed many people, I don't think I'll be quite as terrified or as angry.'

Geoff gave me one of his tongue-in-cheek looks. 'Or maybe if life has been really good for you, you'll be extra disappointed on leaving.'

Then suddenly I recalled. 'Do you remember our track meets in school, Geoff?'

'Yeah, vaguely.'

'Well, I used to be a high jumper, and we usually got three tries to clear the highest level. That third and last jump was always terribly important: if you cleared it and beat the competition, you went home feeling like a hero; if you failed, well, you were a failure. That last jump was always there; you couldn't avoid it. I think it's sort of like that, Geoff.'

A month or so after the cricket outing, I was having lunch with Richard and his wife Rebecca. I had forgotten how pleasant the setting was there. We were finishing lunch on the patio in their back garden overlooking the Misbourne River, the shade trees along its bank and the ripening wheat fields in the distance.

'Yes, we love it here.' Rebecca said, 'As the seasons progress, there are almost daily changes in the vista. And for Richard, the train station is just under half a mile that way, so he can be at his Holborn office in fifty minutes.'

Richard was the only one of our small high-school clique who made any real money, and for a moment, I savoured what it was like to live in an historic townhouse, with these splendid views, less than an hour from central London.

I put down my coffee cup. 'I have two apologies to offer. First, for inviting myself to this lunch.' I had called Richard to ask him to join me for lunch on a Saturday; he proposed the venue and the date.

Rebecca gave a toss of her head as she folded her napkin. 'Don't be silly, Bertie, we're very glad to see you.'

'And secondly for not bringing Jo with me. She, unfortunately, is on a winter photo shoot in Iceland…Richard, you remember that during the cricket day with Geoff, you mentioned a Hebrew term for faith, which you said is very important to you. If you don't mind, I want to understand more about it.'

Rebecca got up from the table. 'I think I'll leave you men to your discussion.'

I held up a hand. 'No, Rebecca, don't leave on my account. Perhaps you have insights you can add.' Rebecca had the large dark eyes, accentuated by strong eyebrows and cheekbones which, for me, were typical of good-looking Jewish women.

'I think what you're referring to, Bertie, is *emunah* which is an absolute commitment to God, his laws, and integrating Him into one's daily life, so that *emunah* becomes part of one's identity and influences personality.'

'It's a lot more difficult than it may sound, Bertie,' Rebecca said. 'You know that there are over six hundred Jewish laws.'

I couldn't resist a chuckle. 'Supposedly, Christians have only two, but I can't get either one right. So, tell me: how does one achieve *emunah?*'

'For me,' Richard said, 'it's about prayer, meditation and reading scripture.'

'And other religious commentaries,' Rebecca added.

'But you said it is about faith. How does one achieve faith?'

Richard considered me for a time, as if trying to understand my mental blockage. 'I think that the first step is actually <u>deciding</u> that you want to believe in something.' There was a pause. 'Let's take a Christian example: suppose you decided that, for you, it is important to believe that Jesus Christ is the son of God. It doesn't matter why you choose that particular point, but it does matter that it's important to you.'

'OK.'

'Next, you compile all the reasons that Jesus Christ is the son of God. Perhaps you read the New Testament, or what Christian scholars say, or what your priest says. You gather the evidence <u>for</u> your point, and then you consider any evidence <u>against</u> your point. You might say to yourself: *the Jews and the Muslims say that Jesus was prophet, not the son of God, and they say that they believe in only <u>one</u> God* but, in response, you say, *Jesus and God are one*, so you dismiss the evidence against.'

'And that's it? You have faith then?'

'No, you've just laid the foundation,' Richard said. 'As Rebecca mentioned, it's only the beginning. What has to follow is daily prayer, meditation and reading.'

'It also helps if you can share your feelings and beliefs with people who are on, or who have been on a similar path to faith,' Rebecca added.

'And prayer is asking God for help in this?' I asked.

'Yes, but it can be more than that,' Richard said. 'It can involve arguing with God about things you don't understand, or perhaps you don't agree with. And it involves listening with empathy and acuity.'

'To the answer?'

Rebecca stifled a chuckle. 'I haven't heard any audible answers. What I may get if I've been listening with empathy and acuity, as Richard says, is a feeling about the answer—if that's vague enough.'"

"And if I remember right, Uncle Bertie, you asked Jo to share your feelings and beliefs."

"Yes, and she turned me down."

"Was that fair?"

"At the time, I didn't think so, but the more I ruminate about faith, the greater was my conviction that faith is an extremely close and personal relationship with God, and therefore it may be counter-productive to try to emulate the experience of someone else. What I'm saying is that you have to pass Faith 101, getting the basics in hand. Then, you can move on, begin to read, consider, talk to others and pray."

He takes a drink of water and glances at my notebook. "Have we talked about Geoff's illness?"

"Not yet."

"Well, the King's Head pub in Aylesbury had the best fish and chips I know of, and it's where I met with Geoff, whom I hadn't seen in months. I told him that I'd left AtoZ and was a budding writer of children's fiction.

I said, 'What's going on at JG Sports, since you've retired?'

'It's still trading but changed hands. All new staff now.'

We lapsed into silence.

'Bertie, there's something I should tell you.' Awkwardness in his tone and body language prompted me to look into his face, which was reflecting inner pain. 'I've been diagnosed with dementia.'

I caught my breath. 'Oh, my God! I'm so sorry, Geoff!'

He looked down at his hands for a moment. 'I was having trouble remembering things—not the usual things, like people's names, but what I did yesterday and where I am sometimes. I thought, *Well, I'm just getting older*, but Martha suggested I see the GP. I didn't do anything about it for a while, but then I began to worry, too. I thought *I don't want it sneaking up on me*.' He took a long draught of beer. 'The GP gave me some memory tests which I knew I didn't do well on, and she sent me to a special clinic, where they did more tests, including genetics, and they measured blood flow in my neck. They said it's over ninety-five percent probable that I have early onset dementia.'

'I'm so sorry, Geoff. Did they give you some medication?'

'Yes, I'm taking Aricept. It's supposed to slow things down, but I don't notice any difference.'

'Are you planning to do something special—like taking a round-the-world cruise?'

He gave a derisive snort. 'I wouldn't remember what I saw a week after, so I'll save what I have for Martha, so she can take the cruise.'

'This is very hard on both of you.'

'I reckon it's really harder on her.' He paused, his face was uncharacteristically regretful. 'She'll have to put up with my mood swings and my incontinence—at least for a while.' He took another sip of beer. 'I told her that she should decide when I go to the home—there is a good one in South Aylesbury called Pathways—and she should pay no attention to my protests. As for me, I'll just be slipping away, unaware of my accumulating incompetence.'

I reached across the table to touch his arm, this now disabled man who had been my friend for over sixty years, since we were boys. 'Perhaps you should focus on what you like to do and still enjoy, like watching cricket.'

He sighed. 'There's not much on this time of year.'

'But there's plenty on YouTube, Geoff.'

'Oh, yeah. I forgot about that. Good idea.' There was the trace of a smile. 'Nice of you to come and see me, Bertie.'

'I'm thinking that you and Martha should come for lunch now and then. It would give you both a chance to get out of the house.'

'I'm sure she'll remember how to take the underground…What's it called? It has a funny name.'

'The Bakerloo Line.'

When I got home, Jo said, 'He's always been a little too macho for me, Bertie, but I really like Martha, and I know you and Geoff go back a long way. Yes, of course, we can have them for lunch. Any dates proposed?'

'No, just some time next month. I have the impression that their friends are gradually deserting them.'

Jo looked out the window at a passing delivery van. 'Well, I suppose that's to be expected. People are embarrassed around handicapped people: they don't know how to handle the situation socially, and their own wellness makes them feel ashamed.'

I told Jo that Geoff said he would be 'unaware of his accumulating incompetence'. 'That's a terrible way to die,' I added.

'I'm not so sure, Bertie. It seems to me that operative word in that phrase is unaware. If you're unaware you've lost something, it doesn't really matter unless someone reminds you of your loss, and as you've said, nobody wants to do that.' She patted my knee. 'The illness I'm most afraid of is acute rheumatoid arthritis. There's no cure, it's crippling, progressive, and very painful.'

We sat in silence for some time.

'What's on your mind, Bertie?'

'I was just thinking about the soul of someone like Geoff.'

'What about it?'

'Well, do you suppose that the soul is in any way damaged by deterioration of the brain? In other words, are the brain and the soul in any way connected?'

Jo looked out the window, around the room and then at me. "The soul is spirit; the brain is flesh and matter. There's no way they're inter-dependent, but I believe they may connect at a subconscious level. For example, I think our pure conscience may flow from the soul and get diluted by our personality—and desires.'

'So, you don't think a soul has a personality?'

'I believe a soul has an identity. Perhaps that includes a personality.'

'How do you describe the identity of a soul?'

'God's fingerprints.'

'My wife is an extraordinary human being, and I wish I could have ten percent of her faith.'

Chapter 18
Geoff and Rebecca

"Geoff and Martha came for lunch about every six months. I guess it was about three years later that they came for lunch the last time. As I opened the door to let them in, I saw a vacant look in Geoff's eyes, as if he's not sure where he is, while Martha's face relaxed into a smile. Instinctively, I moved to take my friend's hand in welcome, but the touch was perfunctory, without an emotive squeeze. Martha took both of my shoulders and kissed my left and right cheeks: it is greeting enough for two.

'How are you, Geoff?' I asked.

'OK,' he replied, looking past me. He wandered into the living room, where Jo had nearly filled my parents' old shelves with her completed projects. 'A lot of books.'

'The new paperbacks are the proof copies of books that Jo has edited,' I explained.

'See, honey? These are books that Jo has read and corrected for the authors,' Martha said.

'Hmmm.' He turned away to encounter Jo who appeared, tossing her apron on the back of a chair. 'Hello,' he made a modest bow. She kissed one cheek while he was still bent over but was unable to reach his other cheek when he straightened, tall as he is.

We moved to the kitchen where there was the smell of asparagus and roast beef. I opened a bottle of red wine and began to pour the glasses. 'Just half a glass for him, please, Bertie.' I handed the glass to Geoff and he drank it down like a welcome medication.

Geoff's table manners were not as I remembered them; in fact, he was not as I remembered him. He was expansive, full of improbable stories, an eye for the ladies, napkin in his lap, one hand free for gesturing, elbow never touching the table. Now, he was silent, slouched forward, focused on the food, utensils used as necessary tools.

Jo and Martha engaged in chatter about the offspring and cooking.

I tried to draw Geoff out of his submerged existence. 'Have you seen any cricket, Geoff?'

'Cricket?' He scanned the room as if it might be there. 'No.'

'Have you seen Richard lately, Geoff?'

'Richard?' He paused to consider. 'No.'

'Yes, you have, Geoff,' Martha reminded him. 'We went out with Richard and Rebecca for lunch just last week.' Then, parenthetically, 'His short-term memory is not very good.'

'How are they?' I asked.

'Like all of us, they're getting older,' Martha replied. 'Richard has Parkinson's and Rebecca isn't very strong. She said she has cancer.'

Dessert was a chocolate cake – Jo's special recipe – and mixed fresh strawberries, raspberries, pineapple, kiwi, and orange sections.

Geoff had two slices of the cake and pronounced it, 'Very good!'

Over coffee, Martha said: 'May I suggest, Bertie, that you and Geoff go for a walk? He doesn't get enough exercise at home, and I'm always afraid he'll get lost if he goes out alone.'

'Yes, of course, we can have a stroll around King George's Park.'

The park hadn't changed much in seventy years. There were the additions of the Southfields Academy Astroturf football pitches and the sprawling Nuffield Health Centre, where my son, Jeff, used to work. The rest was open grass, football pitches, paved walkways, and, in summer, blankets, picnic baskets and sunbathers. In winter, wrapped-up joggers and walkers. Anytime, at least a dozen dogs, including Leo, who looked forward to seeing some of his friends.

We walked north toward the city. Geoff said, 'You look familiar. Do I know you?'

'Yes, I'm Bertie Smithson. We used to go to school together over there.' I pointed to the east.

'Oh, yes. I remember a Bertie. He was tall and skinny. We used to call him Beanie, 'cause he looked like a string bean.'

'That was me—sixty-five years ago.'

'I remember he was tall, and he used to play goalie.'

'But I wasn't very good.'

Geoff had stopped walking. He was gazing toward the tall apartment blocks in the distance, as if there was a large memory screen there. 'There was a girl called Sandra with long blonde hair and nice tits.'

I scoffed. 'Wasn't she your girlfriend?'

'She'd let me touch her tits; she was proud of 'em, and she always wore pink cotton knickers, but she never let me feel inside.'

'What else do you remember, Geoff?'

He continued on with recollections of classmates and events, some in detail, some obscure, and many only misty. I did not comment or prompt as these disassembled scenes of youth tumbled out until a referee at the academy blew a shrill whistle. The memories suddenly faded away.

We walked on in silence for a while, Leo beside me, glancing up at Geoff occasionally, as if there was something curious about him.

'You know how to get back?' he asked.

'Yes, I know the way.'

Jo, Leo and I walked them to the Earlsfield train station. There were hugs and feelings of sadness exchanged as the train arrived.

'Thank you so much.'

'Bye now. Stay in touch.'

We watched as the red taillights grew smaller in the distance.

I told Jo about Geoff's remembrances of his youth. 'It's so sad,' she said. 'He was never my cup of tea, but he was always so entertaining, so full of life. It's like the butterfly has disappeared and left behind only a dry chrysalis.'

'And I suppose it's very difficult for Martha,' I said.

'Very. He can't help her with any of the housework or the cooking. He sits in front of the television or wanders around the house, doesn't do a good job dressing himself, and is incontinent. There is a retiree to whom she gives ten pounds for walking with him for an hour and a half every day. She thinks they spend most of the time in Sainsbury's drinking coffee, but at least she can get away and out of the house.'

'Did she say anything about a care home?'

'Yes, but as long as he knows who she is, she's decided to keep him with her. I suppose money is an issue for them.

I said, 'It must be unspeakable not to be recognised by the intimate, half-a-century-long, love of your life.'

'Or worse yet: to be wrongly suspected of mistreatment by that same insensate, love of your life. It really is the devil at his worst.'"

I sat for a moment with my granduncle and aunt's words echoing in my head. "Do you think that Aunt Jo is right when she implies that the devil causes dementia?"

Uncle Bertie takes a deep breath. "I don't know, Sarah, but if one looks back at human history, it seems remarkable to me that human beings, using science, have been able to overcome one disease after another. Leprosy, polio, tuberculosis, the plague and a host of other diseases are gone now, and many more are stalemated. Where did the science come from? Probably it was always there, waiting to be discovered. From what we know about the personalities of God and the devil, who would have helped us discover medical science? Certainly not the devil. He would just use our illnesses to make life miserable for us, so maybe Jo is right in that sense."

"How about Richard, Uncle Bertie?"

"Well, he called to tell me that Rebecca had passed away. I said how sorry I was. 'You must be devastated. Rebecca was such a special lady.'

'I'm managing to hold together. You may remember she had treatment for cancer several years ago.'

'Yes, I remember, and I thought it was in remission.'

'It was. But it suddenly returned with a vengeance.' There was a muffled snuffle.

'I'm so sorry, Richard.'

'The funeral is tomorrow at the Blythe Funeral Home in High Wycombe…if you can be there…'

'Yes, of course I'll be there. What time, Richard?'

I had never been to a Jewish funeral before and didn't know what to expect.

It was formal and sombre, both at the funeral home and at the graveside. Many prayers were in Hebrew; most mourners were dressed in black, and women had their white handkerchiefs tucked in their sleeves or crumpled in hand. It was a regretful ceremony, without room for thankful memories, placing the soul of a loved one or friend in the hands of an all-mighty God to whom we all must answer.

Richard's house was crowded with mourners, and I learnt that during *shiva*, the seven-day, initial period of mourning, Richard would remain at home receiving the comfort of family and friends. His children had an additional *shloshim*, one month of mourning, for the loss of a parent. This was followed by eleven-months of mourning, if Richard was to follow Jewish tradition.

I found it all but impossible to capture Richard's attention long enough to interact with him in the expressions of grief, so after a brief hug and an expression of my sorrow, I departed.

But on my way home, I decided that my attendance at Rebecca's funeral was not a sufficient expression of the importance to me of their friendship. I'd like to have is a couple of hours with Richard in a relaxed environment, where we can be distracted, if we wish, by an activity which Richard would enjoy, and where he can release his feelings and be comforted.

The ideal activity would be a one-day cricket match between, say, England and India or Pakistan. But it is out of cricket season now, and whatever I select on YouTube, he might have already seen. What then?

American baseball. Cricket fans like to look down their noses at the 'poor, colonial imitation of cricket', but the truth is that we know little about baseball and tend to be offended by Americans who tell us that observing cricket is 'like watching paint dry'. I suspect that most of us have some curiosity about this sport which is watched by over a hundred million Americans every year."

"So, did you fly to the States, Uncle Bertie?" I ask.

"No, I found an old game 4 of the World Series, New York Yankees versus the Los Angeles Dodgers, on YouTube. There's a lot of scoring in the game, plenty of action and excitement. Jo served us beer, hot dogs, popcorn and ice cream. With the sound turned up, the announcer commentating, and the crowd cheering, it was almost like being there.

Richard could relax and enjoy himself, and he told me how he first met Rebecca in year one of primary school.

'I miss her terribly,' he confessed.

'I'm sure that's true. Have you ever tried to imagine what your life would have been like if Rebecca hadn't been sitting in the seat in front of you?'

'No, I only know it wouldn't have been nearly as good.'

'So, you've been pretty lucky, Richard.'

There was a wisp of a smile. 'I know what you're saying, Bertie: I should be thankful and focused on all the good memories, rather than lamenting my loss.'

Our attention turned to the screen. There was the crack of a hit to deep centre field. Would it carry into the stands? No. The centre fielder made a leap up the wall, made the catch, and hurled the ball toward second base.

'One thing I'll always remember,' Richard said, 'and I can tell you this now: we never slept in pyjamas—starting with our honeymoon—Rebecca's idea. It wasn't really about sex—sometimes, of course, it was, but that's not the point. There were no barriers between us, and it was nice to know that her naked body was right there. It created an enduring atmosphere of intimacy.'

By the end of the sixth inning, the score was tied at six all. 'Pretty exciting game,' Richard said.

We had finished the hot dogs – with a little help from Leo – and had started on the Magnum bars from which Leo had been excluded. Ever hopeful, he lay at our feet, alert to any falling crumbs.

'Years ago, Richard, we were talking about what you called *the world to come* and, at the time, you said you were ambivalent about the concept. Is that still the case?'

'I remember we were talking about *Olam Habah*.' He paused for a moment. 'No, I am no longer ambivalent, and it's not just because as I approach the end of my life, the concept seems more favourable. Rebecca was brought up in an environment which believed in *Olam Habah*, but she, herself, was quite sceptical, and all through our married life, we were what you might call non-believers, though we were, in other respects, devout Jews. In the last few weeks of her life, when the cancer had spread, Rebecca had many dreams, and some that she called *visions*. Mostly, they were extraordinary dreams: improbable scenarios related in some way to the past, but some sounded to me like passages from the Torah written by one of the prophets. For example, in one she saw mighty Yahweh, surrounded with clouds of fire, sitting in his Temple in Jerusalem before its destruction. There were vast crowds of spirits shouting and singing, and in the crowd, she saw her parents. They beckoned to her. This and perhaps half a dozen similar visions gave her great comfort at the end of her life.'

'And Rebecca's visions have convinced you, as well?'

'I was pleased for the comfort the visions gave her, but for me, the process was more logical. I believe that we individuals are created by God in the sense that He gives us life, and I find it difficult to believe that a benevolent God would allow his creation to be extinguished when it has learnt so much and has such capacity to do good—unless, of course, it has done something to displease Him.'

'So, you believe that all life arises from God?'

'Yes. I'm not certain that He creates each individual life—including an amoeba for instance—but I believe He holds the keys to all life-creating processes.'"

"I love that story, Uncle Bertie. You know, I've never seen a baseball game."

"Well, I'll try to arrange for us to go to one during our next trip to the States if it's during the season."

I look down at my notes. "How did you feel about Richard's suggestion that God is the author of all life?"

"I thought it was an interesting idea, and shortly after that discussion with Richard, I had one of my talks with Father Anthony."

"You spoke with Father Anthony on a regular basis?"

"Not regularly. Maybe once or twice a year. When a session ended, he would suggest that I think about a particular topic, and in this case, he suggested Spirits. When I had settled into his visitor's chair, he asked what I had concluded. I said, 'It seems to me that the universe is composed of matter, energy, space, and time; we all know about these things, and Einstein tells us that matter and energy are interchangeable. Then, I began thinking about life—I mean the general state— which, I think, is more than energy and matter.'

'How do you define life Bertie?'

'That's not easy, but I would say it consists of at least one cell which is able to reproduce itself, convert chemicals to energy, grow, adapt to changing conditions, and survive.' I paused for a moment. 'I have read that there are three steps for life to arise naturally: one: chemicals form short polymer chains; two: short polymer chains form long polymer chains; three: long polymer chains form cells.' Father Anthony gave me an indulgent smile. 'The problem is step three,' I continued. 'Steps one and two take place in the laboratory; step three never has, and there are over a dozen theories of how step three can happen.' His smile widened. 'But no one has ever proven his theory, and no one has ever created life from scratch.'

'Do you think that anyone will <u>ever</u> succeed in creating life—as you put it— from scratch?'

'No, I don't.'

'So, what is your conclusion?'

'I think that my previous list of ingredients of the universe is incomplete. We have to add something which I'm going to call 'spirit', which I define as inherently undetectable life.'

Father Anthony regarded me doubtfully. 'Have you forgotten, Bertie, that the Holy Spirit is called *the giver of life*?'

'I think when I first heard that, I must have been about six, and having categorised it useless religious stuff, I promptly forgot it.'

'In John 6:63, Jesus says: *What gives life is God's Spirit; man's power is no use at all.*'

So, all my profound and dedicated thinking over the past years could have been unnecessary if I had just read John chapter six. But, sceptic that I am, I would not have been satisfied with just the recorded words of Jesus.

'Sorry, Father, as an agnostic, it works better for me to make a discovery on my own and then to have it confirmed by Jesus, than, sixty years ago, to have put my faith in Jesus' words.'

'I admire your search, Bertie. So, you have concluded that there is spirit— undetectable life. Is God anywhere in this spirit?'

'Perhaps, but I haven't discovered that yet.'

I suppose Father Anthony considered me slow and stubborn. Perhaps I am, but Jo was right: I had to find my own way to an answer. To be led will certainly open the path to doubt and rejection."

Chapter 19
Cousins George and Rosetta

"I was looking at some photo albums yesterday, and there was a picture of Rosetta in her wedding dress, but I never heard the whole story about her."

My granduncle laces his fingers and considers. "I think for the purposes of the memoir, we ought to start with her father."

"OK."

"Jo was preparing dinner for Carol-Ann, me and our first cousin, George Barnstable, who had arrived, unexpectedly, from Leeds. He had been living there ever since his mother, my father's sister, took up with a Barnstable and married him. She made the unfortunate decision of relocating to Leeds, of all places. I have only a foggy memory of George's mother, Georgina, and neither Carol-Ann nor I had ever laid eyes on George until he walked through the door, dressed in mismatched tweed, lace-up leather boots, and a suede cap. Quite a tall, solid fellow, with hazel eyes, a grey goatee and more comprehensible version of a Scottish accent, I judged him to be about my age.

Being uncertain of the drinking habits of northerners, I inquired as to his preferences, to which he replied, 'I'd like a single malt, old chap.'

Luckily, I found a half-empty bottle of Glenfiddich, labelled '10 years' that must have been in the cupboard for at least a decade.

He sniffed the glass, swirled it, took a sip and nodded noncommittally. 'So, Carol-Ann, you ask what brings me to London.' He paused to scan our faces. 'Well, I'm here to purchase a residence. My house in Leeds is for sale. I'd like to get a little closer to family; I have just one daughter—marriageable age—and I have some business interests.'

Carol-Ann suggested: 'Can you refresh us on the genealogy of your side of the family, George?'

He rubbed his hands together. 'My father, Gregory Barnstaple, originally from Leeds, was a classical tenor, who sang minor roles, in the chorus at Leeds opera and at weddings, funerals and other events.'

He reached into a decrepit briefcase at his feet and pulled out a CD. 'In fact, I have here one of his CD's, which is a steal at £13.99.' He lay in carefully on the table, where it remained until his departure.

'I was married to Maria del Conte, a rather beautiful, but tempestuous woman, of Sicilian origin, who died of women's cancer ten months ago.' Jo murmured condolences. 'Thank you. As I say, she was possessed of an erratic, but strong will, and I sometimes found it in the best interests of my sanity to take a leave of absence from home for a week or two. Fortunately, this was possible, owing to my singing engagements around the country, as I have followed in my father's footsteps: in my case as a baritone singing in touring musicals.'

'Have you ever sung in London, George?' I asked.

'Oh, my goodness, on many occasions!'

'Why haven't you let us know of your performances?' Carol-Ann asked. 'I, for one, would have liked to hear you sing.'

'Well, you know, life on stage can be somewhat hectic, and as to hearing me sing, I happen to have a CD of my most popular roles. It is only £15.99.' He placed it on the table, where it remained with its predecessor.

Jo reminded, 'You said you have a daughter, George?'

"I have had only the one child, Rosetta, who is thirty-three and a half, and who, unfortunately has inherited her mother's temperament. As a flutist, some of her emotions can be subsumed in music when she plays with the Leeds Chamber Orchestra."

'You have quite a musical family, George,' I observed.

'Yes, quite right, old chap. In fact, Maria was a coloratura soprano who sang occasionally at Leeds but mostly she taught voice at the Leeds Academy.'

Carol-Ann asked, 'Have you any brothers or sisters, George?'

'At one time, we were four. I had two younger brothers and a younger sister. My sister got married and moved to New Zealand about twenty-five years ago. My next younger brother developed an acute fondness for highland blends and succumbed to liver failure. My younger brother was in the military and was killed in Northern Ireland during The Troubles.'

'Are you still in touch with your sister?'

'Yes, I get a card from her every Christmas.'

'George, we may be able to help you with your house hunting,' I said. 'As it happens, our son Michael and his wife have an excellent local estate agency.'

'Yes, well, I've already engaged Foxx's to look for us around this area.'

'You mentioned business interests as one of your motivations for moving to London,' Carol-Ann said. 'Were you referring to your singing career?'

'Well, of course if I can hook up with a London agent, my singing career would be boosted by more opportunities, but I was actually thinking about my sideline, which is piano tuning. My thinking is that London being somewhat wealthier than Leeds, there is a greater density of pianos which are out of tune.'

Jo had a sour face as she washed the dishes. 'I didn't like him at all. Did you notice that he didn't ask a single question about what any of the three of us do? I'll bet he did some research on the entire family—we're all on Facebook, after all. I'll bet he found Michael and Smithson's, did a little further checking, and found that Foxx's asks for one percent less commission.'

'You know what they say about northerners?' I asked, dishtowel in hand. 'They're Scots bereft of their generosity. By the way, did he leave those CDs?'

'Are you kidding?' Jo asked. 'I think that he's actually targeting you, Carol-Ann. You've got the musical branch of the family. You know the London music scene well, your kids are all musical.'

'That's a good point, Jo,' I said, 'and isn't Albert also a piano tuner?'

Carol-Ann, hands on hips, asked, 'What are you two suggesting?'

Jo said, 'I think he wants to ride your coattails.'

Carol-Ann scowled, 'What's wrong with that? After all, he is family. Said he admired our frequent family get-togethers.'

It was Jo's turn to scowl. 'Fishing for an invitation.'

'Well, I think we should invite George and his daughter to come on a Sunday,' Carol-Ann said, 'so we can get to know his daughter and find out what help they need.'

'George says he wants you to write to the agents based in London on his behalf,' I told Carol-Ann on the phone, my cousin's typewritten letter in my hand.

'Yeah, I know, he mentioned the same thing to me when he came to dinner at my house.'

'How do you feel about it?' I asked.

She hesitated, probably seeking a neutral response. 'I don't mind, particularly, except I think he could have taken me out to lunch.'

'What does he want you to say in these letters?'

There was another pause. 'Well, you know that he has an excellent voice, an outstanding repertoire and great charisma.'

I was wide eyed. 'Is that literally what he asked for?'

'Well, to be fair, that's the way he describes himself.'

'How many times have you heard him sing?'

'I haven't.'

'Carol-Ann, you're being used! Apart from how being used makes you feel, you have a reputation to maintain, and I think you'd be taking a significant risk giving a glowing testimonial, performance unheard. What commitment have you made?'

'I told him I'd consider it.' A moment's silence. 'Before you get too tough, Bertie, remember he's family and blood is thicker than...'

'Vinegar!' I interrupted.

'I'm not...'

I interrupted again: 'I think I should drop him a note and say that you'll be happy to write to the agents once you've attended one of his performances. I don't like my sister being used!'

Today, I received a typewritten response to my polite, handwritten note: 'Dear Cousin Albert, I am appearing in *Oklahoma!* at the Swan Theatre, High Wycombe on the 24th through the 26th and at the Yvonne Arnaud, Guildford on the 28th through the 30th. Cordially, George Barnstaple.'

I sent a text to his mobile phone: 'Dear George, Carol-Ann and I would be happy to attend your performance on the 26th. Can you have two good seats allocated to us? If so, we look forward to seeing (and hearing) you. Best wishes, Bertie.'

Two days later, I received a text from the Swan ticket office informing me that seats C15 and C16 have been allocated to us on the 26th.

I had to admit that George, with hair dyed brown and made up to look thirty years younger, was well cast as Jud Fry, the surly antagonist in *Oklahoma!,* but I also conceded that George had a resonant, emotive baritone, and sinister magnetism as an actor.

George and Rosetta arrived for the family Sunday lunch, and after cadging himself a full beaker of Glenfiddich, while Rosetta went to the kitchen in search of womenfolk, George looked about for a likely family member to engage in conversation."

I start to laugh. "Uncle Bertie, I remember that. Cousin George comes over to me and starts to reveal the details of his family tragedies, which include the deaths of his wife and both of his brothers. Why he picked on me, I haven't any idea. I must have been about sixteen at the time."

"Well, you're a pretty lass with an engaging personality, and I suspect that he was a lonely old man."

"He started out with the details of his late wife. 'Maria was very ill,' he leant closer and, in a stage whisper, informed me, 'The cancer took hold and wouldn't let go. The chemo took all her hair—I mean all, and the radiotherapy made her incontinent. And the pain! It was terrible.'

'I'm sorry to hear that George.'

'But you don't know the half of it, Sarah!' He went on in clinical detail. 'I just had to get away. Fortunately, I had a contract to fill.'

He continued, breathlessly, to make sure I was completely informed about his brother who died of alcoholism and the brother who was killed in Northern Ireland – 'an IRA sniper shot him in the head; he died just like that,' he snapped his fingers.

He told me that he attended none of the three funerals: 'I had to be on stage, you know, Sarah. My sister took care of all that.'

Fortunately, I was called to help set the table and I escaped him, but I was trying to understand how someone could avoid the death of a wife and two brothers and yet have a morbid interest in death.

After Cousin George and Rosetta left, my nan announced, 'I can't believe that fellow! The presumptuousness is outrageous!'

I was very surprised that my nan, who is a great defender of family values, was about to launch an attack on an adult cousin. Sensing, perhaps, that her objectivity may be in doubt, she called Uncle Albert, her son by Raymond, to come and testify: 'Albert, tell us about your conversation with George.'

Uncle Albert had a streak of kindness and truthfulness, as wide as a California motorway, but he also had an off-ramp of caution, which could turn into suspicion.

'Well,' Uncle Albert said, 'George came over to me and wanted to know about my business. I told him that I'm basically a high-end carpenter who repairs stringed instruments, but I could see that he wasn't interested in that. He asked if I was a piano tuner. I said, *yes*, and I was aware that he is also a piano tuner. So then, he started asking me a lot of questions about my turnover, my customers and then he asked to see my customer list. And I said, *Why should I show a potential competitor my customer list?* He turned and walked away.'"

Uncle Bertie says, "I think your nan was absolutely right, Sarah, and I told Albert he had handled the situation perfectly. And, I said to Carol-Ann, 'I think that next time he comes—if there is a next time—I'm going to tell him what the rules are, and that the following Sunday it will be his turn: that we expect him to bring eight chickens worth of legs and breasts for barbecuing, and four bottles of white wine. OK?'

'Absolutely. Incidentally, Bertie,' she said. 'I like his daughter, Rosetta, and I feel sorry for her. She seems like good-hearted, but insecure and somewhat bitter, teenager. She didn't want to move to London. All her friends are in Leeds, but her father insists on moving to London for, she feels, selfish business reasons and to escape the memory of her mother, whom she adored and with whom he couldn't get along.'

Jo joined the conversation. 'I agree with you, Carol-Ann. I also sensed some bitterness, but with an edge of anger. She told me that her mother died a painful, lonely death mainly because the Sicilian side of the family had so many fights with George that they gave up contact with Maria long ago. Rosetta provided most of her mother's round the clock care for six months, while George was away, singing.'

'Is Rosetta actually a flutist with the Leeds Chamber Orchestra?' I asked.

Carol-Ann folded her dish towel. 'Yes, and that's another reason for her not wanting to leave Leeds.'"

"And then, Uncle Bertie, there was the real calamity the following Sunday. Aunt Jo was furious: George and Rosetta had arrived empty handed, having been charged with the provision of eight chickens and four bottles of wine.

When confronted by Aunt Jo, George said, 'Oh, I forgot. Don't you have anything else?'

'I have three hamburgers in the freezer,' Aunt Jo shouted, hands on hips, 'and two bottles of Pepsi. How do you expect me to feed twenty-seven people, short of a miracle from Jesus?'

'You don't have to get so angry, Jo, it was just a mistake.'

'Well, George, you can correct your mistake by hustling over to Sainsbury's for the chicken and wine.'

'Now?'

'Yes, now!'

I was really impressed that Aunt Jo didn't let Cousin George get away with his shenanigans."

"Sarah, it was probably after you left that Sunday," Uncle Bertie says, "that Jo, Carol-Ann and I were having a post-mortem chat in the parlour. 'I had a rather interesting conversation with Rosetta while her father was shopping,' Carol-Ann reported. 'It started with her asking whether I knew of a classical flutist position in London. She apparently has been surveying the musical scene here and is duly impressed. She's also started coming to our church where she seems to have met some nice young people.'

'Can you help her in her musical career, Carol-Ann?' I asked.

'I haven't heard her play, and if I did, I don't know enough about the flute to evaluate her, but we talked about her repertoire, and some of her pieces are regarded as being quite difficult. So, I've given her the names of three conductors I know, and I told her that I'd contact them on her behalf.'

'Does she have a boyfriend in Leeds?' Jo asked.

'No, apparently not. Perhaps she had a boyfriend and broke up with him. She is, I think, quite a pretty girl, in a Latin way: smooth tan, large dark eyes and black hair, and she seems to be reasonably outgoing. The interesting thing,' Carol-Ann continued, 'is that she has taken quite a shine to us—as a family.'

'Probably because she didn't have a good family life,' Jo suggested.

'Perhaps,' Carol-Ann said. 'In any case, she would like to join us for our family lunches whenever her father is away, and she went on to say that she'd like to bring something every time she comes, because she won't be able to fit in the regular rota."

I look over at Uncle Bertie, and I say, "I thought that Rosetta was an attractive and sociable addition to our family gatherings, which she attended about half the time, when her father was out of town. Her long, black hair, neatly plaited into a long pig tail, her large, expressive eyes and sensuous mouth made her seem a nearly adult doll. At the same time, her trendy, satin pantaloons and voluminous blouses identified her as a young sophisticate.

She was certainly grateful for my nan's introduction to the London Chamber Orchestra, where she auditioned and was selected to fill a seat in the wind section where she played both soprano and alto flute. We were all surprised when Carol-Ann brought her violin and sheet music to a lunch, having prompted Rosetta to bring her alto flute, and we were delighted by an un-rehearsed concert, a piece by Vivaldi, featuring violin, flute, piano played by Uncle Albert and tenor vocal by my father, James, a music teacher."

"Yes,' Uncle Bertie says, "we should have more Sunday music concerts. In fact, I have the impression that it was James who, having taken a bit of a fancy to Rosetta, arranged the concert. Throughout the lunch and for much of the afternoon thereafter, the two of them seemed to be engaged in a conspiratorial téte-á-téte, with a generous portion of flirting, finally terminated by a grumpy Anne – your mother: 'Come on, James, we've things to do at home!'"

"Tell me, Uncle Bertie, when did the rumours start? There was apparently a lot of behind the scenes manoeuvring going on to which I was never a party."

"Well, for me, it started when Jo learnt from a private conversation with Carol-Ann that her daughter, Anne, was distraught in the belief that her husband was straying with Rosetta."

I looked at Jo sceptically. 'What evidence does she have?' I asked.

'Nothing conclusive. Just that, as I mentioned, that James and Rosetta looked like two love birds during the last couple of Sunday lunches. James has been insisting that he and Anne should go to London Chamber Orchestra concerts 'To hear our distant cousin play' and going backstage to 'congratulate Rosetta on her performance'. But then my wait for additional evidence is fulfilled. 'There's more, Bertie,' Jo said. 'Anne checked James' phone bill and there are one or two calls to Rosetta every day. She also found a receipt from the Wandsworth Travel Lodge for a night he was supposed to be at a teachers' conference in Birmingham.'

'Has Anne confronted him?' I asked.

'No. She's afraid it's going to turn out to be true. Then, she'll be the one who wrecked the marriage.'

'But that doesn't make sense.'

'It does, in a way, if you think about Anne and James. She's always been timid, and James, who is assertive, holds all the cards.'

'OK, that's a psychological snapshot,' I said, 'but if she were to become aggressive, she might rein in her straying stallion. Besides, doing nothing provides him with space to make his dreams and her nightmares come true.'

We decided to call Carol-Ann, whom we persuaded to have a face-to-face, spine-stiffening session with her daughter.

'He denies that he did anything wrong,' Carol-Ann told us. 'He says that Anne is being paranoid, and that he's only making a distant cousin feel welcome in London. His story is that the teachers' conference was moved to London at the last minute because of transport problems. He had planned to come home for the night, but since there was an early start the next morning, and he was in a workshop until ten pm, he decided to take the room that had been reserved for him.'

I said, 'Just because she's paranoid, doesn't mean he's not out to screw someone.'

'That's not helpful, Bertie,' Jo said.

'OK, let me suggest this,' I said. 'Why don't you, Carol-Ann, have a meeting with Rosetta? You could say you'd like to hear how her career is going, having nominated her for the Chamber Orchestra, and she'll certainly agree to meet with you—maybe even have lunch.'

'And then what?' Jo prompted.

'I don't think I would present Anne's charges. I think I would tell her some lies about James. You have noticed he is very attentive to her; that this fits into a pattern of past behaviour where he tries to seduce attractive women. Invariably, though, he leaves the woman stranded when Anne finds out, because he's quite dedicated to his family; that you suggest Rosetta's giving him the cold shoulder, which may be in her best interests.'

'But that's not true!' Carol-Ann protested.

'Some of it is besides, who cares?' I said. 'Nobody's going to tell James what you said, and it'll probably be enough to make Rosetta cautious.'

'Well, I had lunch with Rosetta today,' Carol-Ann reported. 'She was very grateful for the help in getting the seat in the Chamber Orchestra. She started getting quite nervous when I said that James appears to be paying her a lot of attention. I think she was afraid about what might be coming, but when I made no accusations and started to talk about James' fictional past misdeeds, I sensed a shift in her mood from being defensive about possible censure, to concern for her own welfare. At some point, she said that 'nothing had happened' between them, but she didn't look me in the eye when she said it. She said that James is quite aggressive, and would it be possible for someone in the family to have a talk with James? Your name was mentioned, Bertie.'

I said, 'It's a good idea that somebody talks to James, but shouldn't it be Raymond?'

There was a long pause on the phone, until Carol-Ann said, 'First of all, Bertie, Anne isn't Raymond's daughter, as you know, and secondly, even though

I could coach him, he will probably lapse into judgemental mode. So, will you please talk to James in a fatherly, clear, but oblique way?'

Fatherly? Yes, I could do that. Clear but oblique? Not so sure.

I called James and told him that I'd like to meet him at a pub at about five-thirty to get his input on some musical aspirations I had. This was not entirely a falsehood, as I'd been thinking about Gerri's point about a fulfilling vocation, and perhaps I could take up something musical. A doubtful proposition, but it proved to be effective bait for James, the music teacher.

Having settled in at a distant table with our pints, I explained to James that I was thinking of retiring from AtoZ, and had decided I needed something new to keep me busy, and that, having neglected music all my life, did he think I could learn to play my mother's old piano?

We discussed the piano, the guitar, and singing as my 'old age pursuits'. None was greeted with effusive enthusiasm, but he gave me the names and contact details of three teachers. We lapsed into small talk.

I said, 'By the way, James, I noticed that you seem to be developing a particularly good relationship with Rosetta.'

'Well, she's a lonely lady, new to London, and I just want to help her get her feet on the ground.'

More likely feet in the air. 'Yes, well several others have remarked on the relationship.'

'What do you mean, Uncle Bertie?' He asked sharply.

'Oh, goodness! I'm not suggesting anything amiss, but you know, James, how people are: they love a good gossip, and what starts out as a little flirting is recast as a torrid affair.'

'Certainly, there's no torrid affair,' he said, indignantly. 'We're just friendly, distant cousins.'

'Of course you are, James. I have always had the greatest respect for you, as does the entire family, I'm sure.' I paused for several moments. 'The trouble is…'

'What, Uncle Bertie?'

I casted a long, heavy sigh. 'Well, the difficulty is, James, that gossip can stain someone's reputation, and of course—though I know that's not the case here—if there turned out to be a grain of truth in the rumours…' I looked around for a proper example. "It would be like a publican serving counterfeit beer.'

He was irritated. 'Well, that certainly isn't the case here.'

'I'm sure it's not, James, I'm sure it's not.' I scratched my head. 'You know, speaking off the record, I have the impression that George has a bit of a problem with Rosetta.' James was suddenly paying close attention. 'We all know that George is anxious to see Rosetta married,' I continued, 'and he's probably so anxious that if he gets the scent of a possible suitor, he'd move heaven and earth to make it happen.' James was chewing his lower lip.

'Then there's the other consideration…' I paused briefly. 'Nowadays, children are more exposed to the rumour mill than we adults are because of social media. You know how it is: a school bully hears some gossip in his family, he exaggerates it, and posts it online where all the kids read it and take it as fact.'

His eyes flickered from me to the pub room and back to me, considering, perhaps, the possible consequences of surly, guerrilla warfare with his three children. 'Who asked you to talk to me, Uncle Bertie?'

'Let's just say a family member.'

'Was it Anne?'

'No, James, it wasn't Anne. Have I made my point?'

'I think so.'

The following Sunday, I noticed that James spent most of his time with Anne and you kids, while Rosetta was preoccupied with Carol-Ann, Jo and Gerri. This confirmed my belief that a family, in order to maintain the sanctity of its values, could exert considerably more disciplinary leverage than an individual."

"Mom and I thank you for that, Uncle Bertie," I say. "At the time your mother died, could you have visualised yourself handling the problems with George and Rosetta the way you did?"

"No. My pet philosopher at that time was Charlie Brown, who said, 'There is no problem too big and too complex that it can't be run away from'."

"And your pet philosopher now?"

"Josephine Smithson, who says, 'for the wayward, a kick in the arse can focus the mind'."

Tongue in cheek, I ask, "And you recommend the Smithson Philosophy for the maintenance of family unity?"

"Absolutely! Without it, others would have forgotten to bring their Sunday food offerings, and instead of conviviality we would have descended into bickering. Moreover, Rosetta would probably be your step-mother."

Chapter 20
Mr Lalitha

"Uncle Bertie, you've mentioned your friend Richard, Father Anthony, and the Professor as being influences on your spiritual development. Is there anyone else?"

"Yes, there was Mr Lalitha." He adjusts his position and looks across the rooftops. "It started with Jo sending me out to get some fresh spices for a chicken curry. 'I'm pretty sure I don't have any cumin, saffron or chilli,' she said. 'Don't get cumin powder, get the seeds, black seeds, not brown, if possible, and the chilli should be flakes.'

So, I set out with the intention of going to the local Tesco, but then I remembered that there was a closer local fruit and vegetable market: Maharaja something. Even better. They should have Indian spices.

Maharaja's Best was not much bigger than the old huckster's truck, but under the red and white striped awning was a sloping display of every ordinary, and many exotic fruits and vegetables, some of which looked distinctly inedible. Inside the shop, there was barely room for three customers between the counter and shelves packed to the ceiling with jars, cans, bottles and boxes. Seated behind the counter and illuminated by a single fluorescent light was the proprietor: a small, brown-skinned man with a mat of glossy black hair. 'Good day to you, sir,' he announced in a lilting Indian accent, 'What can I do for you?'

'Well, I'm looking for some spices.' I surveyed the shelves for the presence of small bottles or packets.

'Let me help you, sir,' he said, turning down the miniature TV on which a kaleidoscopic dance is playing, and squeezed out of his lair. At that point, I discovered that he was stooped and apparently quite old, but with a face stretched tight in a smile. 'The spices are here,' he said, pointing to a corner display. 'What do you require?'

'Black cumin seeds, chilli flakes and saffron.'

He removed two small bottles and two packets from the shelves, studied them for a moment and then turned to me.

'I judge you to be quite a discerning cook, sir.'

'It's my wife who is the cook. She makes an excellent curry.'

'I see. In that case, she would probably like to have some of these.' From behind the counter, he retrieved a frond of yellow-green leaves – like bay leaves, but tender.

Sensing my uncertainty, he said, 'They're fresh curry leaves, sir, not to be confused with curry powder which is a mixture of five spices. These leaves, when fresh, add a delightful flavour and aroma to her curry.'

'And how much are they?'

'For a new customer like you, sir, they are a welcome gift from the Maharaja. Now, may I ask about the saffron? I have two offerings of saffron: Spanish Sierra saffron in this yellow package and Kashmiri Mongra saffron in this purple package. This Spanish saffron is what you might call 'diluted', and the Kashmiri is full strength.' He held out the two packages for me to examine.'

'What is the difference in price, Mr Maharaja?'

There was a deep, bass laugh. 'I am not a maharaja, sir; my name is Lalitha. My son is a marketing consultant, and he thought of the name to represent quality,' bashfully adding, 'He works for Price Waterhouse.' And, collecting his thoughts: 'This Spanish saffron is ten pounds and it has ten grams of saffron, and this Kashmiri package contains five grams and it is also ten pounds. If you wish more, I think I have some three-ounce packages.'

'No more, thanks.' I considered the two packages: the yellow plastic sackett and the little purple box with gold lettering. 'How much saffron is needed to make a curry for three?'

'Two grams of the Mongra would be plenty, sir.'

He wrapped my purchases, including the purple Mongra, in tan paper, sealing it with cello tape.

'So, are you from Kashmir, Mr Lalitha?'

'No, sir, I am from Kerala and I am a Hindu. Kashmir is mostly Muslim. I went there once. It is a very beautiful place, particularly in summer when there is no fighting.'

'Mr Lalitha, my name is Bertie. I have often wondered about the Hindu religion; it seems very exotic to me.'

He took a deep breath and fixed his eyes on the ceiling. 'Well, Mr Bertie, I should tell you that Hinduism is about nothing in particular. It is, rather, about a way of life." He counted off the points on his fingers. 'Honesty, doing no harm to living things, virtuous pursuit of wealth, enjoyment of life, and the achievement of perfect spiritual peace.'

A long-standing question occurred to me. 'Is there a principal Hindu god?'

'Mr Bertie, there are many Hindu gods. As a Hindu, it is possible to be monotheistic, polytheistic, atheist or agnostic.'

'And I think I read that Hindus can choose a personal god.'

'Yes, it is possible if your strand of Hinduism recognises gods, and then your choice may be influenced by the sacred scriptures of your strand, your caste and your family tradition.'

'You mention scripture, Mr Lalita: is there a central scripture which represents the Hindu faith?'

'There are many diverse scriptures, Mr Bertie, and we Hindus argue about them all the time, so there is no unifying creed.'

I was confused by what sounds like an adhocracy. 'So, what principles do all Hindus have in common?'

'We believe that every living thing has an eternal soul. We share some festivals, rituals and cosmology.'

I asked, 'What do Hindus think about the cosmos?'

'We believe that time is infinite, and the universe is cyclic, which means that the current cycle of the universe was preceded by an infinite number of cycles and will be followed by another infinite number.'

'Mmm. An interesting concept…You say that every living thing has an immortal soul. Does that mean that Hindus believe in reincarnation?'

'We believe that life is a series of actions which we call *karma*, and that good karma leads to improvement in one's current life, or a better life in samsara, the nearly infinite cycle of re-birth. Bad karma has the opposite effects.'

So, like Christians, they seemed to believe in good and evil. 'OK, but who decides what one will be in the next life?'

'Hindus do not concern themselves with that question. It is a matter for the cosmos.'

I could see it was time for me to go.

'Where have you been, Bertie?' Jo looked up from her book. 'Just on a search for ingredients?'

'Do you know that little Indian shop near the station on Culvert Road?' I lay down the small white package and the curry frond, which she picked up and passed it under her nose.

'What is this?'

I explained the curry leaf and the choice of saffron.

'But how much do I use? One leaf or two?'

'I haven't any idea; Mr Lalitha gave me a brief dissertation on Hinduism.'

'By request, I assume. Give me the highlights.'

I sat down with a gesture of indifference. 'It's more a way of life than a religion.'

'Well, that should suit you even better.'"

"I assume that was the first of several visits to Mr Lalitha," I say.

"Yes, on my second visit, I showed him this." Uncle Bertie takes an exquisite, life-size porcelain lotus flower down from a shelf. It has concentric circles of pink petals with white highlights surrounding a collection of yellow stamen around the central stigma. He places it in my hand.

"This is beautiful! Where did you get it?"

"It belonged to my mother. There was a note in her handwriting with it that said it belonged, originally to her great, great grandfather who was stationed in Kolkata with the East India Company. Mr Lalitha said it is probably from a famous, seventeenth-century ceramic artist who lived in Jaipur. That's his signature on the back."

"The lotus has special significance, Uncle Bertie, what is it?"

"Mr Lalitha told me that the lotus is a symbol of spirituality and of reincarnation. It rises from the muck at the bottom of a lake and produces this beautiful, pure flower. He said this particular flower was probably part of a household devotional shrine."

He places the flower on the table and continues to study it, a smile on his face, his head moving from side to side. "I've talked quite bit with Mr Lalitha about spirits and I believe that each of us has a spirit that survives death."

I stare at my granduncle in amazement for some moments. "Wow!"

"Yes, I know. It's quite an accomplishment. The gift from my mother and a Hindu spice merchant."

"So…are you going to…?"

"Become a Hindu? No. There's a lot that was still missing for me, and Hinduism doesn't have the answers." Uncle Bertie sits, his hands folded in contemplation for a time. "It was shortly after my first meeting with Mr Lalitha that I had a session with Father Anthony on the subject of the universe, and I told him I rather like the Hindu concept of a universe which is unlimited in time or space.'

'And what, for you, Bertie, is the purpose of the universe?' he asked.

'That is quite difficult to say, but I have read that it has something to do with existence.' He observed me patiently over the rim of his cup. 'The point is either something exists or it doesn't. If nothing exists, we wouldn't be here. If only some things exist, that would call into question why some are missing. So, I believe that the universe represents complete existence. It has all the elements from which anything can be made.'

'OK. What about time? You mentioned that it is infinite.'

'Yes, it has to be infinite, because if it's finite, then, at some point the universe would cease to exist.'

'So, Bertie, what do you believe happened before the big bang that scientists like to talk about. Did nothing exist before the big bang?'

'Well, we know the universe is expanding from the big bang. I think what will happen in many billion years is that it will start to contract. It will keep on contracting until it becomes a tiny ball of everything, which is unstable, and we have another big bang. This has happened billions of times in the past and it will happen countless billions of times in the future.'

'OK, why all this expansion and contraction?'

'Because change is necessary for the universe to exist. If the universe never did anything, but was always exactly the same, would it actually exist? How do we know if a thing actually exists if it never changes and we can never change? All we would have then is a theory. So, I believe that the universe and everything in it is in constant motion. There is nothing that doesn't move sometime.'

'But, why is *the tiny ball of everything*, as you put it, unstable, and why the expansion and contraction?'

'I don't know, Father. Understanding such things is far beyond my capacity, but maybe someday another Einstein will postulate a General Theory of Change that will explain everything.'"

The next morning, he is in a reflective mood as he sips his tea. "You haven't experienced this, Sarah, but when one's spouse—or partner—becomes ill with something that could be life threatening, you become so worried that you can't focus properly on anything else that's going on around you.

Jo said, 'Bertie, I think I can feel a lump here.' She had just exited from the shower and was biting her lip. She unwrapped her towel and pinches the flesh under her right breast. I could see nothing but a still-beautiful breast, but her worry was contagious. I felt a series of shivers down my back. She sat next to me and pointed to the suspect area. Clumsily, I began a manual assessment, trying to isolate the concern. 'Can you feel it?'

'Yes, I think so. Yes. About the size of my little fingernail, round, not hard, but firmer than the surroundings.' She nodded. Her lips had turned white and there were furrows on her brow. I took her hands.

'When was the last time you had a mammogram?' I asked.

'I think it was about a year ago.'

'Let's get you to the GP.'

Jo had a mammogram followed by a biopsy. The twenty-six days between initial discovery and official diagnosis were crazy oscillations in our shared mood. Jo had a biting sore on her lip, and my fingernails had become inexplicably short and ragged. We assured each other that it was probably just a cyst, but sleep was difficult for both of us. As the process unfolded from our exam to GP's scrutiny to mammogram to biopsy to surgeon's assessment, the optimism faded and fear took control.

Miss Khoury, a grey haired, kindly faced surgeon in her mid-fifties, wore a starched white jacket, a dark blue, knee-length skirt, thick tights, and spoke with a Middle Eastern accent. 'Mrs Smithson, I'm afraid the lump you have identified in your right breast is a malignancy, but it is not particularly large, and I doubt that your lymph nodes are involved.' Further discussion revealed that it was a middle-grade cancer, neither aggressive nor lazy. As to the options, Miss Khory said, 'First of all, doing nothing is not an option. A radical mastectomy, which some women might opt for, is, in my opinion, a bit extreme unless you have a genetic disposition. That leaves surgery, radiotherapy and chemotherapy in some combination as being the most likely options.'

'I've never had a gene test,' Jo said, 'but my mother and grandmothers didn't have breast cancer.'

'OK, we'll get you tested.'

'Miss Khoury,' Jo said, 'I've read about a procedure that involves surgical removal and live tissue reconstruction at the same time. Is that possible?'

The surgeon looked down at Jo's file. 'Your profession is listed as fashion model, Mrs Smithson. Are you still active?'

'No, not much anymore, but I just like the idea of returning things to nearly normal, if you see what I mean.'

'Yes, it would be possible. The procedure is longer, as you would expect, and that carries slightly more risk. The healing process is longer. We would remove tissue from your abdomen or buttocks, which would leave a permanent mark, even after the tissue has had a chance to regenerate. To be on the safe side, there would also be some radiotherapy.'

Jo's jaw was set. 'Let's plan on that and the gene test.'

On the way home, I said, 'I hope I didn't influence your decision, Jo.'

'What are you talking about?'

'Well, for example, if you're OK with a simple lumpectomy, I'm certainly OK with that.'

She turned to study me for a moment. 'Bertie, I just want to do this thing right and get back to normal.'

Which didn't really answer my question: how much of her selection of reconstructive surgery was motivated by her desire to return her breast to please me and how much was to restore her own self-image?

Given that Jo's mother died in her thirties of alcohol poisoning, her maternal grandmother had been lost in the mists of time, and her paternal grandmother was always an unknown person, I could understand Jo's dismissiveness of the surgeon's question on family history, and her interest in a gene test.

I sat on the rigid plastic chair next to Jo's bed on the women's surgical ward at St George's. She was transferred to another bed and wheeled away to surgery nearly an hour ago. I'd finished reading *The Guardian*. Actually, I laid it out on that wheeled bed table, and turned the pages four or five times. The bed on the right had the curtains drawn; on the left was a grey-haired woman whom I was afraid had died until the nurse said something to her. The woman across the aisle had her TV on, but she appeared to be sleeping and next to her was a whole dark-dressed family surrounding the bed of a young woman slumped down in her bed. No one had moved in the last hour.

Miss Khoury had said the surgery would take about three hours. There was no clock on the ward. I consulted my watch constantly, but the second hand seems to be suffering from inertia. What could I do to make the time pass more quickly? Nothing. This was the first time that either of us had major surgery. Jo

177

gave me a weak smile as she was wheeled away, and that was after she had a sedative. The trouble was that I couldn't avoid thinking about all the things that could go wrong: cardiac arrest, overdose of anaesthesia, discovery of a huge tumour, rupture of an artery, thrombosis…And there was nobody there to calm my electrified nerves, and nowhere to go.

Finally! Three hours and forty-seven minutes later, my Jo was back and smiling. A kiss never felt so good. 'I'm fine, Bertie, I'm fine. Just a little sore right now.'

Over the next days, the pain ramped up and gradually declined. Jo had her radiotherapy. We made plans to go away to the Lake District.

Miss Khoury said, "You look fine, Josephine, and I think there's every chance we've beaten the cancer, so go and enjoy your holiday."

Forty-seven years ago, Jo and I were at the Inn on the Square in Keswick. We had been married in St Christopher's the day before, and a week in the Lake District offered just the transition we thought we needed: a comfortable, economical hotel with good food, a splendid wilderness setting a few hours by train from chaotic London, and plenty of local distractions. Besides, neither of us had ever seen the famous Lake District.

We were truly smitten, hardly able to keep from touching each other, though, at Jo's insistence, the ultimate touching was reserved for any time after the ceremony, yet we recognised that plans, grand (like how to launch Jo's career) and minor (who was to sleep on which side of the bed) were required. We thought we knew each other well, but many small unknowns were unaccounted for: who were our respective dentists, for example?

Then, we retired to our room at nine in the evenings and were seldom seen in the dining room before ten the next morning. After breakfast, we would stroll through the open-air market, examining much but buying only trinkets, and returning for a leisurely lunch. There was often the need for a lengthy afternoon nap, but we took the air with a walk down to Derwentwater before dinner. It was a week in which, happily, all our arriving objectives were satisfied, but, unexpectedly, departing objectives were also required; that, we learnt, is marriage.

After Jo's surgery, we both felt the need to escape, to rest, and to get in touch with each other. I doubted that we'd spend as much time in the bedroom as we did thirty-eight years ago. Then, there were hormone-inflamed libidos, so much suppressed desire, so much to learn and to explore. Now, the desire, unsuppressed, was still there, but for me, it was more about assuring Jo that she was still the beautiful, desirable woman she always was, and for Jo, it was finding reassurance that while lovemaking may have lost some of its erotic glow, it had lost none of its brilliant, emotional halo.

She was understandably protective of her right side, and I paid it only gentle lip service when, in fact, the surgeon deserved the subtitle of 'sculptor', so faithfully was its curvature restored, marred only by thin, red scalpel lines. Her left got more of my attention. I had always marvelled at the shape and smooth, rounded curving of a woman's breasts. In my years of bachelorhood, I personally studied many wonderful examples, but on night one, after the ceremony, Jo became the gold standard.

The difference in the levels of our experience at making love could have become an issue between us, but I don't believe it ever mattered to either of us. I suppose one could theorise that it played a subconscious role in Jo's brief fling, and in my decision not to take up the implied offer by that woman: what was her name?

When we are on our second honeymoon in the Lake District, Jo and I took the eight-mile, scenic walk around Derwentwater at an introspective pace. The black surface of the lake was a mirror for the green forest and the rounded hills on the far side, as well as a lazy sailboat with its white, slack sail.

'I'm not so sure about this new assignment I have,' Jo said. 'He has such a big ego—it seems that his advance of a million pounds has gone to his head—and I'm afraid he's going to turn out to be a control freak.'

I had a mental picture of Lord Benjamin of Salton, the ex-Labour prime minister, and erstwhile mover-and-shaker of British politics, with his shoulder-length white hair, grey moustache and penetrating blue eyes. 'And you've talked to his publisher?'

'Yes, Mercury have given me the ghost-writing contract.'

'But have you discussed who's going to do what in the writing process?'

'They said, *You guys work it out.* And, in a way, Bertie, we've already done that: he's going to talk, I'm going to ask questions, I'm going to record our sessions, and draft the manuscript, which he'll comment on. John Sessions at Mercury will *adjudicate.*"

I considered Jo's concern. 'You're worried that, for example, he'll want to include stuff in which the average reader will have no interest and leave out the embarrassing bits?'

'Exactly. He may spoil of his chances for a bestselling biography by gratifying his ego.'

I reflected on the process by which Jo got this project. Lord Benjamin and Mercury Publishing had reached an impasse about who would do the ghost-writing – fortunately, his lordship recognised that he couldn't do it alone. Jeffrey got wind of the dilemma and approached the Labour peer on his mother's behalf. On meeting Josephine, Lord Benjamin took a shine to her; Mercury checked her references and her previous work and said 'OK'.

'What else, Jo?'

'His wife. She seems nice enough, but she's always around: making tea, rearranging sofa pillows.'

'Sounds like she wants to make sure he's behaving himself—after all, there's an attractive woman with her husband, and politicians don't have the best reputation for their conduct with women.'

She sighed. 'Including His Lordship.'

'You've got a tough assignment, Jo: getting the crucial truth out of a philandering man while, as a very attractive woman, keeping him at least double arms-length.' She turned her trusting smile on me. 'You'll be fine, Jo. If he offers you a margarita, just give it a pass.'

Over fish and chips in a pub at the south end of the lake, Jo confided, 'You know, Bertie, I'm not scheduled to get my name on the cover of the book: like— *My Story as told to Josephine Smithson.*'

'I can understand that, Jo. You're not Oprah…yet. But I think you deserve a specific mention. When the manuscript is finished, you can ask His Lordship to go to bat for you with Mercury. As a last resort, you could waive some of your fee for well-deserved recognition.'

It was very important to me, Sarah, that Jo had a big success in this project with Lord Benjamin: it would do wonders for her self-esteem, which was negative her entire childhood. Raising three successful children was a feather in her cap. Modelling, her cherished ambition as a child, is hard work, and countless images in hundreds of catalogues are simply recycled. And editing helped pay off the mortgage, but it, too, is hard work for thankless clients.

At the age of fifty-nine, Jo needed and deserved a singular, life-affirming success."

"It was a success," I say.

"Yes, Sarah, it sold about three quarters of a million hard copies as well as e-book and audio versions, but best of all, it says *As Told to Josephine Smithson* on the cover."

"Which led to her current assignment."

"Yes, the ex-Tory Prime Minister, David Galloway, has selected Jo to write his official biography, which will feature a decade in the Royal Air Force, three decades in politics, many friends in high places, and a scandal or two."

"Aunt Jo must be very happy."

"She is, but she also gets stressed over deadlines and discussions with David on what to include and how events should be presented, even though he almost always concedes that she is right. Something I hadn't realised before about finding the right vocation is that it should be stressful and challenging. If it isn't, it's boring."

Chapter 21
Margaret

I look at my notes, reviewing family members noted. "Uncle Bertie, I've never heard the complete story about Margaret—bits and pieces, yes, but never the whole thing."

"I doubt that anyone but Margaret—and Nelson—have the complete picture, but I'll tell you what I know."

"Carol-Ann called me during Raymond's illness. 'Margaret's been arrested,' she informed me in a disapproving tone. I was surprised: Margaret always struck me as a goodie-two-shoes. 'Apparently it's something about misappropriated funds at the council. Raymond got a call from Nelson,' she continued, 'who wanted to know if Poppa Ray could stand surety for her bail. Raymond gave me the three thousand cash deposit, and I went down to the court to sign the papers.'

'Have you seen Margaret?' I asked.

'Yes, briefly. Not a word of thanks. She kept angrily protesting her innocence and saying it was all a mistake by the council.'

'She's never been one of your favourite people. When is the trial?'

'Her lawyer says it'll be sometime next month. In the meantime, she's been suspended from work. I guess the council doesn't want to precipitate a counter suit by firing her outright.' Carol-Ann fell silent for a moment. 'I suppose you're right, Bertie: I was never particularly fond of Margaret. Partly because she is a rather remote step daughter-in-law, and she's so aggressive.'

Carol-Ann was certainly right in her characterisation of Margaret, who seemed to consider herself several rungs higher on the social ladder than any of us plebeian Smithsons. Margaret, her late husband, Brucie, and their son, Nelson, considered themselves more a part of Raymond's non-existent lineage than Carol-Ann's, although the rationale for this displacement was never clear: Raymond has no siblings. Although, after Brucie's death, Margaret and Nelson would almost always appear for Sunday lunch and at Seaford; it invariably felt as if they had something better to do but were under an obscure obligation to be with us. And Raymond, as much as he was constitutionally able, tried to pamper his daughter-in-law and grandson.

By now, Margaret would be in her early sixties; she has never re-married, nor is there any sign of a male friend, though it stretches my credibility to conceive of such a relationship with a self-respecting man: Brucie was entirely under Margaret's thumb. She had worked in the benefits department of the council for almost forty years – for about half that time as a manager, though I don't suppose she enjoyed any great popularity.

Nelson was, for me, somewhat unfathomable: quiet, almost supine on most occasions, but I had known him to be rough and impatient when he felt challenged. Perhaps this volatility led to his moving out of his mother's flat into a small, rented accommodation when he graduated from high school. For some years, he worked as an Asda cashier while he was studying for an IT degree. Now, I understand he is working for an IT consultancy and has moved into a single, high rise flat.

Of course, Jo and I had to attend the trial. Raymond said he was too ill. Carol-Ann, who is now in her late sixties, and has re-invented herself as a part-time consultant to the same theatre company, was also present.

Margaret, her hair unkempt and wearing a grey track suit, was sitting with her barrister before the bar. There was no sign of Nelson, which lead me to believe that the historically warm mother-son relationship had suffered a chill.

The judge read out the fraud and theft charges. On being asked how she pleaded, Margaret responded: 'Not guilty'.

The prosecuting barrister began with a summary of the council's case: Margaret Hotchkis – her married name – was alleged to have set up a fictitious benefit account in favour of a Jerome Johnston who died eighteen years ago, but who miraculously reappeared eight years later when the account was opened. Disbursements had been £1,048.51 per month for one hundred and twenty-three months, a total of £128,966.73. The funds had been removed from the TSB Bank account in the name of Jerome Johnston in regular increments of £100 by means of access to ATMs via a Visa debit card, also in the name of Jerome Johnston.

According to the council's head of the benefits department, the fraudulent benefit account was discovered during a data-gathering exercise in which two Jerome Johnstons, separated by eight-years' time, were discovered. The council's witness also testified that there are two pieces of evidence that Margaret Hotchkis personally opened the account: one – the transaction was completed from a PC assigned to her; and two – the council's document which authorises the opening of benefit accounts had her signature on it.

Margaret, having been sworn in, testified that she had no recollection of opening an account in favour of Jerome Johnston, whom she said she didn't know. She said she had no knowledge of the Jerome Johnston who withdrew the cash. She asked to see the authorisation document, and on having seen it, she denied that it was her signature, although she acknowledged that her name was typed below the signature.

The prosecuting barrister then called a Mrs Evelyn Bloom, who was sworn in. Mrs Bloom testified that she sat next to Mrs Hotchkis in the council office, and that Mrs Hotchkis asked her to review and sign the authorisation for an account for Jerome Johnston. Continuing, she said that since two signatures are required, it was not unusual to be asked to review a file with which she wasn't familiar, but which looked in order. She, therefore, signed the authorisation, although she did not see Mrs Hotchkis sign. Asked about Mrs Hotchkis' attendance in the office on the day the account was opened, Mrs Bloom said: 'Mrs Hotchkis was present, and I didn't see anyone else using her computer. Besides, we all have personal passwords.'

The judge called the barristers to the bench for a conference which we couldn't hear, and which lasted fifteen minutes. He then announced the trial was to be adjourned for ten days. Before closing the trial, he advised Margaret that, 'If you are found guilty, you can anticipate a lengthy custodial sentence.'

Neither Jo, nor Carol-Ann, nor I could figure out why there was the conference with the judge, or why he didn't pass sentence immediately. Raymond said, 'It's a political stitch-up. Margaret has pissed off someone high up in the council, and they're trying to put her away. Probably she knows too much about a real case of fraud. The judge has seen through it, and he's giving the prosecution a chance to drop the charges.'

I didn't say so, but this seemed like Raymond's wishful thinking.

The following Friday evening, Carol-Ann called: 'Raymond is very distraught. He wants to see you. He won't tell me what the problem is.'

I found him propped up by several pillows, looking gaunter and more ashen-faced than ever, wearing a black-and-blue striped nightshirt. 'What is it, Ray?'

Pleadingly, he asked: 'Can you lend me five thousand in cash, Bertie?'

I decided to make a joke of it. 'Don't tell me the mafia's after you, Raymond.'

He leant back on the pillows, considering, then looked away. 'It's so stupid and unnecessary! If they had just asked me, I could have solved it for them. I didn't know. How can I be responsible?'

There was a long silence. 'Raymond, who is *they*?'

His mouth and jaw worked sporadically, as if chewing. 'Nelson and his mother.'

Enlightenment flashed with an inaudible thunderclap. 'So, Nelson is the new Jerome Johnston.'

'He was such a good boy. Following in my footsteps.'

'And you need the five thousand for his bail?'

'Probably, his mother talked him into it. She likely demanded a cut.'

'How did they catch him?'

'CCTV.'

'So, he's confessed?' Raymond nodded. 'And Margaret, also?' Another nod.

I sat at the foot of the bed, next to a bony foot, and patted a scrawny thigh. 'Raymond, this is nothing to do with you.'

He glared at me. 'They're my kith and kin, Albert!'

'Perhaps so, Ray, but they made their decisions, without asking you, and sometimes a wise man will distance himself from criminals so as not to be contaminated…if you see what I mean.'

He was chewing on the thought which seemed to be particularly sinewy. Angrily, he asked, 'You mean: just let them rot?'

'There's no danger of that, Raymond. As far as I know, Margaret is—thanks to you—still at home awaiting trial, and Nelson will be housed in custody being served three square meals a day.'

'So, you won't loan me the five thousand?'

'No, Raymond, I'm afraid not.'

Margaret and Nelson each received a four-year sentence in Wandsworth Prison, conditioned on full repayment of the funds. With good behaviour, they'd be out in two years, with a prison record.

We learnt that Margaret's flat was to be sold, with the proceeds to repay the council; Nelson's rented flat was to be evacuated.

'Bertie, could you and Jo come help me?' Carol-Ann asked. 'I've got to clear out their flats.'

'But, Carol-Ann,' I asked, 'what did they do with the money?'

'She said she couldn't really say…Which I suppose is one way of saying, It's none of your business.'

'Well,' I said, tongue-in-cheek, 'we've got to be on the lookout for jewellery and stock certificates.'

We went through Margaret's flat with forensic care. Inside a drawer of her vanity, there was a keepsake box, with an envelope containing a birthday card inscribed, *Happy birthday, Mum. Love you, Nelson.* There was also a diamond bracelet – at least they look like diamonds. The card was undated.

We debated what to do: report it, get it valued, or store it separately? Carol-Ann decided: 'Let's pretend we never found it.'

The furniture was consigned to two different auction houses to be sold. There was a pile of stuff to be picked up by a charity collection service, and another to be collected by a rubbish company. The rest, including the keepsake box, was packed in storage cartons for collection by ABC Storage.

Nelson's flat was easier, as it was rented furnished. There were two bags of rubbish, which I took down to the bin; two large cartons of clothes for ABC Storage; and one carton of personal effects, including a camera and a laptop, which had been returned by the police. Curious, I pressed the start button. Moments later, the desktop appeared; no password was requested. There was an assortment of social media icons, but no emails. In *Documents, Photos,* there was a file marked South Africa which contained about fifty holiday pictures featuring Margaret and Nelson, of eight years ago. There was also a large collection of photos of nude women. Some would be considered legal pornography; interestingly, none of the women appeared younger than mid-fifties, and none of them was Margaret. Jo and Carol-Ann threw up their hands in dismay and shock.

There was an, 'Oh, my God!' from Jo, and 'Do you suppose there was an incestuous…' from Carol-Ann.

'More likely,' I interrupted, 'he has some kind of fixation on older women.'

'And on Margaret, in particular,' Carol-Ann added.

Jo said, 'Yes, but we don't know that.'

'In any case,' a grimacing Carol-Ann added, 'Raymond is not to know about this. It would kill him.'

I concluded that two lonesome people were looking for some consolation in life, and they decided, together, that the consolation was money. What did they spend it on? And how did the money work out for them? Two years in Wandsworth Prison, before probation, and a life-long stain on their reputations.

At the time that Margaret and Nelson were sentenced, we knew that Raymond's cancer had spread. It was in his lungs and there was a suspicious lesion in his brain. There was nothing the doctors could offer except more chemotherapy. He turned that down.

I felt that I should go and see Ray after the housecleaning, about which he knew, but in which he had no interest.

Sitting in the living room in the late afternoon gloom, he hadn't shaved in some time, so his chin, covered with grey hair, seemed dirty. His dark eyes were submerged in grey sockets, and his skin was waxy pale. The considerable weight loss was apparent in his bony cheeks and his spidery hands. He was wearing a black and white Fulham football warm-up set, which Carol-Ann must have just washed.

'Hello, Bertie,' he murmured and sat up, turning off the un-watched TV. I asked if he would like a cup of tea; he shook his head, gesturing at the used tea tray on the table. The room was quite dark, but I made no move to switch on a light, assuming that he preferred the gloaming and the medicinal smell.

'How are you feeling, Raymond?'

He shifted his position slightly. 'Lousy. Doctors say I'm goin' to die.'

'Doctors have been wrong before. Besides, maybe this is the time to enjoy your family. You've got Carol-Ann, the children and grandchildren.'

He gave a derisive snort. 'When I'm six feet under, Carol-Ann will find herself a new fancy man. I used to be the hot ticket that Carol-Ann needed, but not anymore.'

'Well, we're all getting a little older.'

'And as for Margaret and Nelson,' he added, 'they both let me down. Margaret has always been stupid, and Nelson's broken his moral compass. I thought he would take after me. Be a big businessman. But no.' He glared into the distant gloom. 'And the council? They're just incompetent and meddlesome.'

I was left with the impression that the only injured party in all of this was Raymond.

He looked vacantly around the room. 'The thing I don't understand is why this happens to me. I'm only seventy-five—been healthy all my life—I expected to live 'til at least eighty-five. It seems damn unfair to be taken away before I have a chance to make a name for myself.'

'But I thought you were an important businessman.'

'Hell, Bertie, that was twenty years ago. I had three dry cleaning businesses that were making good money. Only problem was keeping decent staff for a tuppence. I had to go 'round checkin' on 'em all the time. This big service company showed up; offered me a good price for 'em, and I sold. Never looked back. Invested the money in rental properties. I didn't make a big splash on the high street or buy a football club or write a book. I should have done.'

I said, 'You can still write a book, Raymond—maybe with a ghost writer— with a flash title like *How I Took People to the Cleaners*. Or maybe you could start one of those business guru columns in the newspaper, you know, like the guy who owns all the corner shoemakers writes.'

'Nah. I used to read his column. It's all love-your-employees-and-your-customers and do it like the Harvard Business Review says. You can't make real money doin' that shit!'

Raymond's cancer was a great, dark pall resting on top of this tragedy, and tightening its insidious grip on him. He no longer had the essential emotional strength, let alone the physical or intellectual fortitude. No longer was the vital question, 'Why me?'. There was now no question worthy of consideration. Two days later, he was dead."

"I remember his death, Uncle Bertie; it was awful. Why did he have to die like that?"

He ponders, tilting his head from side to side. "It seems to me, Sarah, that his situation was similar to mine. He had no vocation, other than as a Fulham football fan; as far as I know, he never went to church; and he didn't have a real family connection."

"He was always present on Sundays and at Seaford."

"Yes, I know," he responds, "but what did he get out of it? As far as I could tell, it was just another time-filler for an otherwise vacant man."

A vacant man. I had never thought of my step-grandfather as a 'vacant man'. "I think I see what you mean," I say. "He seemed to care about Brucie and Margaret and Nelson, but he just wanted them to shine in his image, rather than to create special identities of their own."

"How was his relationship with you?"

"There never was one. In fact, I think he disapproved of me."

"That doesn't surprise me," Uncle Bertie says.

I suddenly have a heavy weight on my shoulders and no strength or energy. "It must be terrible," I hear myself saying, "to feel that one's life has been wasted."

"It was two years later that Margaret and Nelson were released from prison," he continues. "I understand that they had a hard time getting their feet on the ground. They were both able to get jobs in Sainsbury's, she as a baker and he as a shelf-filler, both with some overtime opportunities. There was no local council accommodation available. They were put on a waiting list for a one-bedroom flat in Birmingham, but when they both had jobs, they were eligible for income support and housing allowance. They were able to find a two-bedroom flat above a busy off-license on the high street in Tooting, a ten-minute bus ride south of Wandsworth.

Margaret approached Carol-Ann to find out whether the Sunday lunches were still held at my place. Carol-Ann told her, 'You'll have to check with Bertie.'

I found it interesting that Margaret took a tangential approach, suggesting that she was unsure whether they would be welcome to re-join the family. Carol-Ann passed the buck to me, which lead me to conclude that she was opposed to a permanent reunion. When I asked her, she was evasive: 'I don't know, Bertie; on the one hand, I don't like the idea of the grandchildren, in particular, consorting with convicted criminals; on the other hand, they have been punished and are no longer outlaws. You decide.'

I decided to take a poll, and interestingly, the grandchildren were largely in favour of 'forgive and forget', while their parents were more risk averse, and took the view: 'We're not going to benefit from their attendance, so why invite them back?'

When Margaret came to see me, I gave her the parents' view, and I said, 'Margaret, my first concern is financial, and I want you to be totally honest with me, with the understanding that whatever you say will be between us alone.'

'OK.'

'Do you or Nelson have any money left over from the embezzlement?'

'My solicitor told the council there was nothing left.'

'But I'm asking <u>you</u> to tell <u>me</u> how much is left. Please bear two things in mind. First, several of us went through your flat when you were convicted; we found a diamond bracelet. Second, hell hath no fury like an Uncle Bertie lied to.'

We stared fixedly at each other for perhaps twenty seconds. She looked away, biting her lip. Was she going to cry? 'I can give you an exact figure tomorrow.'

'Good. You can also tell me how much of it will be given to which charities?'

'You…you said your first concern is financial.'

'Yes, my second concern is what benefits—obviously not financial—you can bring to the family on your return. Why should we have you back? Figure it out, then call me.'

She obviously hadn't expected such a narrow pathway back to the family, and she started to cry. 'Oh, Bertie, that seems so unfair! Nelson and I have been punished; we are sorry for what we did; we'll have no money and no real jobs. We desperately need the emotional support of our family.'

'I understand that, Margaret, but why should it be a one-way street? You must know that you have soiled the reputation of the family, and now you want us to provide you with emotional support?'

There was a gust of honest, distraught weeping. 'It doesn't sound very Christian, Bertie.'

'I'm sure you've heard of tough-love, Margaret. That's where we are. You've doubtless done a lot of thinking in prison: now, you should do some imaginative thinking.'

I received a letter marked 'personal' the following day. It was signed by Margaret and Nelson. It contained the final settlement with the council in which Margaret's equity in her flat, and cash from Margaret's bank account were used to offset the value of the fraud plus interest. Also attached were Margaret's and Nelson's bank statements, which together show a residual value of one thousand six hundred and thirty-one pounds after paying two months deposit on the Tooting flat and living expenses since their release. Finally, there is a jeweller's valuation of the bracelet at three thousand six hundred pounds. The cover letter said that they have about one thousand pounds worth of clothing, the bracelet and one thousand pounds in cash which they proposed to give to shelter and two local charities.

It suddenly occurred to me that the tangible value which Margaret and Nelson placed on being members of the Smithson family was over five thousand pounds. Moreover, their proposed re-entry fee to the family would leave them with just six hundred pounds. We were indeed a valuable group of people, but not so valuable that we reduced our members to penury. I told Margaret that it would be sufficient to give the bracelet and the clothing to charity, and that we looked forward to hearing her proposal about what they could do with or for the family.

On a Friday evening, two weeks later, Margaret asked to see me, and Jo left us alone in the living room. Margaret seemed spent, but anxious. There was no colour in her face. She was thin, and at sixty-one, she looked seventy. We drank tea and chatted politely about her work as a baker.

'Bertie, I have an idea for the way Nelson and I can work on a project with the family to our mutual advantage.' I inclined my head. 'You know,' she continued, more vigorously, 'that there is a great deal of interest in this country about reducing recidivism and re-integrating prisoners into productive society, and...' she hurried on, 'I am thinking of publicising the work that Nelson and I do together with the family—work which will benefit the family as well as us. For example, we might stage a community art project in memory of Jason, or we could join a clean-up project for the River Wandle. I've talked to the editor of the Wandsworth monthly magazine, and he has agreed to run at least three examples. It would be favourable publicity for charity work that the family believes in. Naturally, you would have final say-so on the copy I submit to the editor. It will also help the two of us to regain acceptance in the community.' She leant forward, her lips tightly compressed, and her hands clasped at her waist.

I liked Margaret's proposal not just for the reasons she suggested, but also because it would enhance values of reconciliation and teamwork which I think are important in a family. 'I think you've got a good idea, Margaret. May I suggest that next Sunday, you and Nelson come along, apologise for the hurt you have done to the family, and outline your overall amity plan? Then, you can describe several specific projects which you'd like to work on with family members. May I suggest that you're more likely to have an enthusiastic response from the grandchildren? The parents may sign on later.'

'Thank you so much, Bertie!' She seized my hand to shake it, and for a split second, I was afraid she was going to kiss it.

'I'm sure you understand, Margaret,' I added, 'that all this depends on your honesty and good will.'

'Yes, of course, Bertie.' She gave me a farewell hug before departing."

"I remember the Sunday they came to present their proposal," I say. "It started with a very nervous Margaret apologising over and over. She said they made a stupid mistake in taking the money. She said they were both feeling down, and they decided that they ought to take a nice holiday. But they ended up only taking the one holiday, buying clothes, a bracelet and putting the money in the bank. She explained about the reimbursement of the council, and that they were giving the clothing, and the bracelet that Nelson had bought her to charity. They will have only sixteen hundred pounds and no significant assets. Then Nelson got up and said they were looking for volunteers to help them clean up the Wandle. When a couple of us raised our hands, he stared to cry. Then both of them – and even some of us – were crying. At the end he said, 'Thank you so much for taking us back!' Uncle Bertie, they'll remember that for the rest of their lives."

Chapter 22
The Alpha Course

"Sarah, I've got to take Leo to the vet this morning. He's been very slow lately, and this morning he had an accident, which is very unusual. I should be back in about an hour, and we can carry on then."

I give him a smile and a nod. Leo hasn't followed us up to the second floor for several months now. I suspect he may have arthritis. After all, he is in his mid-teens. When I see him occasionally on my way out of the house, he looks at me mournfully from his bed in the kitchen as if to say, Sorry, Sarah, I can't make it up the stairs anymore. You take good care of him, will you? Leo is such a good natured, sociable dog, and he thinks his master hung the moon.

Our subject today, is going to be the Alpha Course at St Christopher's, which I'm surprised he agreed to, given his somewhat distant relationship with the church. It's been on at St Barts, but Jenny and I haven't signed up for it yet.

He flops down into his chair, looking the other way and hiding his face. His posture suggests exhaustion. "Uncle Bertie, are you all right?"

Gradually, he turns to face me, red-eyed, his hair all askew, his lips compressed and lifeless. "I had to put Leo down."

"Oh, Uncle Bertie, I'm so sorry!" Suddenly, a knot bursts inside me and I am on the edge of tears. *He loved that dog so much and they were real friends.*

"I had to carry him to the car. He didn't want to walk. In the vet's office, he just wanted to lie down. Usually, he sits watching the vet in case there's a treat coming. She tried getting him to stand, but his back legs didn't seem to be working. 'Arthritis in the back legs is very common in retrievers,' she said. When I told her about his accident this morning, she said that dogs feel a kind of shame when they can't control themselves and make a mess. She examined him carefully, and said, "I think he is ready to go, Mr Smithson.' I started to cry. I didn't know what to do or say. 'I'm sorry, Mr Smithson; he'll be in a better place.'

'OK,' I said.

'Perhaps you'd like to say goodbye,' she said.

I sat on the floor with his head in my lap, stroking him. His eyes were closed. The vet gave him a shot. He trembled and then relaxed. His bladder emptied…I just started to cry, and I couldn't stop. They let me out the back way. When I got home, Jo and I had a cry together."

I get up, kneel beside him and put my arm around his shoulders. We hug each other for a while, each of us sobbing gently.

He pulls a handkerchief from his pocket and offers it to me. I return it. He wipes his face, blows his nose. He sits, breathing deeply for a minute. He stands up, looks down at his pant leg with a wry face. "I've got to change my trousers."

When he returns, he sits looking at the spot on the floor next to him where Leo used to lie. "Funny," he says. "It feels like he's still there."

"Maybe he is," I say.

"Do you think so?"

"Why not?"

We have a cup of tea. "We were going to talk about the Alpha Course," he says. I nod. "Well, I usually glance through the weekly church bulletin to see if there's anything interesting. This week I see an announcement of the Alpha Course which will start next month and run for twelve weeks. I have a strange feeling of unfinished business about the announcement – as if I have an unfulfilled obligation and must take some action. I try to dismiss the thought, but the feeling persists like a good wine. I have seen announcements before of Alpha Courses, and I'm aware that the course is about life, faith, and purpose, but I've side-stepped the opportunities, thinking that twelve weeks is too long. Now the words; Life, Faith and Purpose resonate unexpectedly with me. The announcement says, 'Alpha is a series of sessions exploring the Christian faith. Each talk looks at a different question around faith and is designed to create conversation. Alpha is run all around the globe, and everyone's welcome. It runs in cafés, churches, universities, homes – you name it. No two Alphas look the same, but generally they have three key things in common: food, a talk and good conversation.'

On the way home, I said to Jo, 'I think I might sign up for that Alpha Course.' Jo turned to look at me. 'Really?'

'It is interesting, and I think you'll enjoy it.'

'You've been, haven't you, Jo?'

'Yes, and I'm going to be running this one.'

Oh, my God! How was this going to work: being on the same course with my wife who's always refused to discuss her faith with me? I could feel her eyes probing me. 'What is it, Bertie?'

'If you're going to be the leader, maybe I ought to drop out.'

'Nonsense! We'll be in different discussion groups.'

The grandmotherly greeter at the door of the vaulted church hall was a familiar face, but there is no name to go with it until is see 'Dorothy' on her name tag. She equipped me with a marking pen, and I became 'Bertie' to the 'Harry' who patted his tag into place. 'This is my first Alpha course,' I confessed.

'Mine as well,' Harry, who is in his mid-thirties and still wearing a grey suit from work, told me with a smile. 'My self-improvement assignment—from my wife.'

'So, can I assume that your wife has attended previously?'

'Oh, yes, she wouldn't miss a course.' He turned toward a small group. 'That's my wife Cindy, in the green jumper, over there.' The lady indicated was a youngish redhead, who was gesturing volubly to her colleagues. 'She is a discussion group leader, and she's persuaded me that I've been missing out on what can be an extraordinary event.'

The conversation drifted into family and work as others introduced themselves and we form a small klatch.

Jo described the routines we would be following, and said, 'Please remember that there are no right or wrong opinions about faith. If you have doubts, feel free to express them in your small groups. We want everybody to feel that they are being heard and understood, and that no one feels marginalised for having a different view.'

She then introduced Father Anthony, who spoke briefly about the many forms of faith, mentioning King David, the worshipful sinner, Saul/Paul, the persecutor – evangelist, and Zacchaeus, the tax collector who climbed the tree. He then offered a prayer that we all would reach a new level of spiritual awareness of ourselves through patience, thoughtful listening and empathetic exchange of ideas.

As I was standing in the queue for dinner, Father Anthony came over. 'Bertie, I'm glad to see you here.'

'I thought it was about time, Father.'

'Well, I hope you'll speak up in your small group, Bertie. Many of the attendees could benefit from hearing your doubts.'

'In what way, Father?'

'In my experience, unexamined faith tends to be fragile. Enjoy your dinner, Bertie.' I suppose he meant that some of the congregation were committed, unseeing, to their faith.

We were each asked to put five pounds (or whatever you wish to contribute) into a collection basket for the dinner, so I was not expecting much beyond a cheese sandwich and coffee, but to my happy surprise, I found that we were being served spaghetti Bolognese, salad, rolls, brownies and fresh fruit. But it was not the spag-bol that one has come to expect: overcooked cheap spaghetti with beef-flavoured tomato sauce; it was al dente, durum wheat pasta, with fresh-cooked tomatoes, lots of ground beef and plenty of Parmesan cheese.

A round of applause was given to the two ladies who prepared this dinner for thirty-one of us seated at five round tables clustered together.

'Those of you who would like coffee or tea should get it now and return to your seats,' Jo announced. 'We're going to watch the video of a talk by Nicky Gumbel: the vicar of Holy Trinity Brompton church.'

I was sceptical. The title Is there more to life than this? flashed on the screen. More than what? As random young people were interviewed, it became clear that the 'this' is seeing friends, going out, having a lie-in, working: living an ordinary life. Then Nicky Gumbel appeared on screen. He was an attractive but otherwise ordinary man dressed in a navy-blue sweater and jeans, who said that he came from a non-believing family and that he himself hated going to church. He remembered feeling that something was missing and always looking forward to a future happening. There were questions he was asking himself: why am I here on earth? What is the point of my life? What is the meaning of my life that death cannot destroy?

Gumbel said that we all seek an infinitely loving, unending relationship with God. That statement startled me like the sudden appearance of a robin on my windowsill. Is that what I'm seeking? Infinitely loving sounds good, if I could ever find it. And un-ending sounds perfect. Gumbel made the point that Jesus was the lens through which we can see God, the world and ourselves. I get that. God can seem distant and obscure; Jesus was flesh and blood. Gumbel acknowledged that many very bright people considered themselves to be atheists, but they were far outnumbered by the believers who had examined the evidence for Jesus, his teaching and his resurrection. In my experience, that seems to be true. The vicar quoted Jesus: "I am the way (to God); I am the truth (existential truth); and I am the life (the eternal life you seek)."

He concluded by saying, 'This is true and it's absolutely relevant…the most important point to take away from this course is that God loves you enormously.' There was something thrilling in that assertion. It was a warm, and lasting electric charge that lifted me, body and mind.

Well, I had to admit that Nicky Gumbel was a very credible and persuasive speaker; he had certainly got me thinking.

Jo suggested that we move our tables apart, so as not to disturb each other and convene our small group discussions.

The moderator of my small group was the animated, red-head Cindy, whose husband was not among the other five of us. I was feeling anxious about being called upon to account for myself in this environment, which seemed devout in its acceptance of the message we had heard. There were two older – probably widowed – women, Rosemarie and Winifred, whom I had seen in church many times, but with whom I had not spoken a word. There was Gustav, overweight, middle-aged, and eastern European by his accent. He was still dressed in clean work coveralls; and a pretty young woman, Judy, with no left-hand rings who may be a university student.

Cindy began with a prayer asking God to be with us, then she asked: 'How do you feel about the question: is there more to life than this?'

Rosemarie and Winifred looked benevolently at the other three of us but said nothing.

'I think it's a good question for the politicians," Gustav volunteered, "they not doin' much to help other than the rich folks.'

'Some people my age probably wonder about it,' Judy said in an uncertain tone. 'I mean some people are experimenting with drugs and alcohol.' Her voice trailed off.

'How about you, Bertie, what are your thoughts?' Cindy asked.

'Oh, my,' I paused to consider. 'I never asked myself the question that way.' I looked around. 'It's more a gnawing feeling I get now and then—maybe it's age-related. You wonder if there's a God and how you should approach Him.'

'Yes, in my case it was age-related,' Rosemarie said. 'You begin to think: have I lived the best life I could, and that's where the church comes in, giving you a chance to think and pray.'

Cindy asked, 'What do you think Jesus meant when he said, I am the way, the truth and the life?'

'I figure he was saying he was the son of God,' Gustav volunteered.

'Well, when he speaks about the way,' Winifred suggested, 'I believe he is talking about a path to follow, a direction to take, following him, and it's also about a way to behave: loving God and your neighbour.'

'Truth is an interesting one,' Rosemarie said, 'particularly in this age where there is a lot of fake news.'

Judy added, 'But weren't there a lot of false prophets in Jesus' time?'

'Yes, there were, Judy,' Cindy said. 'So, how do we understand what He means by truth?'

I found myself saying, 'He must mean the important, permanent truth, not just the current facts. I think we have to understand it in the context of an eternal universe.'

Rosemarie said, 'I agree, Bertie.'

The conversation continued, fluidly, with only the occasional nudge from Cindy, for what seemed like twenty minutes, but what was actually an hour. On reflection, I found that the lubricant of the session was more the willingness of the participants to express very personal doubts, beliefs and feelings than it was the expert facilitation by Cindy.

Jo told me that she had a difficult group to manage. 'They were, by turns, either reticent to talk or eager to disagree with each other. I think there may be some personal history between some of the participants.'

I mentioned my group to Jo. 'Well, Winifred and Rosemarie are always in church together,' she said, 'and I think they know as much about the bible as Father Anthony.'

"If that's the case, why do they come to the course?'

'I don't know. Maybe it's partly to show off, to socialise, to find out what's going on, and something to do.'

I said, 'That fellow, Gustav, didn't seem very bright.'

'I think he works at the self-storage warehouse, so maybe you're right, but you might have noticed: he's always in church, second pew, at the end.'

'But if he's so committed, why does he need the course?'

'Bertie, there are some people who take to religion with great ease at an emotional and spiritual level, but they haven't a clue at an intellectual level about facts or doctrine. He probably just wants to learn.'

'And then there was Judy, who seems like a shy college student.'

'I don't know Judy. She may be away from home, new to the area, and looking for a church home.' She considered me for a moment. 'What did you think, Bertie?'

'I was surprised at how good it was. The dinner was very good. The speaker was articulate and credible—a rare combination. And the whole atmosphere was open and relaxed: I didn't feel under any pressure at all, and I found myself wanting to open my mind and participate.'

In a session called *How can I have faith?*, Nicky Gumbel showed a beautiful, old painting by William Holman Hunt in which Jesus was seen carrying a light and knocking on a door with no external handle and which was covered in vines.

Cindy asked our small group, 'What does that painting say to you about faith?'

Gustav said, 'It means you have to take the initiative. You have to open the door which hasn't been opened before.'

'Yes!' Cindy gestured affirmation with her fist. 'And why would you want to open the door?'

'Because you know and trust Jesus,' Judy responded.

'OK, but how does one get to know and trust Jesus?'

'You just have to read the Bible.'

'Well, it's a little more complicated than that,' Rosemarie suggested, 'In my experience, one has to read beyond the words and really feel the meaning and intention behind them.'

'Can I say,' Winifred added, 'that when I opened the door to Jesus thirty-two years ago, I stopped drinking, and my life changed completely. I became a different person; none of you would like the person I used to be.'

Several of the later sessions were about the Holy Spirit. And I must say that I was uncertain about exactly who he (or she) is. I was pretty happy with the definition I'd heard from time to time: 'Holy Spirit, the Lord, the Giver of Life'. I was comfortable with this because I felt sure that only God could create life.

In the final session, we journeyed out to an ancient abbey in Surrey for a one-day retreat during which we practised what we'd learnt, and to pray for another person in the name of the Holy Spirit.

'If you ask for the Holy Spirit to come to you while you're praying,' Father Anthony said, 'He will come, and eventually, you will be able to feel His presence.'

We were instructed to form pairs to pray. I looked around and there was Gustav. He said, 'Shall we pray together?' I nodded, and he said, 'What shall I pray about for you, Bertie?'

I thought for a moment. 'I suppose that what I would like most of all is a more enlightened faith. What would you like, Gustav?'

'I have prostate cancer and I'm scared. I've just started treatment. Could you pray that the treatment is successful?'

The abbey hall was lit only through the high windows. One could make out the forms of other pairs in the late afternoon dusk. There was only the sound of whispering and the remaining scent of incense.

I was facing Gustav, hands on his shoulders. His head was bowed, my eyes were closed. 'Come, Holy Spirit, come!' I whispered intensely several times. 'Come and be with me while I pray.' While I paused to consider what I should say next, there was an unfamiliar sense of authority and fluency.

I don't remember how long I prayed, but it was at least five minutes.

'Thank you, Bertie. Thank you very much.' He asked what I mean by 'enlightened faith'.

'What I think I mean is believing _and_ understanding.'

He placed both his palms on my head, and began what sounded like a long, soft chant in a foreign language. My eyes were closed, I was in limbo, there was the distant whiff of incense, and only the soothing sound of his prayer, but I began to have a sense of awareness, of asylum, and of completeness that had not left me since.

After the Alpha Course, I went to mass with Jo every Sunday. On the face of it, there was nothing different about this, but now, the experience was different. Previously, my mind would wander to issues about work or the children, and I would sit, respectfully, in the pew trying to develop a practical solution to a problem that was on my mind. Now, I find I don't have time for that when I'm identifying the message from the reading, really listening to what Father Anthony has to say, and following the service word-for-word in the missal.

Could Father Anthony have noticed? I doubt it. But during the coffee service after mass, he asked me, 'Bertie, how would you like to teach fourth year Sunday school? With you being an Alpha graduate and a writer of children's books, you seem like a good fit.'

'But Father, I know almost nothing of scripture, and I've never done any teaching.'

Father Anthony gave me his patient, understanding smile. 'The curriculum is pretty well defined, and I think you'll find that teaching is also learning.'

'Let me think about it.'

I asked Jo whether she thought I could do it. I expected her to say yes, with a caveat or two. She got up, came over and put her arms around me, saying nothing. Then she said, 'Can I teach with you, Bertie?'

It turned out that we would be taking over from a couple who wanted to retire from teaching but had agreed to stay on until a new teacher could be recruited.

There were several of hiccoughs in our first class. I studied the lesson plan carefully, planned out all the activities, and read the background material in the teacher's guide. Having reviewed it all with Jo, I made copies of the materials that the children would be using.

The first problem was that I had forgotten how spontaneous and unruly a group of sixteen ten-year-olds could be. Yes, I've had children and grandchildren that age, but never a such a large collection of friends, whom I was expected to supervise. When you and I do our school readings, Sarah, there was always a teacher there to keep order. Fortunately, Jo, who had taught Sunday school before, acted reflexively to keep order. The second issue was that some of the children were expecting that I would read from a Robbie book. I had to disappoint. Instead, I read the first paragraph of chapter three in the year four book *Who Was Jesus?* We then turned the reading over to the students.

'What did you learn about Jesus?' I asked.

'That he was a carpenter.'

'What did carpenters do in those days?' I asked.

'They didn't just saw wood, they made houses.'

'That's good. Now on these sheets see if you can identify all the skills that house builders have today that Jesus must have had to build houses then.'

There were some errors of inclusion like 'electrician' and errors of exclusion like 'roofing thatcher'.

Jo asked them to fit 'carpenter' onto a Roman hierarchy chart from slave to emperor, and it took a while for the children to see that this was a skilled job, but quite lowly in status. 'And why,' Jo asked, 'do you think God would have wanted

His Son to be a carpenter, rather than an emperor or a slave?' Again, there was considerable debate, but a consensus emerges: God wanted His Son to be a respected, ordinary man.

'And why?' I asked, 'was it good for Jesus to start his mission as a carpenter?' This was more difficult, and we talked through the wide social interaction that house builders like Jesus had. Finally, one quiet, but attentive boy raised his hand. 'Yes, Joey.'

'Because Jesus learnt a lot about people. What they needed and what their problems were.'"

"Uncle Bertie, when I heard that you were teaching year four Sunday school, I couldn't believe it, and I had to see for myself. I went to St Christopher's, and asked where the year four class was. I peeked in, then I went in and closed the door behind me. I held my index finger up to my lips, so you would know not to introduce me, went to the back of the room and sat down."

"Yes, Jo and I knew what you were up to, so, we just carried on with the class."

"I sat there and watched until the class was over, reflecting on what I was seeing versus what I had experienced at the age of your kids. I mean, I enjoyed Sunday school, and I learnt quite a lot in spite of all the random misbehaviour. But this was something else. These kids were engaged, and they were really soaking it up. There was whispering, but it was helpful whispering. There was fidgeting, but it was seeking-the-answer fidgeting. They enjoyed the class and they'll remember it."

"Thanks, Sarah, Jo and I are enjoying it, too, and Father Anthony was right: I'm learning some good stuff…Can we call it quits for today? I'm a little tired."

There is no colour in his cheeks and there are dark circles under his eyes. "Are you all right, Uncle Bertie?"

"Yeah, I'm OK. Just a little tired."

Chapter 23
Cancer

We take a few days off from the memoir sessions. When we return to his second-floor office, he sits in his chair and for some moments, gazes at Leo's spot on the floor next to him. "Strange, you know, how the mind can play tricks on you."

"What tricks?" I ask.

"Well, since the Alpha Course and the prayers with the Holy Spirit and Leo's passing, I seem to be drifting a bit into what the Professor called the Fourth Dimension."

"That was the spiritual dimension wasn't it?" He nods. "What have you experienced?"

"It's odd. Sometimes at night I have the feeling that Leo is lying on the foot of our bed. Odd, because he was never allowed to do that. He always slept in the kitchen. When I reach down to check, of course he's not there. I go back to sleep, and I wake up thinking there's something against my leg, but there isn't. And then, a couple of times I was going down to the ground floor past the first-floor landing, where Leo often slept so he could have bird's eye view of the front door. I was about to go right across the landing when something made me stop. For a second, I thought I was going to trip over Leo, but he wasn't there."

"So, what do you think it was?" I ask.

"I don't know, but that wasn't all. I find myself thinking about my mother lately, but I hardly ever think about her as it's been thirty-three years since she died. Recently, she seems to want to have a conversation with me, and it started out with questions about Jason. Why didn't I try to find him a job? I explained that I suggested lots of options to him, but that he seemed to have given up. The discussion would continue. She wasn't being critical. It was as if she was trying to understand how I felt at the time. There were issues about Carol-Ann and Michael that she wanted to pursue. It was really weird, Sarah."

"Sounds like dreams," I say.

"But I was wide awake at the time, and sometimes it felt like she was in the same room with me. It wasn't a remote discussion…What do you think, Sarah?"

"Could it be a more interactive version of Father Anthony's email?" I suggest.

"That's what it seemed like, but I've never had that experience before."

"Neither have I."

When, mindful that he's been ill, I ask Uncle Bertie how he's feeling, he admits to having lingering headaches behind his right eye, and while two large ibuprofens relieve the pain, more recently, it is only moderated. He confesses to having peculiar sensations of impending imbalance, as if he had too much to drink and is uncertain of where the horizon might be.

Yesterday after breakfast, he apparently was suddenly seized with nausea and barely was able to reach the downstairs loo. Jo insisted that he see Dr Rumford, the GP.

He tells me, "Unlike Raymond, who was convinced that doctors are bad for your health, I have no objection to seeing a doctor as long as I can't be accused of hypochondria. But one of the problems I have with Doctor Mort is that he makes me into a ninny by fussing about my health. Perhaps it's my fault for having told him about my nightmares of the doctor with the grey crew cut.

I mentioned my symptoms, which by now include several bouts of nausea, to Dr Mort. He scrutinised my eyes, took my blood pressure, and required me to walk along a line in the flooring, placing each foot exactly in the centre of the line. I found this quite difficult.

Jo said, 'Doctor, I've noticed that lately he is a little forgetful.'

I objected to this, but Jo mentioned three pieces of evidence, and I admitted that I was not aware of this. 'But I don't think I'm sliding into dementia,' I said.

Dr Mort ignored my diagnosis and contemplated the framed medical certificate hanging above his computer screen.

'Bertie, I'm going to refer you to the neurology department at St Georges. They will call you to make an appointment.'

'What do you think it could be, Mort?'

'Well, it could be nothing much, but they will probably want to do a brain scan.'

I was not going to let him off that easily. 'So, you think there might be something wrong in my brain?'

He frowned in irritation. 'Well, you might have had what we call a TIA—a trans ischemic attack—a mini stroke, which is quite common, and the symptoms of which disappear.'

My symptoms were gathering strength, rather than dissipating. 'And, what could it be at the other end of the spectrum?'

'I would really need to see an MRI to comment further, Bertie.'

Could this be it, approaching? The day when I <u>know</u> that my life will end. Strangely, I was not worried about an end. For me, there was only a transition, not really an end. What made me apprehensive was the means of that transition. Would it be lengthy? Would it be painful? (I've never been very good at pain.) Would I be a burden on others?

Jo appeared unconcerned. She was cheerful, and sympathetic. 'It'll probably turn out to be some minor thing, Bertie. You've always been healthy.'

Outpatients' appointments at St George's called me the following Tuesday. I could see Dr Grankovski in three weeks' time. Disappointed with the long wait, I told the secretary that I would be happy with an earlier appointment if there was a cancellation.

During the three-week wait, I was out in front of the house replacing long-deceased geraniums in the ground floor window boxes with some blue, yellow and white winter pansies. I was dressed in a heavy wool sweater, paint-stained denim jacket, old jeans, rubber boots, my favourite, brown-tweed flat cap and rough gloves. I probably looked like an old, down-on-his-luck burglar. My work bench, a broom, dustbin, trays of pansies and assorted garden tools surrounded me, as I busily extracted the geranium skeletons.

'I am asking all the neighbours…' a voice said from the sidewalk behind me. I turned and found an attractive black woman, perhaps in her mid-thirties, well-dressed, with a plump-face and a patient smile. 'I have been asking them if they think that the Bible is relevant today.' She paused.

I noticed that there are two little girls with her. The older girl, about eight, was standing a few feet away from her mother and was staring at me with large dark eyes.

The woman had her head cocked to one side and her hands clasped in front of her as if my response was a matter of importance. *She must be doing the Lord's work.* 'Yes, I think it's relevant,' I said.

The girl glanced anxiously at her mother now and then, but her inquisitive focus was on me as the woman read from a Bible. As it became clear that I was listening to her mother and interested in what she was reading, the child's hands fell to her sides and she smiled at me. Probably, this was what mother and daughters do on a sunny Thursday afternoon in Wandsworth: preach the Gospel, and I suspect that in many cases, the woman was rudely rebuffed by her would-be convert. These insulting rejections must be painful for the child, to see her mother apparently dismissed as a nuisance, and I dare say that the child had trouble understanding her mother's stubbornness in persisting in this lost cause.

I was sincerely enjoying my role in this small drama, removing my hat and gloves, facing the woman with rapt attention, and answering her questions with enthusiasm. Now and then I gave an extra little nod to the child, who, by now, sensed that something good was happening. Most of all, I wanted this little girl to know that her mother was not a crazy, wilful eccentric, and that sometimes in doing a good thing, you were rejected.

It turned out that Dr Grankowski was actually Professor Doctor Ivan Grankowski, a senior instructor in medicine at King's College London, and after my consultation, I asked him whether he preferred to be called 'Doctor' or 'Professor'. He said, 'By all means, call me *Professor*. It distinguishes me from the run-of-the-mill doctor.'

I said, 'I should have guessed. Admiral Lord Horatio Nelson preferred to be called *Admiral* rather than *Lord*.'

The professor was a small energetic man with a neatly trimmed grey moustache and goatee. Frequently, there was a sparkle in his eyes when he engaged in humour or irony. He was dressed in a three-piece, blue-striped suit, off-white shirt and narrow black tie. The suit jacket was over the back of his chair and his sleeves were rolled up to his biceps.

Having taken a lengthy oral history of my health, he examined me with needles and tuning forks, looked in my eyes, had me catch a ball, and assessed my balance.

'All right, we'll send you for an MRI now, and I'll see you at…' he consulted his computer screen '…two-thirty on Friday with a full report.'

There was something about this little Napoleon of a man that gave me confidence. I sensed his skills, intelligence and trustworthiness, and I believed in his care.

'I'm afraid it's not good news, Mr Smithson,' the professor told me on Friday. 'You have a tumour about the size of a tennis ball at the front of your left brain. Unfortunately, it is almost certainly malignant.' He went on to point out the tumour in various MRI sections, explaining its structure. When I asked him how long I've had it, he told me, 'You've probably had it for less than a year. This is a glioblastoma which can grow very rapidly in the white matter of the brain and can reach a large size before showing any symptoms.'

'What is the treatment?' I asked.

'Surgical removal is essential. Without it, your life expectancy would be about three months. But it is impossible to remove more than about 98% of the malignant matter surgically, even using a dye marker. The reason for this is that malignant cells are imbedded in the brain outside the main tumour, and new tumours are generated, but the regeneration process can be slowed with radiotherapy.' I sat thinking and looking at the image of my newly discovered adversary, a white blob. Somehow, it didn't seem so sinister. *It doesn't seem like the devil's creation. It's just something that went wrong in the enormous complexity inside my brain.*

I took a deep breath and released it, hands folded in my lap. 'What about chemotherapy?'

'The problem for chemotherapy with tumours that start in the brain is the blood-brain barrier makes it difficult for the treatment to reach the tumour. These tumours also have a unique cellular structure which makes them relatively resistant to chemotherapy.'

I looked at him for some moments. 'What is my prognosis, Professor?'

'I would say you have a year, at best, but we can make you quite comfortable after your surgery; the pressure on your brain from the tumour will have gone and won't return until quite late.'

'So, the pain I have will be quite manageable?"

'Yes, that shouldn't be a cause for concern.'

Leaning forward and biting my lower lip, I asked, 'Will I need nursing care at some point, and will I be able to stay at home?'

Professor Granlowski, perhaps sensing my anxiety, said, 'I think you'll be able to stay at home, though you'll probably be in bed for the last couple of weeks. Nursing care may or may not be needed.'

'I will…' Jo began. Her hands were clenched white and her eyes brimming. 'I'll be taking good care of Bertie, Professor.'

In eight days' time, I was to see Mr David Collingwood, the neurosurgeon who would remove the tumour.

On the way home, Jo said, 'I want to make love with you, Bertie. I want to get as close to you as I can for as long as I can.'

'Yes. I agree.' I took her hand and smiled at her. 'Wasn't it St Paul who said that we no longer have use of our bodies in heaven—assuming that one gets to heaven—so we might as well make good use of them here.'

Jo couldn't supress a chuckle. 'He did say that, but I don't remember him suggesting that we make use of them here.'

I gave a shrug. 'So, that's my prescription.'

As I parked the car, I said, 'I'm not shocked by the diagnosis. It feels ordained in accordance with some universal formula. There is no point in protestation, anger or lamentation. What is needed from me is using my time lovingly and productively.'

'I'm not shocked,' she said, 'but I feel hurt. How can I not feel hurt? But I'm not angry at God. I just wish He had given you to me for ten more years, so that I could have gone first.'

We sat in the car for a time, shoulder-to-shoulder, holding hands.

Mr David Collingwood must be six feet five, and he seemed spindly and all long bones, including his hands, which he used to gesticulate while he talked. He was blonde, mid-forties, with a square jaw, but I wondered about his hands. Are they delicate enough for the intricacy of brain surgery?

He was explaining the surgical procedure. When he paused, I asked, 'Do you play the piano, David?'

Perhaps he had noticed that my eyes had been following his gestures. 'No, but I used to make ship models until I became a surgeon. Nothing packaged, mind you. Some years ago, I made a model of HMS Victory, Nelson's flagship. I used to stock quite a variety of fine, soft woods in various colours, and, of course, I used to buy the miniature cannons. I'm rather proud of her.' On the rear wall, he pointed to a framed photo of the 104-gun, three-decker, with all her canvas set.

'Well,' I said, 'you certainly have me outclassed. I just made packaged balsa wood military aircraft.'

He laughed. 'Actually, Bertie, many surgeons nowadays use microscopes and robotics in their work. Robotics deleverage the movement of the surgeon's hand to make the positioning of the instrument more precise, and microscopes permit us to see in more detail. But having said that, I've always liked to work with my hands, except, of course, boxing.'

I gave a chuckle. He turned to a computer graphic of a human head, and with his mouse, he cut and removed a piece of the skull. 'You'll notice that I've avoided cutting the forehead, so that there is no visible scar.'

'For me, a scar on my forehead is not a concern.'

'I understand, but, post operatively, it's good to feel pretty much intact.'

'How long does the procedure take?'

'About six hours, and we'll keep you here in the hospital for a couple of days for observation.'

I met the anaesthetist after I reported to St George's and was assigned a bed. Dr Krishnamurthy was a small, business-like man who assured me, with a sideways nod of his head, that Mr Collingwood was a very good surgeon and that, 'we will take good care of you'. He collected my legal release form, scanned my medical history, and told me he would see me shortly.

Having a general anaesthetic would be a new experience for me. Jo said, 'You'll be talking to the anaesthetist while he's fooling around with the cannula in your arm,' and he'll say, 'I'm going to put you to sleep now', and then, bang, you're out. There's nothing gradual about it. Then you kind of slide into consciousness, and you realise that you're still you, and the world is still there, except that you're in a hospital recovery room.'

I can't help but wonder whether my transition to an afterlife – assuming that there is such a thing – will be similar.

'How are you feeling Mr Smithson?' There was a white space with corners, some murmured conversation, a sharp, medicinal smell and a pale female face – probably a nurse. I could hear people moving about. I was lying in a bed. Nothing bad, just floating with a slight headache.

'Yes. I'm OK.'

'That's good. We'll take you back to the ward soon. Your wife has been asking about you.'

Josephine! I had an image of her waiting by the bedside as the hours passed, looking at her watch, asking the nurses, disquiet unresolved, moving to the waiting area outside recovery, until a recovery room nurse promised to come out with periodic updates. My Josephine!

There she was now, in person, beside the bed with the porters moving it. She was triumphant on the brink of tears, looking at me, searching for my hand under the bed linen. My Josephine!

'Bertie, you look like you've been wounded in battle.'

I reached up and patted the thick layer of gauze on my head. 'Is there any blood?'

'No. Your head is completely bandaged. How does it feel?'

'It feels a little sore. Probably my scalp. Brains don't have any nerves.' I looked around and found that I was completely enclosed in blue curtains. 'Why don't you draw the curtains so we can see what's going on?' She made a one-hundred-and-eighty-degree sweep of the curtains. We sat, holding hands, watching the activity on the ward. 'Jo, I'd like some tea.'

Radiotherapy consumed me almost completely for seven weeks, five days per week, two hours a day when you include travel and waiting time. But then one must include the hour and a half nap that I must have because, for some reason, having your body bombarded for forty-two minutes by an intense beam of x-rays is exhausting.

The procedure itself was neither painful nor physically demanding. I lay on a table with my head in the centre of a huge white donut, and a radiologist, using red laser pinpoints, lined my head up exactly, according to plan. The plan had been prepared by David Collingwood, using measurements taken during my surgery of the tumour and its precise location. 'What we want to do,' he explained, 'is to direct the most intense beam at the periphery of the tumour where there are some residual cells, and then cover the area outside the periphery with a less intensive beam where there are rogue cells we want to destroy.'

I was alone in the treatment room with the enormous, noisy Siemens machine, which made loud mechanical groaning and softer whirring noises as it went about its invisible business, all but drowning out the soothing background music.

Two female radiologists sat in the shielded, adjacent room monitoring an array of computer screens.

Having little else to do, I cheered the machine on: *go, get those bloody cancer cells, Siemens! There! That's it; you got that one. There's one over there. Get it!*

The machine came to a stop, the door was opened, and the radiologists wished me well, I changed into street clothes, and Jo took me home for lunch.

I was not completely OK. I didn't have headaches, but my balance was not trustworthy, so Jo stood watchfully beside me. My memory was unreliable, particularly about what happened yesterday, and of nouns and verbs I didn't often use.

I particularly like to look at the photo albums of Seaford. There are pictures dating back to when I was five and my parents started going. That was seventy-two years ago, and Jo has collected on her iPad hours of smart phone videos that family have shot over the years. Some are funny, a few are sad, but they all bring back memories. If it's not raining, Jo and I take a walk around King George's Park. There is a bench near the Southfields Academy's all-weather pitch where I can watch the kids playing football. The huge gingko trees are shedding their leaves now; the poplars have already done so. It's that time of year when the trains are delayed for leaves on the track.

There's always family around, and friends drop in now and then. When you come over, we work on a new book, but I leave most of the doing to you. Father Anthony and I enjoy having a cup of tea and a theological conversation; he's pretty much retired now. Richard and Martha come to see me, together. I am surprised. Of course, they've known each other for years, but since they've both lost spouses, maybe they've decided to get together. They don't say so. It's good to see them animated and happy together.

Just after Christmas, I have another MRI and Dr Grankowski says there are numerous tumours now, and he's going to prescribe a powerful analgesic.

There are district nurses that come several times a day to give me morphine. I sleep most of the time."

Chapter 24
Farewell

When I arrive at the Old Homestead on a February morning, Jo opens the door. Her eyes are pink, her face powder is blotched, and she is biting her lip.

"Bertie died in his sleep, beside me, last night. He made not a sound, but he stopped breathing and that woke me up."

"Oh, no!" I fling my arms around her and we both weep. Arms around each other, we make our way to the kitchen, where she pours me tea from a pot, and we sit at the table.

"It's such a huge loss," I say, paying no attention to the tears wetting my cheeks and my jumper.

"You know, Sarah, I don't think he has left me. Perhaps I am imagining, but I only miss his physical presence: my thoughts are being shared, and I can speak with him in the sense that I know exactly what he would say."

Uncle Bertie's funeral service, at St Christopher's was unusual in several respects. There was a small brazier on the altar burning incense in a wispy column, just as Jo thought he would have liked. The church organ was silent in favour of an awesome audio presentation of Richard Elliott on the eleven thousand six hundred pipe Mormon Tabernacle Organ, beginning with Elgar's Nimrod, and concluding with Pachebel's Canon in D. As far as I know, Uncle Bertie never cared particularly about flowers, but at the insistence of Carol-Ann, there were two grand arrangements of white carnations.

Father Anthony performed the service and gave the main eulogy. He spoke about Bertie's religious doubts and how 'through persistent search and listening to the tiny spark of God within each of us, he found his Lord.'

There were a lot of family members who wanted to talk about Bertie. Jo decided to limit the family speakers to Margaret, and me. I was surprised, but of course I didn't question her decision. I spoke about Bertie's extraordinary talent for creating magical prose that set fire to children's imaginations. But I said it was much more than talent that made him successful. 'It was the depth of his love for children, and his drive to engage with them as a writer, as a reader and as a Sunday school teacher.'

At first, I thought that Margaret was nervous, but then I saw the tears in her eyes and her white knuckles gripping the lectern. Her jaw was set firmly. She began speaking about her dismissive attitude toward family before being imprisoned, and how, when she was paroled, 'being part of a caring family became essential to Nelson's and my mental health. Without it, we would have crashed into nothing.' Then, she said that Bertie had imposed some conditions on their re-admittance to the family, that he called it 'tough-love' and this has made her resentful as being un-Christian and unfair. At this point there were tears streaming down her face. She said, 'I have come to realise that without love, a family is worthless, but without an element of toughness, a loving family cannot love.' She paused to wipe her eyes. 'And so Nelson and I would like to send Bertie our thanks and wish him farewell.' She paused to smile at the congregation. 'And I pray that the Good Lord offers him tough love.'

We all boarded a large boat in Newhaven on a windy March day. It had been raining most of the morning, and now, under low, flying clouds we headed out into the English Channel off Seaford. There is a one metre swell topped with white spume rocking the boat, and the seabirds are flying low. As the captain turns the boat across the wind, the sun reaches momentarily through the clouds, and Jeffrey, standing in the bow, releases his father's ashes into the wind.

For some time, the figure of the Professor has been something of an enigma to me. He was obviously a wise man, but why would an elderly black ex-bus driver, on a state pension be called Professor? Jo and Carol-Ann both say they never met him, although Carol-Ann remembers her mother talking about him. Probably, Bertie also remembered his mother talking about the Professor. Did this Professor really have an MBE? I decide to check the archives at the Council. Did a George Jenkins receive an MBE about twenty years ago? The clerk calls me back a week later. 'No, but there was a George Jenkins who received the award thirty-one years ago.'

OK. So, maybe the Professor was mixed up on his dates. I ask, 'What can you tell me about Mr Jenkins?'

'He was retired from Transport for London in 1975 and lived in the Prince Henry Estate. He received a state pension until his death 6 April 1996.'

'Are you sure the date of death is correct?'

'Yes, ma'am. I'm looking at a copy of his death certificate.'

But, my great grandmother died in late April 1996, so how could the Professor have attended her funeral?

I ask Carol-Ann and Jo. My nan says, 'Interesting question. I have no idea.'

Jo says, 'You and I know, Sarah, that Bertie had an amazing imagination, and I can also tell you that he had a lot of dreams. Maybe the Professor was caught up in some combination of the two.'

We're all together on a Sunday at the Old Homestead two months after the funeral. Jo lives here alone as her late mother-in-law did for twenty-four years. I don't think Jo is lonely. I've noticed that sometimes when she looks disengaged and pensive, her lips are moving as if she's talking to someone. So, I think she's still close to Bertie. She enjoys the Sunday lunches, and insists on doing all the cooking provided that the grandchildren set the tables and the adults clear afterwards. She loves all the grandchildren – hers and Carol-Ann's – and she keeps up to date on all the adults, face-to-face or by phone. We thought she would become the matriarch of the family, but it's not quite the same without Bertie. Jo only gets involved if there's an important disagreement. Cathy, acting for Jeffrey, keeps things running smoothly.

One thing that Jo particularly enjoys is hearing vignettes about Bertie. Since I worked and travelled with him for seven years, I'm often called on to tell one. Like the time I was chatting a mile-a-minute with a lovely old black bartender in New Orleans. He asked me if the man with me was my grandfather. Bertie says, 'No. I'm her script writer.'

Actually, Jo is quite busy visiting with David Galloway and completing his biography. She tells me that Galloway's publisher has two other possible biographies for her, both in America: interviewing a West Coast philanthropist in his sea-side mansion, or an aging country music star in her Nashville chateau. When I ask her how she is doing, she says, 'Well enough, Sarah. I've got everything I need except Bertie in person.'

Carol-Ann hasn't changed, except she has given up her consultancy role with the theatre company. Bertie told me this story about his sister that happened several months after Raymond's death. "Jo tells me she went over to Carol-Ann's to give her a book she had been reading. She said, 'There's something strange going on, Bertie. There was a man there sitting on the sofa watching TV. Carol-Ann introduced him as Luigi somebody-or-other, who plays the cello.'

I asked her, 'What's strange about it that?'

Jo said, 'I saw the same man with Carol-Ann last week—in Sainsbury's—they were loading up a trolley together, and he's not a member of the Wandle String Quartet.'

So, Raymond was gone, and my seventy-one-year-old sister had a man in the house.

I got on the phone and arranged an immediate introduction. Luigi Demarco is an affable, middle-aged Italian, perhaps a little laid-back, and the first cello in the small orchestra at Carol-Ann's theatre company. He is attractive, fit, well-presented, has no children and no wedding ring.

Carol-Ann said, 'I've known Luigi for twenty years.'

'Twenty-two, darlin',' Luigi corrected her.

'I was alone, so was he, we're good friends, so now we're together.'

'That makes sense,' I said.

Luigi asked, 'Would you like to hear some live music to go with your tea?'

'Yes, of course.'

The cello and violin were produced, and we were treated to some sprightly Bach by two musicians who are clearly in tune.

Later, Jo said, 'Well, I suppose they're just two lonely, kindred spirits.'

'I wouldn't bet on it.'

'Oh, come on, Bertie. She's seventy-one.'

'My sister, bless her lusty heart, has never been without a man since she was sixteen. She may look and act like a spinster, but she isn't."

Jeffrey is still in Parliament as a junior business minister. He says, 'It's the perfect role for me. It's obscure enough that I don't get caught in the political crossfire but elevated enough above the back benches so I can see what's really going on. When his brother teases him about becoming Prime Minister, he says, 'Mike, there is a good thing and there's too much of a good thing. It's important to know the difference, because being Prime Minister fits into the latter category.'

Michael has become more laid back with a ticklish sense of humour. There are now five Smithson's offices in Wandsworth, and Michael says he's having to fight off take-over proposals from the large chains. 'I'm too young to retire, and the only other job worth having is Member of Parliament, but my brother's standing in the way.' I have the impression that he's become a mover and shaker in Wandsworth – not a councillor, but certainly he knows them all, as well as the management of the Housing and Planning Departments. I ask him about the possibility of expanding into other districts. He says, 'I've had a look north of the river into Fulham, but it's so posh over there that I couldn't possibly fit in. It's just not me.'

Elizabeth is a newsreader on the BBC News top team. She's a little too serious for me, but she has two very pretty and lively teenage daughters at the Academy, and a lovely husband who used to be a city banker, but now runs a homeless charity in East London.

Jenny, God bless her, hasn't changed. She's still at St Georges and has been elected a vice president of the Royal Academy of Nursing. Thankfully, she is, as ever, my rock. I try to inject a little silly shine into her life.

My parents are more relaxed about the vicissitudes of life as they have grown older together. There's a particular story about my father at Rosetta's wedding. Uncle Bertie gave Rosetta away to a tall Greek named Dionysus, an oboe player in her chamber orchestra. Dionysus is a free spirit with a lot of Greek expatriate friends, and he wanted to have some Greek music at his wedding. Of course, he'd met my father when he was introduced to the family at a Sunday lunch. My father agreed to arrange an *entekhno*, a classical genre of Greek music with rhythm and melody from folk music, for flute (Rosetta), oboe (Dionysus), violin (Carol-Ann), cello (Luigi), and piano (Albert). There were about three dozen of Dionysus' friends there, and as the music began, they performed a Greek folk dance, arms linked, bodies swaying, feet shifting quickly. Adventurous English guests joined the linked Greek line and imitated its movements. Other guests began to clap rhythmically and shout encouragement. The room filled with delightful sound and energy.

Uncle Bertie was watching, standing next to my father and me, and he asked where the musicians got the music. Dad explained he has composition software where one can input an original piece, select the instruments you want to use, and the PC will produce an arrangement for the instruments selected.

"So, what we're listening to is the world premier?" Uncle Bertie asked.

Dad laughed. "I suppose you could say that. Music brings people together."

"Yes, and I suppose it brought the bride and groom together." Uncle Bertie said.

Dad gazed at the musicians. "Think they will be happy together."

I tried to sense his feelings about attending his ex-lover's wedding for which he arranged the music. He had a wistful, almost melancholy look on his face. Uncle Bertie must have noticed, too; he said, "You can be proud of our family and your music, James."

Dad gave Uncle Bertie a quick smile. "Yes, I am content."

That falls short, I think, of being truly happy: the impossible dream of somehow starting his life over again with Rosetta. It's so like my father, always seeking perfection. But if he had divorced Mum and married Rosetta, he would be unhappy because his children would be mad at him.

In my case, I feel truly happy that most people accept me for what I am: a gay Christian artist in a beautiful relationship. And I know Uncle Bertie was happy in his faith, in his family and in his books for children.

The End